MURDER ON THE COAST

A 1920s Cozy Mystery

A Lady Felicity Quick Mystery
Book 5

ROSIE HUNT

ISBN: 9789083290652

With thanks to early readers Peggy Craddock, Federica De Dominicis, Kel Hodgkins, Nancy, and others

Editing by Effie Wilson

Cover art by DLR Cover Designs

For a dear friend.

It's an honour to be killed off in a book, I promise.

A Note on Language

This book is written in British English. There are two reasons for this:

- the story is set in England, and
- I, the author, am British.

Part of my British writing style is the use of s where z is used in American English. For example: hospitalise instead of hospitalize, and idolise instead of idolize.

However, you may have noticed that in the blurbs and marketing for this book, it's called a cozy mystery and not a cosy mystery.

This is because the American spelling is standard for the genre. Spelling it this way helps people (and algorithms) recognise my book more easily.

But outside of book genres, it's cosy all the way.

Cast of Characters

Quick family

Lady Felicity Quick, journalist and occasional amateur detective

Pip, Felicity's Yorkshire Terrier

Lord Jasper Quick, Earl of Denbury, editor-in-chief of the Western Daily News and Felicity's brother

Residents of Ashdene

The Honourable Mrs Isabella Mountvernon, widow and arts patron

Beetle, Isabella's Briard

Mr Chivers, butler

Mrs Rawling, housekeeper

Ottermouth's artistic community

Mr Lawrence Whitburn, artist

Mr Martin Granger, artist

The Honourable Miss Audrey Lawson, companion to Martin

Mr Harold Prothero, art dealer

Miss Elizabeth Prothero, student and Harold's daughter

Mr Nigel Davies, gallery assistant

Mr James Halliday, art collector

Ottermouth's fishing community

Captain Edward Dunn, fisherman and skipper of the fishing trawler, the Maggie

Mrs Margaret Dunn, wife of Edward

Miss Thora Dunn, daughter of Edward and Margaret

Mr Colin Reynolds, fisherman

Mrs Grace Campbell, widow

Mr William Seddon, war veteran

Others

Mr Alexander Cooper, reporter for the Western Daily News and friend of Felicity

Mr Joseph Ferris, lighthouse keeper

Constable Henry Thompson, police officer

Officer Roger Marshall, Customs and Excise agent

Detective Inspector Sands, police detective

The captivating shoreline setting is not the only element that contributes to the allure of this exquisite oil painting: a solitary female figure dominates the composition.

Her gaze turns over her shoulder, encountering that of the viewer, as if entranced by an ethereal connection. What message does she wish to convey? Or does the artist's own revelation lie within her vulnerable expression?

From the unpublished catalogue prepared for the exhibition, Ottermouth: A Retrospective
Spring 1922

Extract from the Western Daily News, 1922

Fugitive Spotted On The Continent

Subject of interest in Ottermouth fiasco seen in Spain

EXETER, 4 April — Spanish police have contacted the Devon County Constabulary to report a reliable sighting of a fugitive wanted for questioning. The individual is linked to the tragic tangle of events that occurred in the Devonshire village of Ottermouth last month.

This newspaper understands that His Majesty's Customs and Excise are keen to interview the same individual. Representatives from the police and customs will travel to Bilbao to investigate separately.

The drama of the wrongdoing in once-peaceful Ottermouth has captured the nation's attention. As the newspaper closest to the action, the Western Daily News shall continue to provide you with only the most credible and timely information as the culprits are brought to justice.

Chapter One

OTTERMOUTH, SOUTH DEVON, 23 MARCH 1922

As cotton clouds scudded across the sky and briny air blustered in off the sea, Lady Felicity Quick, reporter for the Western Daily News and occasional amateur detective, held onto the brim of her straw picture hat and admired the view. Despite being Devon born and raised, Felicity wasn't especially familiar with either of the county's coastlines. Yet now was not the time for sight-seeing.

Pip, Felicity's three-year-old Yorkshire Terrier, was ahead of her on the clifftop path that ran from the heights of Ashdene down into Ottermouth. Turning towards his mistress, the little dog lifted an inquisitive paw, his blue-and-tan fur swept by the wind.

"You're absolutely right," said Felicity, addressing the faithful Yorkie. "We mustn't be late for our appointment." Mr Alexander Cooper was a fellow reporter at the Western Daily News. After several adventures together and many meetings over tea and buns, Felicity now considered Alex a close friend, and he was due to arrive in Ottermouth at any moment.

In her tightly laced Oxfords, Felicity confidently navigated the steep, stony path worn into the red earth of an undulating clifftop meadow. Bees buzzed around the milky froth of the blossoming blackthorn that separated the field from the cliff's edge. A generous pleat in the back of her moss-green woollen skirt allowed Felicity to climb a set of wooden stiles in a dense hedgerow extending inland. Having scurried under the stiles, Pip bounded ahead, chasing a Red Admiral as Ottermouth came fully into view.

Framed by jagged coastline and patches of woodland, its picturesque harbour lined with colourful fishermen's cottages, Ottermouth was a village worthy of any chocolate box lid. It was, nevertheless, a queer location for an art exhibition.

Over land, from just about any direction, Ottermouth was a slow and lengthy trek along inhospitable lanes barely suitable for a motor. The village was more easily accessed by water. Felicity had opted for the ferry from Kingswear, although the journey had been far from comfortable.

Despite its remoteness, or perhaps because of it, Ottermouth had become a haven for artists, especially painters enamoured by the coast and its residents. The artistic allure of the village was partly why Felicity had braved the boat ride to Ottermouth, and upon arrival, the views certainly didn't disappoint. But Felicity wasn't in Ottermouth to sketch or paint.

The coastal path swept sharply downwards, narrowing as it dipped past orange sandstone crags. Felicity put out a hand to steady herself. She was both grateful and resigned to being in Ottermouth. Reporting on an art exhibition was closer to her old role as a writer for the society pages than to her chosen career as a news journalist. Yet her fate could have been much worse.

Following the dramatic events at Grimstow House just a couple of months before, Felicity and Lord Jasper Quick — the editor-in-chief of the Western Daily News and Felicity's elder brother — had met at the newspaper's Exeter offices to discuss her future. Felicity had arrived at the meeting ready to fight for her job, and in a sense, she'd done just that. Only not in the way she expected.

Through the fug of his pipe smoke and against the

background clatter of typewriters, Jasper expressed that though it would impact the paper's circulation numbers — for Felicity was a popular journalist, particularly among female readers — Felicity would have Jasper's full support as she stepped away from her duties as a reporter to focus on sleuthing.

Her brother's encouragement towards a career change had caught Felicity quite off-guard.

Until that point, Jasper had disapproved of Felicity muddling herself into the solving of crimes. While it was true she'd been involved in several cases, the thought of abandoning her career as a journalist hadn't entered Felicity's mind.

Felicity and Jasper's late father hadn't allowed Felicity to even consider a career as a reporter. He'd considered work in general an unsuitable pursuit for women, let alone newspaper work. After her broader-minded brother became the editor of the family paper, Felicity was at last given the opportunity to write — albeit only for the society pages, which nearly ended Felicity's career in journalism through sheer boredom.

Achieving the position of news reporter had been hard won. She wouldn't give up on it easily.

Felicity had therefore vehemently insisted on her wish to remain at the Western Daily News and her absence of interest in setting up as a private detective. Jasper had narrowed his eyes and pressed his fingertips together, his chestnut moustache twitching. Then he suggested the assignment in Ottermouth.

The assignment had less to do with serious news reporting and more to do with a promise Jasper had made to a dear friend lost in the war. Desperate to cling onto her job, Felicity had nevertheless jumped at the opportunity.

Continuing along the rocky path into Ottermouth, the sea breeze sweeping her bobbed curls across her cheeks, Felicity couldn't help wondering. Had her brother duped her into accepting a tedious assignment? The mere idea of writing up paintings and conversing with art enthusiasts was enough to make Felicity stifle a yawn.

Yet she had every reason to be satisfied with her situation. Felicity's career as a journalist was back on track, and soon enough, she'd be catching up with Alex over a warm cheese scone at the cosy village inn. What was there to grumble about?

Far below, the tide swooshed rhythmically across the pebbled shore of a rugged little cove. Pip paused ahead as Felicity made her way down the steep, uneven path. The angle of the little dog's tufted head seemed to say, *Can't you go any faster?*

"I assure you I'm doing my best," said Felicity, picking up speed as the stony path gave way to a cobbled track dotted with squat, slate-roofed cottages. A hanging sign announcing *The Dolphin* came quickly into view, although the accompanying illustration looked more like a menacing sea monster than a sleek, aquatic mammal. Scooping Pip under her arm, Felicity pushed open the door and stepped inside.

For a village as small as Ottermouth, the inn's bar was exceedingly full. A large group of men took up most of the rather dim space, gathered mainly around a broad wooden table littered with empty bowls, heels of bread, and tankards of drink. The men represented a broad spectrum of ages. Some were clean shaven, some even full-bearded, all arranged between stools, benches, and standing. Many wore overalls or the thick, cable-knit jumpers associated with seafarers. Some were more smartly dressed, including a policeman of advanced age in the customary dark-blue uniform.

Felicity closed the inn's door behind her. Pip's little black nose twitched. The aromas of tobacco smoke and a richly seasoned fish stew mingled with decades' worth of ale sloshed onto floorboards.

Some of the men looked up at Felicity as she entered. A couple of them even smiled at her, including a striking man of around twenty-five with shining brown curls and a grey jumper. The rest of the inn's patrons kept their eyes on their drinks, their conversations too mumbled to be overheard.

With a polite smile, Felicity didn't allow her attention to linger on the men. As a stranger in the village, it was especially important to create a good first impression, and she didn't need to stare to know there was no sign of Alex.

"Lady Felicity?" Behind the bar, a silver-haired, severe-looking man with an eye patch rubbed a pewter tanker with a linen cloth.

Confirming her identity, Felicity greeted the innkeeper. He nodded towards a small table pushed against the wall with two empty, mismatched seats. Atop the table, a smeary piece of paper bore the word *Quick* in a slanted scrawl.

Ashdene's housekeeper had offered to make the reservation on Felicity's behalf. The inn as an appropriate location for a meeting between friends had been suggested by the Honourable Mrs Isabella Mountvernon, the owner and primary resident of Ashdene, the grand Victorian villa at which Felicity was staying while in Ottermouth.

Isabella had been widowed when Jasper's dear friend, Major Timothy Mountvernon, lost his life under withering artillery fire during a daring manoeuvre near Amiens. Although not a creator herself, Isabella was a passionate art enthusiast and a generous patron of Ottermouth's artistic scene.

Felicity thanked the innkeeper and tucked Pip onto her lap as she sat down at the table. The mottled leaded window beside the seat hardly afforded a view of the cobbled street outside, let alone of the sea. Hopefully, Alex had taken the advice to arrive by boat and wasn't now stuck with his motor on some diabolically narrow lane.

"He's not coming, your ladyship." The innkeeper's voice was a flat growl, rising only slightly above the murmur of his patrons' conversations.

Felicity blinked at the innkeeper. "Not coming?"

"The fellow you're meeting. He telephoned. Said he's awful sorry. Caught up with matters in Plymouth."

"Ah." Felicity did her best to hide a surprisingly acute sense of disappointment. Yet such let-downs were to be expected, were they not?

Alex was covering a long-running court case involving a bank manager accused of embezzling his clients' funds. Readers across the region were riveted, especially in Plymouth, where many of the bank's customers lived. While Felicity and Alex were by now good friends, work would always come first. Their commitment to journalism only strengthened their bond.

Felicity stroked Pip's silky back. "In that case…" She hesitated. The Dolphin wasn't somewhere a woman would typically dine alone, but what if the innkeeper had already prepared a luncheon for the booking? The stew's scent was rather tantalising.

A chair screeched over the floorboards on the other side of the room. A man of around twenty with sandy-blond hair and sun-bleached fishing overalls stood up, his glare fixed on a dark-haired man at the other end of the table, who was dressed in a well-cut waistcoat and crisp shirt sleeves.

"I'll not have it!" The sandy-haired lad jabbed a finger at the waistcoated man. "He's dragging Thora into it. He's putting us all at risk. I'll put an end to it. I'll put an end to it right now!"

Felicity stiffened. Pip's ears were pricked.

A man with a weathered face and white stubble rose to his feet. "Calm yourself, Col." He placed a hand on the agitated young man's arm. "This isn't how we solve things."

Was the situation dangerous? Felicity looked for the innkeeper, keen to gauge his reaction, but he was no longer behind the bar. He'd disappeared.

The man in the waistcoat stood up, his arms folded over his chest. He was perhaps a few years older than Col. "Go ahead." He smirked as he approached the angry young man. "Put an end to it, as you say. I'd like to see you try."

With a grunt, Col reached into the front pocket of his overalls and drew out a knife. The small, sharp blade glinted in the dim light.

Charming and *atmospheric* were words Isabella had used to describe the Dolphin Inn. Had she ever visited the establishment herself?

Her heart pounding with alarm, Felicity looked at the policeman for his reaction. He leaned back in his chair, his eyes narrow and watchful, but he made no move to intervene.

Col shook off the older man's grasp. He turned, the knife slack at his side, as though ready to walk away. Then he twisted and lunged. Seizing the starched collar of the dark-haired man's shirt, Col pushed the tip of his knife beneath his antagonist's chin. "Oh, I'll do it." Col's voice shook as the knife quivered. "I'll do it all right!"

Chapter Two

With Pip clutched to her chest, Felicity was edging towards the inn's door when the man with the shining brown curls rose calmly to his feet.

"Gentlemen, please." His voice was deep and velvet-like. He put a hand firmly on Col's arm. "There's a lady present," he continued, nodding in Felicity's direction.

Unsure whether to feel reassured or exposed by the attention, Felicity nodded in uncomfortable acknowledgement.

Hesitating for a moment, Col lowered his knife from under the dark-haired man's chin. Straightening his collar, the dark-haired man smirked.

Relief washed through Felicity. A quiet lunch was out of the question, but the threat of violence seemed to have passed.

"Although the decision whether to run a blade through a man ought not rely solely rely on the presence of the fairer sex." The curly-headed man was dressed like a fisherman, but he didn't sound like one.

Col's gaze smouldered with fury as he continued to fixate on his enemy.

"What difference would another scar make?" said the dark-haired man in a mocking tone, his arms still folded over his smartly tailored waistcoat.

The seafarer with the white stubble sank back onto the wooden bench. He tugged hard on Col's sleeve. "Finish your drink." He shoved a tankard across the table as Col landed with a thump back in his seat, the knife still tight in his hand.

With an amused grin, Col's antagonist returned slowly to his seat and drank from his own tankard. A glimmer of a smile passed over the policeman's face. He'd also returned to sipping his drink. Even the innkeeper had reappeared behind the bar, a drying cloth and tankard in his hands as though nothing had happened. Had the danger passed?

The curly haired man with the honeyed voice approached Felicity. "Forgive my enquiring, but you're surely not luncheoning here alone?"

Felicity's heart rate was still settling down. "That wasn't the intention, n-no." She stroked Pip, who had somewhat belatedly begun growling.

The man looked at the note on the table. His curls bounced as he turned his head. "Do you happen to be 'Quick', or was that who you were waiting for?"

The man's grey cable-knit jumper and brown moleskin trousers looked rather unblemished for someone accustomed to a life at sea. Yet to have settled the disagreement so deftly, he was clearly deeply embedded in the local community.

As Felicity introduced herself, the man's amber-golden eyes widened. "Well, fancy that. Bella said she'd introduce you, but I've pipped her to the post. It's wonderful to have you here to cover the exhibition for the paper." He gently ruffled Pip's ears, which did little to calm the Yorkie's growling.

"I am awfully sorry," said Felicity, "but I don't believe we've been introduced."

"I'm Martin." The man's smile was extremely charming. "Martin Granger."

The pause that followed felt loaded with expectation. Was

Felicity supposed to recognise the name? Once, she might have mumbled a response, feigning familiarity to ease her interlocutor's discomfort. While age and experience — particularly her experiences over the past year — had eased Felicity's urge to please even complete strangers, she would always remain polite.

"A pleasure to meet you, Mr Granger," she said, returning Martin's smile. Pip, at last, ceased his growling.

The man blinked. "I'm the painter." His charming smile had disappeared. "I'm Eustace Granger's son." He was adamant Felicity must recognise him.

Then it hit her. "Why, yes. Of course."

Felicity had made efforts to research the art scene in Ottermouth. She was determined to do her best for her career and for the widow of her brother's friend. She had, however, fallen asleep several times while trying to get through a book that contained more pictures than text.

"Forgive me, Mr Granger," she continued. "The new exhibition focuses on your late father's work, if I'm not mistaken. He was one of the founding artists here in Ottermouth, was he not?"

Martin pushed an errant curl back from his forehead. "That's correct. He was. Had he stayed with us for longer, who knows what he might have achieved? I only hope I'm not struck down before I reach my full potential."

Martin's father had perhaps succumbed during the same influenza outbreak that had claimed Felicity's own father and many more lives besides, but it wasn't a topic for a first meeting.

Eyes flicked up from the fisherman's table. While the earlier tensions seemed to have evaporated, Felicity no longer felt entirely comfortable at the inn.

"Shall we step outside?" Martin seemingly sensed Felicity's unease.

"Let's." With her appetite having deserted her, and considering Alex's cancellation, the opportunity to interview Martin was welcome. The Grangers were central to the articles

Felicity would write while in Ottermouth, and her notebook and trusty mechanical pencil were, as usual, in her skirt pocket.

Martin held the door open as Felicity stepped out and set Pip on the cobbles. The inn's sign creaked softly in the salty breeze. Felicity adjusted her hat's brim against the pale sun.

"I suppose you mistook me for a fisherman." Martin smiled grimly, still disturbed by Felicity's not having recognised him. "I'm completely integrated into the local fishing community, you see. Just as my father was. There's no other way to do it. If you want to capture their way of life, you need the access."

Felicity recalled a photo she'd seen in the book that had put her to sleep several times. Taken at the turn of the century, the photo captured a man dressed in scruffy sea-faring clothes with a pipe clenched in his teeth and a sketchbook on his lap. The subject of his work was a group of women outside a row of sturdy cottages typical of Ottermouth. The women were mending crab pots, concentrated on their work as though there weren't an artist present.

Felicity reached for her notebook. "Your father—" she began.

"Excuse me." The words were grunted by a young man in shabby, paint-smeared workwear with dark, tousled hair as he rather rudely pushed between Felicity and Martin to enter the inn. He had a sketchbook tucked under his arm.

Felicity stepped back to avoid colliding with the surly fellow, but he caught Martin's elbow as he passed. Martin said nothing, but the glare he gave the man's back as he disappeared into the Dolphin could have melted stone.

"I say." Martin turned to Felicity with a smile, any trace of antipathy suddenly gone. "Why not make your way straight to the gallery? The whole gang is there, getting ready for the exhibition. They'll be thrilled to see you, I'm sure."

Felicity nodded. "Thank you. I shall do just that." Her schedule was rather flexible, and she'd planned to visit the gallery after lunch with Alex, although she couldn't help reflecting upon Martin's sudden keenness to be rid of her.

"The gallery's beside the harbour. Can't miss it. Big old thing. Used to be a boat shed." Martin was already pushing the inn door open, his foot on the stone step. "We'll see each other later tonight." A charming smile set his amber eyes sparkling.

Before Felicity could ask for details, the door to the inn swung shut. Martin had disappeared back inside.

Pip lifted his nose in the direction of the Dolphin, the gleam in the Yorkie's eyes echoing Felicity's own curiosity.

What exactly had Martin meant by 'we'll see each other later tonight'?

Chapter Three

Turning her back on the Dolphin Inn, Felicity continued along Ottermouth's cobbled streets towards the harbour, Pip bounding ahead as grey-and-white gulls swooped and cried above them. It was perhaps a good thing Alex hadn't made their appointment. If and when he arrived in Ottermouth, Felicity would arrange for them to meet elsewhere.

Sea-going craft of various sizes and purposes bobbed on their moorings in Ottermouth's harbour. Their rigging knocked and clinked in the breeze. There were simple wooden rowing boats and sleek yachts with dark, gleaming hulls. A large, rugged trawler, designed for days or even weeks at sea, was the only commercial fishing vessel present. A thick harbour arm built from roughly hewn sandstone and topped with a walkway protected the boats from the worst of the Channel's weather.

A row of squat cottages lined one side of the harbour. Outside the dwellings were women, children, and several cats, their coats a patchwork of ginger and tabby. Feline eyes watched Pip warily from atop piles of brine-bleached crates as needles dived in and out of a large net spread across several laps, perhaps repairing tears from the trawler's most recent mission.

Hardly anyone looked up as Felicity passed, although she did meet the gaze of a woman in an ill-fitting brown dress with tangled grey hair. Seated by herself, she was eating winkles and tossing the shells into the water of the harbour. Her glare made Felicity uncomfortable, but then perhaps Felicity had been staring too long herself. She smiled politely and returned her gaze to the cobbles ahead.

The gallery was, as Martin had said, difficult to miss. Set at the far end of the harbour overlooking a stone slipway, the voluminous wooden shed looked freshly painted in a deep, glossy green. Its entrance was an enormous set of doors through which presumably boats used to be hauled for repairs. Upon passing inside, however, any resemblance to a boat shed ended.

The interior walls were covered in artworks — oil paintings, watercolours, charcoal sketches, Felicity couldn't quite keep up — with temporary dividers creating even more hanging space. Pedestals had been set out for sculptures and pots. A shade of paint somewhere between beige and grey covered every surface, from the concrete floor to the high metal-beamed ceiling, allowing milky sunlight filtered through clerestory windows to brighten the space without dazzling.

For a small village in such a remote location, the gallery was a remarkable sight.

"Can I help you?" A man of about twenty-five approached from behind one of the temporary walls. He had black pomaded hair and wore a sharply cut grey suit with a navy-and-gold bow tie. He gave Pip — who was tucked under Felicity's arm — a wary look. "The exhibition isn't open to the public yet," he added rather haughtily.

"Oh, Nigel. Do you really not know who this is?"

Nigel frowned with confusion and pulled his chin into his bow tie as the Honourable Mrs Isabella Mountvernon swept through a doorway at the back of the gallery in a shimmering green gown. "Cici, darling," she purred, her large-beaded jewellery clacking and her dark brown hair streaming from the loose bun as she surged towards Felicity.

Nigel stood back as Isabella warmly clasped Felicity's hands, kissed her on both cheeks, and scratched Pip under the chin.

Despite meeting her for the first time only the previous day, Felicity was captivated by Isabella's instant familiarity and warmth. While Ottermouth and its artists were of moderate interest to the readers of the Western Daily News, Jasper had stated plainly that it was primarily for Isabella's sake that he wanted the exhibition covered in such detail. Isabella's charm made Felicity's job all the easier.

Isabella beamed at Felicity. "I wasn't expecting you here so soon. Allow me to introduce you to Harry. Harry, darling? Won't you come and meet our intrepid reporter?"

A portly man in a finely tailored suit with a silk cravat and a tiny gold pince-nez appeared from behind a cabinet displaying a collection of painted plates. Close behind him was an upright young woman with pale brown hair. She wore a prim, dropped-waist dress in claret-coloured velvet and was perhaps a couple of years Felicity's junior. In contrast to Isabella, she had no warmth in her expression.

The man with the pince-nez extended a hand. "Harold Prothero. Art dealer. Very pleased to make your acquaintance, Lady Felicity. Mrs Mountvernon had informed us you'd be visiting the gallery today. It's an honour to have you here to cover our little exhibition."

"Little?" Isabella grimaced with playful displeasure.

Nigel looked genuinely affronted.

"This is the most important art event to take place in Devon since…" continued Isabella. "Well, since the very existence of art itself."

"Err. Yes." Harold's cheeks grew pink. Isabella's enthusiasm seemed to bewilder him. "May I introduce my daughter, your ladyship?"

The young woman in the claret dress stepped forward. "Elizabeth Prothero. Pleased to meet you." She extended a slender hand, which was cold and limp. Pip sniffed the air, although Felicity couldn't detect even a hint of perfume on the young woman.

There came a clearing of the throat. The man in the bow tie who had attempted to repel Felicity upon her entrance into the gallery raised his thin, dark eyebrows expectantly at the portly art dealer.

"Why, yes." Harold Prothero gestured towards the younger man. "And this is Mr Nigel Davies. My right-hand man, so to speak."

Nigel stepped forward, his handshake warm and even a little too tight, his attitude towards Felicity having undergone a reversal. "It's indeed an honour to make your acquaintance." Nigel span towards Harold. "Mr Whitburn was just here briefly. He continues to insist his works aren't for sale." The art dealer's assistant threw a disdainful glance at a large and dramatic oil painting of a boat crashing through waves. Next to it was a canvas in a similar energetic and realistic style, depicting men hauling nets onto a ship by moonlight, sea spray glittering all around them. The paintings were rather striking.

Nigel sighed. "He's lending them to us for viewing only. Out of respect for the local people."

"Ah." Harold took a handkerchief out of his pocket and mopped his brow, despite it not being particularly warm in the gallery. "I see."

Had it been Mr Whitburn who'd pushed past Felicity and Martin to enter the inn? He'd had a sketchbook under his arm, and the wilful and abrasive attitude was a match.

"I find it admirable." Elizabeth folded her arms and regarded the oil paintings in question with an air of satisfaction. "Mr Whitburn is standing up for his principles."

Harold gazed at the same paintings, his brow pinched. "I suppose Mr Whitburn doesn't have the success of this exhibition among his concerns." His expression lightened as he turned his gaze from the paintings to his daughter. "Not that it need be a concern of yours, my dear. You've got your studies to think about."

Isabella sighed deeply, her arms folded as she, too, contemplated the dramatic works in oil. "Mr Whitburn is a talented artist, and there are so few of his works on the market. It would have been quite the coup."

Felicity stroked Pip's tufted ears and frowned slightly. Had she missed something in falling asleep one too many times while researching Ottermouth? "Forgive my ignorance, but I thought the Grangers were the focus of the exhibition?"

"Oh, they are, darling." Isabella's reassurance came quickly. "They absolutely are. Both father and son. I've got buyers coming from all over for them." She glanced sheepishly at Harold. "I didn't promise any Whitburns, of course." Isabella fiddled with one of her beaded necklaces. "I'll have to think of some other way of keeping the collectors satisfied. Ottermouth could be the next Pont-Aven. The next Worpswede, even."

Not having ever heard of Pont-Aven or Worpswede, Felicity reached into her pocket for her notebook. It was high time she became serious and methodical about understanding Ottermouth's art scene, but a clatter of boots over the gallery's concrete floor made everyone turn.

A tall, broad-shouldered man in a dark blue uniform with brass buttons — like a policeman but with a peaked cap — came to a frowning halt with his hands on his hips.

Harold's eyes widened. Isabella drew a hand to her chest. Elizabeth swallowed nervously.

"Miss Prothero?" The new arrival looked between the women in the room. "I'm here to speak to Miss Elizabeth Prothero."

Elizabeth stepped forward, her delicate fingers knotted. "Y-yes?"

"Officer Roger Marshall of His Majesty's Customs and Excise." The uniformed man's booming voice could likely be heard down the street. "You found a package washed up on the beach, as I understand it?"

"Ah, well." A flush of pink coloured Elizabeth's pale cheeks. "Shall we step into my father's office to talk?" She ushered the customs officer towards the back of the gallery.

Harold mopped his forehead with his handkerchief. Nigel looked mildly amused.

Isabella strode towards Harold. "She didn't, did she?" she hissed. "I mean, Lizzie didn't report it? We told her not to. Not to that uniformed buffoon, of all people."

Harold didn't look at Isabella. His gaze was fixed on where his daughter and the customs officer had disappeared into the gallery's back office. "She's not always one for doing what she's told is my Lizzie. I have only myself to blame for that, I suppose."

With Pip still tucked under her arm, for the gallery's contents were no doubt unique and irreplaceable, Felicity edged forward. She spoke in hushed tones. "Would it be terribly rude of me if I were to enquire what that was about?"

Harold blinked, his lips drawn downwards. Isabella waved a hand, bracelets clacking. "It has nothing whatever to do with the exhibition, you understand."

Nigel cleared his throat. "Officer Marshall is conducting an investigation into—"

"I'll tell you what, Cici." Wrapping her arm through Felicity's, Isabella began walking with her towards the gallery doors. "What say we leave Harold and Mr Davies to continue getting things ready for the big day tomorrow, and you and I return to Ashdene? There are the preparations to oversee for my little soirée, and I could so do with your help."

"There's to be a little soirée?" It was the first mention of a social event Felicity had heard, and it made her stomach sink.

Chapter Four

Between choosing dresses, tasting hors d'oeuvres, and speaking to eager guests arriving early at Ashdene for Isabella's soirée, Felicity somehow found time for a telephone call but found Alex unreachable. That was, of course, absolutely fine. Felicity didn't begrudge Alex his focus on his work, and her motivation for wondering if he might make the soirée wasn't entirely selfless.

At Isabella's mention of the event, Felicity had flashbacks to her time as a society journalist. Polite but dull conversation and attention to the details of clothes and food had formed the mainstay of her work. While Felicity had been grateful for her job at the paper and knew such problems to be trifling in the grand scheme of things, the tedium could be unbearable.

Yet, somehow, Felicity had almost survived the soirée.

If she could endure another hour, it would not be completely rude to announce she was tired and withdraw upstairs. Pip was likely already asleep on her bed. Or perhaps he was off causing mischief in the company of Isabella's dog Beetle. A Briard, Beetle was a relaxed French sheepdog who, like Pip, had a keen sense of fun.

With her gloved arms folded over a sparkling, sleeveless dress

Isabella had loaned to her, the pale yellow clashing awfully with her auburn curls, Felicity squinted and lifted her glass as though deep in thought. She'd positioned herself close to a large canvas delicately lit by electric lamps on curved brass fittings in Ashdene's main salon. The painting depicted a typical Ottermouth fishing scene, and Felicity's tactic seemed to be working.

As the genteel hubbub of the soirée continued behind her, no art buyer down from London approached to tell Felicity how splendidly quaint it was to visit her home county. No industrialist drew near to invite her out on their boat — although it seemed there wasn't an art collector in Ottermouth without a sailing yacht. Even Isabella sailed regularly, and Felicity had already declined several boat trip suggestions. As proven on the ferry from Kingswear, Felicity didn't have very good sea legs.

Taking a sip of her tonic water, Felicity shivered. The salon's generous French doors had been opened onto a large paved terrace, beyond which the moon hung above the dark, glittering sea. Stairs descended from the terrace into Ashdene's lush gardens, many of the exotic specimens having been established during the villa's construction in the previous century. The fresh air helped clear the cigarette and pipe smoke from the room, but it was only March, and the sea air made it very cool indeed.

A light flashed intermittently on a distant headland. Was there a lighthouse on the coastline? Felicity didn't remember seeing one.

The chatter and laughter of the gathering swelled behind Felicity as she continued to squint at the painting. A row of women not unlike those she'd seen earlier beside the harbour were depicted mending crab pots. Felicity was standing too close to appreciate the canvas' overall effect. She could, however, see the direction of the brush strokes in the oil.

What was it that sent people so gaga about paintings that they spent great fortunes on them? Had Alex been there, he would have had a wise word to say on the matter. They might even have laughed at things together.

"It's a Granger."

Felicity hadn't noticed the approach of a tall, neatly groomed grey-haired man in a well-cut brown suit. He held a crystal tumbler that glinted under the painting's lights.

"A Eustace Granger, of course," he added with a subtle smile. "There's a frankness to his work that's unlike any other artist's." His accent was distinctly American. "James Halliday." The man extended a hand, which Felicity accepted. As she introduced herself, the man nodded. "Bella told me who you are. It's an honour to have a reporter of your calibre writing up the exhibition."

Smiling politely, Felicity felt a twinge of guilt. She might have tried harder to be more sociable. She'd agreed to the assignment in Ottermouth and was committed to getting her reporting career back on track. Isabella was also thoroughly lovely and clearly cared a great deal about the local art scene.

"It's an honour to have been invited to report on the exhibition," said Felicity with sincerity. "I shall do my best to spotlight the artistic talent and passion here in Ottermouth." Her stay in the village would be limited to just a day or two. It wasn't a tremendous sacrifice to make.

"Speaking of artistic talent." James turned. Ashdene's butler was showing Martin Granger into the salon.

Martin's fisherman's jumper had been replaced by a slim-fitting navy double-breasted suit. A paisley pocket square and his still-unruly curls hinted at his creative tendencies. A woman with pale blonde hair in silky waves and a smoke-grey dress smiled nervously at his side.

Isabella released herself from a gaggle of guests by the fireplace and flew to the new arrival, beads clattering, chiffon wafting. "Marty, darling. Thrilled you made it. Come, there's someone you absolutely must meet." Isabella led Martin and his companion towards where Felicity and James were standing.

"Marty, this is Lady Felicity Quick," began Isabella.

Martin held up a hand, cutting the introductions short. He smiled. "Sorry to disappoint, Bella, but Lady Felicity and I already met."

"You did?" Isabella frowned like a disappointed child. She looked between Felicity and Martin. "Why on earth didn't you tell me?"

James clapped Martin on the shoulder. "Martin's father founded the art movement here in Ottermouth. He's the closest we have to royalty in these parts."

"That's over doing it a little, isn't it?" Martin somehow looked both humble and eager for more praise. "Lady Felicity, may I introduce you to Audrey?"

Martin's pale-blonde companion stepped forward to shake Felicity's hand. "How do you do?" Her eyelashes fluttered as she retreated to Martin's side.

Isabella huffed good-naturedly. "The Honourable Miss Audrey Lawson, you mean, Marty darling. Just because you're an artist doesn't mean you can forget the norms of politeness. Although I suppose you'd be quite forgiven for not knowing Audrey had any type of honour." Isabella mumbled this last part and Audrey seemed not to notice. Felicity had perhaps been the only one to hear. The comment seemed at odds with Isabella's warmth and good-naturedness.

Harold Prothero arrived at the little gathering in front of the painting, his daughter Elizabeth in tow, Felicity's plan for quiet solitude now rightfully in tatters. Harold's bow tie seemed a little tight, his neck and jowls bulging and flushed. Elizabeth looked quite splendid in a dark green frock.

"I'm awfully sorry to interrupt," said the art dealer, drawing his pince-nez out of the top pocket of his jacket, "but are we discussing *The Crab Pot Menders*? It's part of Mrs Mountvernon's private collection and not for sale. There are several of Eustace Granger's pieces available for purchase at the gallery."

"Father had an extraordinary gift." Martin's tone was deadly serious. "I do what I can, but I'm not a scratch on his genius."

A confused look passed over Audrey's pale features.

"Come now, Marty," said Isabella, falling for what was a rather obvious appeal for praise. "You've more than enough talent. You're an established artist in your own right."

James raised his eyebrows. Whether he agreed with Isabella on this point was hard to say. "Did you wrangle any of Lawrence Whitburn's pieces into the exhibition, Mr Prothero?"

"Yes, yes, we did," replied Harold in a confident tone, his cheeks quickly turning red. "They're not for sale, however. Not just yet. Negotiations are ongoing."

"You'll let me know the moment they go on sale, won't you?" James' tone verged on commanding.

Martin smiled and shook his head. "Whitburn claims to be uninterested in commercial activities, yet insists on driving the price of his works ever higher with this sort of behaviour."

Elizabeth lengthened her neck. "What's wrong with making one's own decisions and taking control of one's life?"

Audrey put a hand on Martin's arm. "Don't be jealous, darling."

Harold winced. He looked from his daughter to James. "Buying and selling works isn't simply about money, of course." He glanced at Isabella, who nodded in earnest agreement.

"Jealous of Whitburn?" Martin had turned his attention to his pale-haired companion. "I'm quite serious, Audrey. Should I be jealous of the man?" His tone was becoming unpleasant.

"Marty." Audrey's mouth opened and closed. "I didn't mean… I'm not saying…"

Isabella hooked her arm through James' in a familiar way that seemed most unaligned with the older gentleman's neat uprightness. "These artists and their temperaments. You know what they're like, Jimmy. Harmless really." She began guiding him to a group of guests that had gone out onto the terrace. "Do you remember my mentioning a print-maker opening a workshop in the village?"

A charming smile returned to Martin's features as he was hailed from the other side of the salon, a group of artists and art collectors beckoning him to join them. As he moved confidently across the room, Audrey hastened along behind him.

Felicity had been left alone with Harold, Elizabeth, and *The Crab Pot Menders*. In light of the discussions just witnessed, the atmosphere was tense.

The art dealer smiled awkwardly. "We were wondering whether to have an exhibition in Ottermouth at all, you know. It's such an out of the way place. But the talent here is undeniable."

Felicity nodded. She didn't have her notebook with her, Isabella having sworn her off pursuing any 'boring newspaper topics' for the evening. The purpose of the soirée was to help relax the artists and — above all — the art collectors, getting everyone in the right frame of mind for the exhibition's opening the next day. Which would presumably hopefully result in multiple sales.

Even without her notebook, Felicity could enrich her understanding of the situation. "This might be an incredibly ignorant thing to ask, Mr Prothero, but how does the exhibition work?"

The portly man's eyebrows furrowed. "I'm not sure I follow, your ladyship."

"It's free for anyone to enter the gallery," said Elizabeth forthrightly. "Anyone can come in and look at the art. It's only fair. Otherwise, the local people would probably never get to see the paintings they're featured in."

"I see," said Felicity. "But the emphasis is on selling the artworks, is it not? And you're the seller, Mr Prothero?"

"Ah. Well." Harold blinked. "I'm the exhibition's organiser. When a work of art is sold—"

Elizabeth turned and glided away, heading towards the

terrace. Did she not want to hear about her father's work, or had something else caught her attention?

Harold paused only briefly to watch his daughter. "When a work of art is sold," he continued, returning his attention to Felicity, "I earn a commission. Most of the selling price goes to the owner. That might be a collector or the artist himself."

Felicity nodded. It was as she thought. "Are you also a collector, Mr Prothero?"

Harold sighed. "Believe it or not, your ladyship, I was once an artist. A ceramicist, in fact. Unfortunately, not a very successful one. When my wife sadly passed, I had to find myself a more stable source of income. Lizzie was still only an infant, and a good nursery nurse does not come cheaply." He smiled with a hint of melancholy, his gaze towards the terrace. "Thankfully, I was much better as a gallerist than as an artist. Although I've done nothing like this before. Never put on an exhibition outside of London, in fact. Mrs Mountvernon convinced me, of course. As is her way."

Out on the terrace, Isabella was telling an engaging story, gesturing wildly with her arms while people around her laughed.

Felicity smiled. "Mrs Mountvernon is a very charming woman."

Harold nodded. "She is. The exhibition's been a year or more in the making, but I must say, I'm quite satisfied with the result."

Felicity searched the terrace for Elizabeth's silhouette but couldn't locate her. "Your daughter's a rather intriguing presence as well."

Harold blinked. "That's kind of you to say so, your ladyship. She's a highly intelligent girl. A little strong-willed, perhaps. She's a calligraphist, you know."

"An artist?" Felicity couldn't hide the surprise in her voice. Somehow, the stiff-backed girl seemed not to be the type.

"Not quite," said Harold with a smile that showed he was proud of his daughter. "Lizzie specialises in ancient manuscripts.

Been accepted for an apprenticeship in Rome starting this summer."

"Congratulations," said Felicity, "to both you and your daughter." She raised her glass of tonic water. "To the success of your endeavours."

The art dealer waved a dismissive hand, despite clearly valuing the encouragement.

Having been on her best behaviour the whole evening, Felicity indulged herself. "Seeing a customs officer stride into the gallery earlier today left me with a number of questions," she began. "Might you be able to satisfy my curiosity, Mr Prothero?" Even if it had nothing to do with reporting on the exhibition, Felicity couldn't resist tugging on such a compelling thread.

The art dealer's mouth gaped for a moment. Then his eyes flew to the terrace. "Lizzie is an earnest, principled young woman. It's understandable she wants to, err… But there's a certain… How can I say it?" Harold took off his pince-nez and returned it to his jacket pocket. "Do bear with me one moment, your ladyship." He scurried towards the terrace.

Having craved solitude, Felicity was now disappointed to have been left alone before the big painting. She sipped her tonic as she waited for the art dealer to return, as he'd left her with the impression he would do so, but Harold was ambushed by Isabella and pulled into an animated discussion between artists and collectors out on the terrace.

Felicity waited some more. Harold didn't once look back at her. Had he deliberately abandoned Felicity? While she didn't take offence, it was rather odd behaviour.

"May I refresh your drink, your ladyship?"

Isabella's butler had approached, proffering a tray of different libations, from wines to spirits. The dim chime of a grandfather clock in the hall could be heard tolling some unthinkable hour.

"No, thank you, Mr Chivers. Would you be kind enough to give Mrs Mountvernon a message from me?"

A roar of laughter went up from the terrace.

"Certainly, your ladyship."

"Please tell her I've retired to bed, and that I'll make an early start in the morning. I should like to be at the gallery well ahead of the opening."

The butler nodded. "I shall let Mrs Mountvernon know, your ladyship."

When Felicity arrived in her allotted guest room, she found two shaggy dogs, one large and one small, asleep on the wide bed. There was only mild protest in the form of whimpering from Beetle and a brief pause in Pip's snoring as she slid between the sheets, but Felicity couldn't sleep straight away.

The package Elizabeth had found, the customs officer's interest in it, and Harold's evasive reaction had heightened her curiosity. Further gentle digging into the matter would keep Felicity's mind stimulated while reporting on the art exhibition. It might give her something more interesting than oil paints and sea scenes to discuss with Alex whenever she saw him next. Or it might not amount to anything at all.

Either way, there was a mystery for Felicity to investigate.

Chapter Five

Ashdene was deadly quiet when Felicity woke, the milky sunshine creeping around the edges of the thick curtains. Beetle was gone, perhaps to join his mistress on her bed. Pip was eager both for breakfast — a sausage for him, scrambled eggs with toast washed down with Ceylon for Felicity — and to go outside. The little Yorkie went tearing off along the coastal path before Felicity closed the gate at the bottom of the house's gardens.

The breeze coming off the sea was gentle but cool. Though the haze on the horizon would no doubt burn off later, it gave the coast an ethereal atmosphere, the promontories further along the coast shrouded in a light mist, the sun a silver ball hanging in a pale grey sky. Felicity felt the morning's chill through her royal-blue wool skirt and jacket, a musketeer hat in a matching shade pulled firmly over her curls. Her lace-up shoes allowing for easy purchase on the stony path, Felicity moved quickly in pursuit of Pip and soon warmed up.

The crunch of her footsteps, the maudlin cry of gulls high overhead, and the gentle hiss of the sea breaking against the rocks below were the only sounds. It was a welcome contrast to the clamour of the soirée the night before. It also boded well for

Felicity's plan to get to the exhibition ahead of anyone else. She was committed to taking her work seriously and keen to write up the works of art on show without being distracted or interrupted. Only then would she allow herself to probe the matter of Elizabeth's package, like a reward for good behaviour.

The path between Ashdene and Ottermouth wriggled along the coast like a snake. As the track dipped steeply, then wound sharply inwards to navigate a small cove, Felicity peered down at the rocks below. The tide was receding, the water swishing over millions of tiny pebbles that made up the foreshore of a shallow beach. The cove was cast in shadow and edged with large rocks that had, at some point, tumbled down the steep granite cliff face.

Felicity stopped on the path above the cove. Further ahead, Pip halted also, lifting a paw, his nose twitching in Felicity's direction.

Below, on the beach, something lay nestled against the rocks. Although dark like the surrounding stone, the item had an entirely different texture to it. Was it a bundle of old rags? Or a package?

Felicity's heartbeat quickened. She hadn't had to go digging. The matter had come to her. Alex had said it more than once. Felicity was a magnet for newspaper scoops.

She retraced her steps to where the path forked and followed a narrow track leading down to the shadowy beach. Pip came barrelling back along the path and went shooting past, flying down the track to the cove.

"Pip, please. Be careful," Felicity implored, for the track wound backwards and forwards in hairpin fashion along an extremely sheer rock face covered in gnarly shrubs and hardy grasses. The Yorkie, however, was not to be deterred.

Long before Felicity made it down the winding track, Pip was on the beach. With his nose to the ground, it took him mere moments to become attracted to the bundle beside the rocks. At last, with both feet on the shingle, Felicity crunched across the beach towards where Pip was sniffing. The sound of the sea was no longer a hiss as it had been from the top of the cliff. Waves roared as the surface of the sea churned silvery blue, the milky haze still clinging to the horizon.

"Pip, what have you found?" Felicity approached, willing to give her eager canine companion credit for his enthusiasm. The Yorkie's tail wagged in response, but he didn't lift his nose from the bundle.

Contrary to the impression from the clifftop, the bundle was rather large and not something one could easily describe as a package. As Felicity drew closer, she saw that the fabric she had assumed to be a ragged wrapping of some kind was in fact clothing. A wet jacket. Wet trousers. A hand.

Felicity gasped.

"Pip," she said warningly, instinct telling her they ought to withdraw, for this was surely something ghastly. But Pip didn't heed the warning, and a voice within Felicity insisted she must advance, insisted she must know.

Gingerly approaching, the tide still roaring, the crunch of her Oxfords on the gravel slowing, Felicity brought a hand up to her jacket collar as she leaned over the bundle. It was a man, his face half pressed into the pebbles, his pallor and blank expression denoting he was no longer among the living.

It was a terrible sight, but most shocking of all was that Felicity recognised him.

The man lying dead on the beach was Martin Granger.

Chapter Six

The morning flew by in a flurry of activity.

The cove was nearer Ottermouth than Ashdene, so Felicity hurried from the beach to the village and found the policeman's cottage, running nearly as fast as Pip.

Grey-moustached Constable Thompson was thankfully a good deal more moved by the news of a body on the foreshore than he had been by a potential knifing in the public house the day before. He hastily pulled on his helmet and dashed off before Felicity could say much beyond her description of where the deceased man lay.

Returning to Ashdene seemed the next logical step. As shaken as Felicity was, Martin's passing on the eve of the exhibition had to be reported in the Western Daily News. Ahead of the write-up, however, Felicity had a duty to share the news with her hostess.

Isabella was in her room and not to be disturbed

"Mrs Mountvernon heard the awful news already, your ladyship," explained the housekeeper, Mrs Rawling. "Mr Davies saw Constable Thompson on his morning walk. Mr Davies promptly informed Mr Prothero, who then telephoned to Mrs Mountvernon."

Felicity couldn't quite fathom how it all occurred before she'd returned to Ashdene, though local information could spread quickly when necessary.

"The exhibition's opening has been cancelled, of course," continued the housekeeper. "Although, that's not the only reason the mistress is so upset, of course."

It was a small comfort to not have to inform Isabella of Martin's passing, but Isabella wasn't the only person who needed to hear the news.

As Felicity sat down at the telephone table under the stairs in Ashdene's entrance hall, her first instinct was to ring up Alex. He would have listened to all the details, offered thoughtful advice, and perhaps even lightened Felicity's mood with a clever remark or two. After all, it wasn't every morning one came across a lifeless form, and Felicity still felt rather shaken. It was, however, Felicity's brother who had to be informed first.

Jasper was in London for high-level discussions with important advertisers. Though unsaid, the extra worry Martin's passing brought was a burden Jasper didn't need. After ensuring Felicity was herself unhurt, Jasper cautiously verified, like the protective yet respectful brother he was, that Felicity wouldn't get too involved in any investigation beyond reporting for the paper.

"I shall focus on my work as a journalist," said Felicity, and she meant it. She'd come to Ottermouth to do just that.

There was a long silence on the line, which crackled slightly.

"I promised Tommy I'd look after Bella whenever needed." Jasper's voice was taut with frustration. "I'm wondering if I shouldn't drop everything and race down there."

Felicity disliked the idea of her brother being saddled with additional concerns. She also didn't particularly want him providing in-person supervision of her duties in Ottermouth. "I shall do everything I can to ensure Isabella is all right."

"You'd do that for me, Cici?" Jasper's voice was hopeful. "Won't it be a terrible distraction from your reporting?"

"I shall manage," asserted Felicity confidently.

Releasing a slow exhale as she hung up the receiver, Felicity remained at the telephone table to write a stop-press style announcement of Martin Granger's passing, which she telephoned into the news desk for the next edition, promising the editor with whom she spoke more to come. Though a slew of locals needed interviewing as soon as possible, Felicity's hand itched to once again pick up the receiver.

As she wavered, a painting on the wall of the hall seized her attention. It was of a girl alone on the beach, her hair dancing in the wind, her gaze cast over her shoulder at the viewer.

Bang! Bang! Bang!

Pip and Beetle bounded into the entrance hall, barking at the visitor who had ignored the prominent doorbell in favour of bashing on the door. Mrs Rawling, who adored dogs and happily kept watch over both Pip and Beetle, corralled the hounds away.

The butler, Mr Chivers, opened the door.

The uniformed customs officer barged inside. "Officer Roger Marshall of His Majesty's Customs and Excise," he boomed by way of introduction, the brass buttons shining on his dark blue jacket. "I'm here to speak to Lady Felicity Quick—" he landed an intense stare on Felicity, who was still seated at the telephone table "—and to Mrs Isabella Mountvernon."

Mr Chivers' measured voice was almost a whisper in comparison. "Mrs Mountvernon is currently indisposed, Officer Marshall. And Lady Felicity…" The butler trailed off, turning towards Felicity for her reaction.

Felicity stood up from the telephone table. "How can I help you, Officer Marshall?" It was expected the authorities would want to interview Felicity, seeing as she'd found the body. Official quotes were also essential for her reporting. Was Martin's passing regarded as accidental or suspicious? The distinction made all the difference.

The butler led Felicity and the customs officer to a small study with a mahogany desk, leather-cushioned chairs, and a view onto a bright green lawn. A collection of watercolours depicting bucolic scenes decorated the walls. Various ceramic creations lined the window sill.

Felicity settled into a chair.

The Customs and Excise man remained standing, his arms folded over his powerful chest. "Found him then, did you?" His manner was clipped and informal.

Felicity nodded. She swallowed. "Not the most pleasant of things one could come across on a beach."

"Just the fellow, was it? Nothing else?"

Felicity shook her head slowly. "Not that I could see."

"How was it you came to be on the beach?" The customs officer's tone was mildly accusatory.

Felicity was unfazed. She had nothing to hide. "I was on my way into Ottermouth to report on the exhibition. I saw something on the shore." As she spoke, Felicity fished her notebook from her skirt pocket. "I thought it might be a package."

Officer Marshall's eyebrows shot up. "Did you now?"

Felicity pressed the top of her mechanical pencil. "Tell me, Officer Marshall. What's known so far about Mr Granger's passing? Was it likely an accident? Or is there more to it than that?"

"Writing this all up for your brother's paper, are you, your ladyship?" A little smile danced on the customs man's lips, as though he found the idea amusing.

The door to the study flew open. Isabella swept in wearing a floor-length turquoise kimono covered in red and gold motifs. Her eyes were raw and pink, and she'd only made a partial attempt to tie back her flowing, dark brown hair.

"Officer Marshall." She spoke bluntly, coming to a stop with her hands on her hips. "First, I'll not have you harassing my guest."

Felicity was actually keen to speak to the customs officer, but to disagree openly with her hostess was not the done thing.

"Second," continued Isabella, "I can't think why in the world you'd want to speak to me about any of this. Marty was an extremely dear friend, and we're all devastated. Can't we be allowed to grieve in peace?"

Officer Marshall turned a narrow-eyed gaze on Isabella. "Mr Granger left Ashdene at what time last night, Mrs Mountvernon?"

Isabella blinked defiantly, her hands still on her hips. "When I organise a party, I don't keep tabs on my guests, Officer Marshall. I encourage a spirit of relaxation and trust."

"You have a boat here in the harbour, do you not? Did anyone go out in it last night?"

Isabella sighed hard. "I'm sorry. What kind of questions are these?"

The customs officer was silent for a moment. "A man is dead, Mrs Mountvernon."

Isabella hugged herself. "But it was just a horrible accident, wasn't it?"

Officer Marshall folded his arms and raised an eyebrow. "There'll be an autopsy. I'll make sure of that. And there's not yet been an inquest."

"What I mean," continued Isabella, "is that I've barely had time to come to terms with the fact I'll never see Marty again, let alone the impact this will have on the whole art movement here." Isabella began pacing. "And I've invested so much… So much of my…"

"Could you not procure information about people's movements last night from the staff here at Ashdene, Officer Marshall?" enquired Felicity. Isabella's current distress was exactly what Jasper would have wanted her shielded from.

The customs officer huffed. "How about I not tell you how to do your job, your ladyship, and you not tell me how to do mine?"

Felicity pulled back her chin. "And may I ask what your job here is, exactly?"

Isabella ceased her pacing and looked with surprise at Felicity. One had to, on occasion, give a person a taste of their own medicine.

Felicity continued. "The local constabulary have a police officer present here in the village. Why are Customs and Excise so interested in Mr Granger's demise?"

Officer Marshall looked vaguely amused. "I can't say too much, your ladyship. Not yet. Discretion is a cornerstone of my work."

Felicity suppressed a disbelieving frown. Was there anyone in the county less discreet than Officer Marshall?

"Although I'd wager that for a woman," continued the customs officer, "you're rather intelligent. I imagine you'll be able to work things out for yourself in due course."

Felicity had already been feeling rather riled by Officer Marshall. But 'for a woman' was absolutely one of her least favourite phrases to hear, especially from a man. It was just as well the door to the study opened before Felicity could respond.

"Constable Thompson, ma'am," announced Isabella's butler, having no choice but to step aside as the grey-moustached policeman ploughed into the room.

"Officer Marshall." Constable Thompson had his helmet under his arm and his chest puffed out. Though shorter than both the customs officer and Isabella, his voice boomed with bluster. "We agreed Mr Granger's death was a matter for the local constabulary and nothing of concern for His Majesty's Customs and Excise, did we not?"

The customs officer frowned. Then smiled. "Did we?"

Isabella's eyes widened. "So I'm free to go?"

The policeman nodded. "Of course you are, Mrs Mountvernon. And may I apologise for the confusion that led to Officer Marshall accosting you in your own home?"

Officer Marshall sneered. "You're the one that's confused, old chap."

"Let's go, Cici." Isabella took Felicity's hand to leave. Felicity rose to her feet but hesitated, curious to see how tensions between the Devon County Constabulary and Customs and Excise might play out.

"Not so fast, Mrs Mountvernon." Officer Marshall stepped forward to block the study door. "I've not finished with you yet."

"Oh, but you have, Officer Marshall," boomed Constable Thompson, pulling the truncheon from his belt and pressing the tip into the customs man's middle. "You've finished your whole business in Ottermouth. Matters here are to be handled by me and the constabulary alone."

Officer Marshall held up his hands in mock surrender. He laughed as he glanced down at Constable Thompson's truncheon. "Are you threatening me?"

Isabella spoke up. "This is my home, Officer Marshall, and you've outstayed your welcome."

Without further protest, Officer Marshall obeyed the dismissal. In departing the study, he gave Felicity a glare that made her skin prickle. Still, she hoped to see him again. A package washing up on the beach was one thing. A body was quite another. Did Officer Marshall suspect a link?

With the customs man gone, Isabella's shoulders fell with relief. "Thank you, Constable."

The policeman reattached his truncheon to his belt. "No, Mrs Mountvernon. I'm the one who's grateful to you, for emphasising how that unpleasant gentleman isn't welcome around these parts."

Isabella sighed deeply. "I feel quite exhausted suddenly."

Felicity put a hand gently on Isabella's arm. "You should probably sit down and settle your nerves."

"Will you take tea with me in the morning room?" Isabella's warm brown eyes sparkled with hope.

Felicity smiled apologetically. "I'm afraid I've interviews to carry out for the paper."

"Of course, Cici. Of course." Isabella nodded but looked dejected.

The policeman cleared his throat. "Before you go off, your ladyship, might I have a word?"

Felicity could refuse Isabella, but she couldn't refuse Constable Thompson. "Naturally," she said.

The butler was summoned to escort Isabella to the morning room, leaving Felicity alone in the study with the policeman. To take advantage of being the first journalist in Ottermouth covering the Martin Granger story, Felicity had to work fast. An audience with the village policeman aligned with this goal.

"You have my full attention, Constable," said Felicity, as they took their seats on either side of the shining desk. "And after I've answered your questions, you'd perhaps be kind enough to answer mine."

The policeman eyed her from across the mahogany desktop. "When you write this business up for your paper, you can say it was an accident."

Felicity blinked. The discussion had veered in an unexpected direction. "Do you not need a statement from me?"

Constable Thompson frowned. "Mr Granger's death was an accident, your ladyship. He fell. From the cliff path. There's no need to go digging into things. It's a tragedy, of course, especially considering all the young lads we lost in the war. But it was an accident."

No journalist worth his or her salt had ever taken a warning against investigating at face value.

Felicity's back straightened. "How do we know it was an accident? There's not been an inquest yet."

The policeman huffed. "Now hold on just a moment. Who said there'll be an inquest?"

"Officer Marshall said he'd demand an autopsy."

The policeman's cheeks reddened. "Officer Marshall holds no authority here, your ladyship."

"Constable Thompson." Despite the policeman's obvious irritation, Felicity's voice was steady. "Mr Granger was a well-known artist. His father was a famous painter. Even if I respect your invitation to report on the incident as though an inquest had already reached its verdict, I won't be the only journalist to come to Ottermouth, and not all publications are as diligent as the Western Daily News. Some even thrive on scandal."

The policeman glared at Felicity from across the desk. "That may be so, your ladyship. But not all reporters have trouble that follows them like you do."

Felicity stiffened. The accusation was harsh and unexpected, but ought she have been surprised? Her reputation had preceded her in the past.

Quickly regaining her composure, Felicity's tone became stern. "Are you insinuating, Constable, that I'm in some way responsible for Mr Granger's untimely passing?"

The policeman shifted in his chair. "You misunderstand me, your ladyship." His frustration was growing. "I only meant—"

The door to the study flew open. Isabella once again swept into the room, her kimono fluttering behind her. Her eyes were puffed, her cheeks wet with tears. She went to Felicity and knelt at her side.

"I can't give up on things. I simply can't." Isabella's voice cracked with grief. "Talk to the artists. Talk to the collectors. Tell their story. Keep the passion alive. Please, Cici. With the exhibition cancelled, you're Ottermouth's only hope."

Felicity put a gentle hand on Isabella's. "Come now. You need rest." She wasn't quite sure how to soothe Isabella, but Felicity had promised her brother she'd do what she could.

"You'll help us, won't you, Cici?" Isabella sniffed. "So much hard work can't suddenly count for nothing, can it?"

The policeman looked warningly at Felicity, his jaw tight.

Felicity patted Isabella's hand. "I shall do my best." Her next move would have to be calculated carefully indeed.

Chapter Seven

The policeman having returned to his duties in the village, and Isabella having been escorted by Mrs Rawling back to bed, Felicity enquired of the butler if he had witnessed Martin leaving the soirée the night before.

"Mr Granger departed towards the end of the evening, your ladyship," confirmed Mr Chivers. "He seemed in good spirits, although not overly merry, if you catch my meaning. He was in the company of the Honourable Miss Audrey Lawson, with whom he'd also arrived."

Audrey Lawson was certainly someone to whom Felicity needed to speak.

"Have the authorities asked for the servants' accounts of the guests' movements?" she asked.

"Not yet, your ladyship. I expect we'll hear again from Constable Thompson in due course."

As Felicity set off at a brisk pace along the cliff path towards Ottermouth, she wondered whether Mr Chivers would, in fact, be interviewed. With the Customs and Excise officer banished, who would challenge the position of the local police that Martin's passing was an accident?

Without slowing her stride, Felicity peered down from the

clifftop, the sea breeze ruffling her curls under the brim of her musketeer hat. The beach where Felicity had found the artist's lifeless form had already been cleared. While the path was a safe distance from the edge, the drop was deadly. It would also have been dark when Martin left Ashdene.

In the context of building Ottermouth's reputation as an artists' haven, an accident was the preferred outcome, was it not?

Approaching the village, the spring sunshine having burnt off the morning's haze, Felicity followed a fork in the track that led away from the village's centre and into the hillside woods. Nestled beneath mature trees in a higgledy-piggledy fashion was an array of cottages. Unlike the neat rows of well-kept fishermen's dwellings beside Ottermouth's harbour, these cottages had a more relaxed appearance. Some might even be described as crumbling. Colourful mosaics, whimsical sculptures, and painted plant pots distracted from the disrepair and created an informal, fanciful atmosphere. The smell of joss sticks wafted on the breeze as the sunshine filtered through the trees, lighting clumps of yolk-yellow primroses.

Martin Granger's recently built arts-and-crafts-style villa was easy to find. Mr Chivers had given Felicity reliable directions. Although not as grand as Ashdene, the house was much larger than the neighbouring cottages, occupying a purposeful clearing in the woods and surrounded by topiary hedges. A sign on the gate read *Halcyon Cottage*, but it was a cottage in name only, for no one would describe the luxurious building as such.

Felicity advanced along the neat brick path and, using a heavy brass knocker, rapped gently on the arch-topped front door. It was here that she hoped to find Audrey Lawson. Audrey could surely confirm whether Martin had gone over the cliff's edge.

Having waited a while, Felicity knocked again. A gust of wind hissed through a nearby stand of trees. Could she hear someone sobbing?

"Audrey's awfully upset. She won't speak to anyone."

Felicity turned. Standing beyond the white wooden gate at the end of the brick path was the man in faded, paint-flecked workwear who had barged into the Dolphin the day before. He wore an oversized navy-blue jumper that was frayed at the neck. He was perhaps slightly older than Felicity but not over twenty-five.

Felicity stepped down from the villa's porch. "Mr Lawrence Whitburn, isn't it?"

Lawrence gave a curt nod, his hands in his pockets. "I know who you are, too, your ladyship." His tone carried a hint of mockery. "He shan't be missed, you know."

Felicity raised her eyebrows. Having barely seen Lawrence and Martin interact, the tension between them had been unmistakable, and here was further proof.

Felicity's notebook remained in her pocket, however. The newspapers' readers wanted facts about Martin's death and opinion that sat well with their sensibilities, which aligned with the adage that one should never speak ill of the dead. Unless the dead had done something despicable, which was not yet proven in Martin's case.

"And I don't mind if Audrey hears me." Lawrence raised his voice for this pronouncement. "She knows it as well. She was with the blighter for one thing only. If she's crying, it's because she feels sorry for herself."

Felicity moved quickly along the path towards Lawrence in the hope he would lower his voice. The shock of death affected people differently, but Lawrence's behaviour was uncalled for. "Might you know anything about Mr Granger's movements last night, Mr Whitburn?"

Lawrence scrunched his brow. "I wasn't at Isabella's event. Surely, you knew that already."

Like everyone else at the soirée, Felicity had noticed Lawrence's absence, but she wouldn't give him the satisfaction. "Do you live nearby?"

Lawrence glanced over his shoulder. "My cottage is just over there."

"Did you happen to see if Mr Granger returned home yesterday evening?" If she could, Felicity would build a picture of Martin's last known movements.

The artist frowned. "When I paint, I do so with my full concentration. Nothing exists but the canvas. I was painting yesterday evening."

"Your artworks are quite in demand, as I understand it."

Lawrence smirked. "I don't paint for other people." Despite his fresh, handsome features, there was a sombre seriousness about him. "Art isn't about money. It's about creation, not consumption."

It wasn't the moment to get drawn into politics. "You've made it quite clear you weren't keen on Mr Granger. May I ask why?"

The wind hissed through the trees as Lawrence regarded Felicity warily. "If I told you he was jealous of me, I don't suppose you'd believe me."

The artist standing before her didn't strike Felicity as the most reliable of witnesses, yet this was a statement she could believe. She'd seen Lawrence's paintings, heard the fuss made about them at the gallery, the discussion about him at the soirée, and Martin's reaction. "You didn't like the man because he was jealous of you? Could you not consider it flattery?"

Lawrence's expression darkened further. "He was no good for this village."

Felicity cocked an eyebrow. "His father founded the artists' community here, did he not? Would you yourself be there had he not done so?"

The remark seemed to irk Lawrence. He stiffened, his eyes darting away. Felicity turned.

A familiar yet unexpected figure was approaching through the trees.

———

Elizabeth Prothero stopped on the forest path, her eyes wide. She had a wicker basket over her arm, a green-and-white checked cloth covering whatever lay within. She wore a long, featureless grey dress. It gave her the aura of a nun.

An almighty gust of wind shook the boughs above.

"Good afternoon, Miss Prothero," said Felicity, raising her voice above the sound of the wind. "Surely you and Mr Whitburn are already acquainted?" She turned towards Lawrence, expecting him to greet Elizabeth. Instead, she saw only his back retreating down the track that led towards the artists' cottages.

"Lady Felicity, good afternoon to you." The spell on Elizabeth had broken. She was now moving purposefully towards Felicity.

Felicity continued to watch Lawrence's retreat. He disappeared from sight, and a cottage door was heard to slam. Had Felicity irked him that much? "What an unusual man," remarked Felicity, more to herself than to Elizabeth.

"Oh," said Elizabeth with a little wave of her hand, coming to a stop at Felicity's side. "These artists."

It was a change in tone compared to the defending of Lawrence Elizabeth had so far done. "You're something of a creator yourself, I understand?"

The girl looked mildly offended. "Calligraphy is a craft, your ladyship. I specialise in the copying of ancient manuscripts. It's the continuation of a tradition. I don't create works of art."

"My apologies." Felicity wondered if she'd ever make sense of the artistic realm. "I meant no offence. How is your father? I heard the exhibition's been cancelled. Was he close to Mr Granger?" Felicity reached into her skirt pocket for her notebook. "Did you know Mr Granger well yourself, Miss Prothero?"

Elizabeth glanced around, repositioning her basket in the crook of her elbow. "Walk with me, would you, your ladyship?" She had a seriousness about her that matched her sober clothing.

"Very well." Felicity was happy to comply if it meant they could talk further.

The two women fell into step, passing the neat topiary creations at the boundary of Martin Granger's property and pressing further into the woods.

After walking in silence, Felicity tried another tack. "I'm gathering reactions for the newspaper. Might I enquire what effect Mr Granger's passing has had on you and your father?" Surely, this manner of enquiry aligned with Isabella asking Felicity to keep the emphasis on Ottermouth's artistic community.

"Father's devastated, of course." Elizabeth spoke distractedly as she scanned the area and came to a stop next to the gnarled trunk of an ancient oak.

Felicity glanced down at a length of bramble caught on her skirt. Elizabeth had led them off the path. "And what are your feelings on the matter, Miss Prothero?"

Seemingly satisfied she and Felicity were alone, Elizabeth lowered her voice to a whisper. "Listen. There's something going on in this village."

Felicity blinked. "I've been told Mr Granger's death was an accident. Do you not believe that was the case?"

Elizabeth gripped the handle of her basket. "Father says I shouldn't meddle, but one cannot turn a blind eye to something one knows isn't right. And now a man is dead."

Felicity drew down her brow. "What is it you're telling me?" But she'd guessed the answer before she'd even asked the question.

"Smuggling is what I'm talking about, your ladyship." Elizabeth fixed Felicity with wide, anxious eyes. "There's smuggling here in Ottermouth."

Chapter Eight

A cold spike of unease ran through Felicity. Of course, she'd hoped for something more interesting than art to report upon in Ottermouth. A body on the beach, the trafficking of contraband, and a potential link between the two was perhaps a tad too much.

Felicity matched Elizabeth's whispered tone. "What do you know?" She left her notebook in her skirt pocket for the young woman was sharing the information in confidence. "The package you found. Has that something to do with it?"

Elizabeth's slender fingers tightened further on the basket handle, her knuckles whitening. "I gave the package to the customs officer without opening it. Father said I oughtn't even to have touched it, but I know it's not correct. Nothing about it is." She swallowed. "You'll do something about it, won't you?"

Felicity recognised the desire to set things right. She also knew the limitations under which she operated. "I'm a journalist, Miss Prothero. My original purpose in Ottermouth was to report on your father's exhibition. My scope has now expanded to cover the passing of Mr Granger. I collect the facts and write them up. Nothing more."

Elizabeth's youthful brow was deeply wrinkled. She looked desperate.

Felicity felt pity for her. Pity and a great deal of curiosity. "Is it your belief Mr Granger's demise is linked to smuggling?"

Elizabeth sighed shakily. "I can't say for sure. I didn't know the fellow well, and I've no proof of anything. That's the whole bother of it. No one will talk, especially not to an outsider like me."

Felicity remembered the uneasy hush that had greeted her in the Dolphin. Constable Thompson's attitude also gave her pause. "Do you imagine people will be more willing to speak to me? I arrived in Ottermouth only the day before yesterday."

Elizabeth gazed squarely at Felicity. "You're a professional reporter, aren't you? And you've been involved in tricky situations before. You'll do a far better job of investigating than I ever could."

Felicity pressed her lips together. She was extremely serious about her work as a journalist, and Martin's passing had to be reported upon. The reputation of Ottermouth's art scene might also be salvaged as far as possible. Where did a probe into smuggling fit into Felicity's duties? The washed-up package found by Elizabeth and the mere presence of Officer Marshall in the village were strong clues. Indeed, ahead of the grim discovery made at the cove, Felicity had given herself permission to dig into these matters.

But was there not also a case for leaving such things alone?

Felicity had never reported upon organised crime before. Networks of such people could be dangerous, and so far, nothing solid linked Martin to any such activities.

A stiff breeze fluttered the corner of the cloth covering Elizabeth's basket. Bread and a pair of apples were revealed. Hastily, the girl tucked the cloth back into the basket.

"Were you on your way to pay a visit, Miss Prothero?"

Elizabeth parted her lips but hesitated.

"The going around here's rather rough, isn't it?"

The interruption came from further up the wooded hillside. A tall, thin man in a trilby hat with a notebook in his hand was fighting his way through the undergrowth.

Felicity recognised him. He was a journalist from one of the big London newspapers. The Empire Examiner, if Felicity wasn't mistaken.

Elizabeth closed her mouth and pulled her basket close.

The man came to a stop, plucking a twig from the lapel of his overcoat. "Had to leave the motor at the top of the hill. Not sure the brakes were up for the descent. Ottermouth's this way, isn't it?"

Felicity nodded. The man hadn't recognised her as a fellow journalist, but she didn't let it get to her. For some men, women would always be practically invisible. "Are you here to report on the passing of Mr Martin Granger?"

"Indeed. Made a beeline over from the Tamar Bank case in Plymouth."

Felicity's heart skipped at the mention. It was the case Alex had been reporting on. "Has the Tamar Bank trial finished?"

"Indeed, it has. Bank manager sentenced to seven years."

Felicity was resolute. She would put a call through to Alex that evening. They had so much upon which to catch up.

"Unlucky to have been in the area," continued the reporter, removing his hat and shaking off a few leaves. "Or lucky, as my editor would have it. Was due to go back up to London today."

"Excuse me, your ladyship." Elizabeth took the interruption as a chance to scurry away. She rejoined the path that wove between the artists' cottages and returned along the same route via which she'd arrived.

"This way to the village, did you say?" The reporter pointed down the hill.

Martin Granger's passing was going to be big news, and to keep the advantage for the Western Morning News, Felicity had to work quickly. Further questions to Elizabeth Prothero would have to wait, but Felicity wasn't out of options. Far from it.

Chapter Nine

A salt-scented breeze blew in from the glittering sea as Felicity sped towards Ottermouth's harbour. With his long legs, the reporter from London had moved faster and was now interviewing Harold Prothero and his assistant in front of the old boat shed's firmly closed doors. Felicity also wished to speak to Harold, but all was not lost. There were other people to interview.

Outside the blue-and-white cottages beside the harbour, women wearing sturdy aprons over dull-coloured dresses continued repair work on a vast expanse of fishing net. Even children were involved in the activity. A girl of around sixteen, with thick reddish-brown hair and sea-green eyes, glanced up at Felicity. Quickly, she returned her gaze to her needlework, as though ashamed of her own curiosity.

Readying her notebook, Felicity approached the net-menders and introduced herself. "Might any of you be willing to speak to the Western Daily News about the unfortunate discovery at the cove earlier this morning?" Felicity asked, looking at the women.

There were two angles to explore. First was the danger posed by the cliffs and sea. How likely was Martin's passing to have been an accident? Second was the question of Martin's relationship with the local fishing community, in which he'd apparently been well-embedded. Would there be a quote or two expressing how much he'd be missed?

The only person to look up was a woman of around fifty with weathered skin and thick wavy grey hair pulled into a bun. Her eyes were the same sea-green as those of the girl who'd looked up at Felicity. The woman tipped her head towards the harbour arm. "Go to the Maggie. Ask for Captain Dunn."

Felicity held the brim of her hat as she turned into the breeze. The large wooden trawler was moored alongside the sturdy sea wall that separated the harbour from the Channel. Though her deep-red sails were furled around her booms, the trawler's deck was alive with activity. On the ship's stern, in large white lettering, the words *MAGGIE — OTTERMOUTH* had been painted.

"Thank you," said Felicity, but the woman had already turned her attention back to the net on her aproned lap.

As she navigated coils of rope, ships' fenders, and other sailing-related debris along the harbour arm, Felicity was overtaken by a small wooden boat on the water below. It weaved between the moored vessels under the confident stroke of oars held by a man in overalls and a faded cap. He was perhaps sixty and had a long, silver-grey beard. Aboard the little boat were sacks of glistening, dark-green seaweed. Felicity knew from her grandmother that seaweed did wonders in the garden. What other uses might it have?

The Maggie's gang plank bobbed slightly with the gentle movement of the tide. Felicity recognised several of the men on deck from the Dolphin Inn, although the sandy-haired knife-wielder was thankfully absent. The lubricating of winches, the caulking of plank seams, and the splicing of ropes were among the activities the men aboard the trawler were engaged in. Odours of tar, oil, and fish filled the air. It was a heady mix.

"Good day," called out Felicity from the harbour wall, her notebook in her hand. "Might I speak with Captain Dunn?"

A man with a deeply lined face and white stubble looked up

from where he sat atop a cleat sharpening a shining fish hook. Felicity recognised him as having tried to calm the situation at the inn. He wore a faded peaked cap that perhaps once was black, a thick navy-blue cable-knit jumper, and an expression that said he preferred not to be disturbed.

On the other side of the harbour, the journalist from London was striding towards Constable Thompson's cottage.

"I'm Lady Felicity Quick, a reporter for the Western Daily News." She spoke rapidly and gave the fisherman no chance to speak. She wanted to at least present herself before being turned away. "You're Captain Dunn, if I'm not mistaken?"

The man nodded almost imperceptibly. He narrowed his eyes.

Felicity continued, undeterred. "In light of the very recent and tragic passing of a local man, might I speak to you or a member of your crew?"

The lines on the captain's face deepened. "No time for that," he growled and went back to sharpening the fishing hook.

A snigger came from behind Felicity.

Sitting on an upturned wooden crate was the dark-haired young man who'd had the knife pressed under his chin during the altercation at the inn. His fashionably garish sleeveless jumper, crisp white shirt, and roomy plus-fours looked out of place among the limpet-encrusted fishing tackle stacked around him. He held a cigarette loosely in one hand, his other hand tucked tightly under his arm.

"I'd wager no one aboard the Maggie has ever read a newspaper," he said with an exhale of smoke.

Captain Dunn threw an ice-cold stare in the young man's direction. Felicity didn't much appreciate his tone either. He was at least talking to her, however.

Felicity introduced herself. "And you are?"

"William Seddon." The young man smiled slyly. He made no effort to stand. "But you can call me Billy."

"Are you a sea-goer yourself, Mr Seddon?" Felicity was keen to keep matters formal. "Might you be interested in commenting on the issue of safety at sea for the Western Daily News?"

Billy's smile lingered on his lips, his brilliantined hair gleaming in the pale sunshine. "I'd be interested in commenting on anything you'd like me to."

His tone sent a quiver of unease through Felicity.

"I'll give you a comment, your ladyship."

Felicity turned. A woman was ascending a set of stone steps that led up from the water. She had tangled grey hair, wore a lumpy brown dress, and Felicity recognised her. She'd been eating shellfish at the harbour's edge the day before. At her side, the woman grasped a sack of shining seaweed.

"You will?" Felicity was relieved to have the opportunity to turn her attention away from Billy, who clearly had no serious interest in assisting her with her reporting. "To whom may I attribute the comment?" Felicity readied her notebook as she approached the woman, lowering her voice so that they might have some privacy.

"Grace Campbell's my name." The woman set her sack down beside her feet, which were shoeless. "And my comment is that no one will talk to you. Not from around here."

Felicity let her pencil and notebook drop to her sides. She was beginning to feel quite peeved. "Are you the designated spokesperson for the village, Mrs Campbell?"

Grace smiled a little. "Far from it. But I know the folk around here." She glanced along the harbour arm. The net-mending woman who had directed Felicity to the Maggie had been watching but now averted her gaze.

"And what makes you so sure no one will speak to me?"

"We read the papers, your ladyship." Grace had warm, deep-green eyes. "We know who you are. And I'd say the general assessment is that you're the type who works with authorities."

Felicity blinked. Had she heard Grace correctly?

Felicity had been accused of going too much her own way at Wolborne House, in Lower Diddleton, at Langton Manor, and in

Ippleford. Even most recently at Grimstow House, where there had been practically no choice in the matter, Felicity had been chided by the police for not awaiting help.

To now be accused of being 'the type that works with authorities', and to have dashed about the whole village and still not have a word written in her notebook — it lit a small but very definite flame within Felicity.

"Forgive me for being obtuse, Mrs Campbell, but was I not supposed to report the finding of Mr Granger on the beach?" Only a thin veneer of politeness covered Felicity's frustration. "Was I supposed to roll the man back into the sea and pretend I never saw him?"

"Few around here would have stopped you, your ladyship." Grace shrugged. "Perhaps I'm speaking too bluntly, but I thought you'd rather hear the truth of it."

Felicity took a steadying breath. There was nothing hostile in Grace's manner, and Felicity regretted the tone she'd taken with her. Grace might not have spoken to her at all. What Elizabeth Prothero had hissed to her in the woods loomed in Felicity's mind. *Smuggling*. It wasn't a word one said aloud, yet the atmosphere on Ottermouth's harbour was heavy with it.

"Lady Felicity. Lady Felicity!" Moving along the harbourside with short, brisk strides in shining patent shoes came Nigel Davies.

Grace picked up her sack of seaweed and set off towards the cottages as Harold Prothero's assistant approached.

"There's been a development, your ladyship," said Nigel breathlessly, without giving Felicity the opportunity to speak. "It's good news. The exhibition is back on."

Felicity raised her eyebrows. "Really?" Martin's body had perhaps not long reached the morgue.

Nigel nodded with enthusiasm. "We'll need a couple of days to reorganise, but we wanted to check you'll be staying in Ottermouth to report. There's not a lot of use going ahead if we don't get the coverage."

Felicity held the brim of her hat as the sea breeze whistled through the rigging of the boats on their moorings. The wall of resistance she'd met along the harbour had triggered something within her. She was determined not to be beaten. If there was any link between the body on the beach and illicit trade, Felicity would uncover it and expose it in the Western Daily News. As a news reporter serious about her career, she wouldn't shy away from the challenge.

"Yes." She gave Nigel a firm nod. "I'm staying to report."

Chapter Ten

It had rained overnight. The slippery path to Seaview Lodge was edged with long, wet grass that swept one's ankles. The track looked down on the shining slate roofs of the village from above the wooded hillside. Beyond, low grey clouds scudded over pewter waves. A fresh, damp wind swayed the treetops.

Felicity was wearing the same moss-green tweed jacket and skirt with a matching felt cloche she'd worn for a pre-breakfast walk with Pip and Beetle. Both dogs had become caked in mud and were now in the care of Ashdene's housekeeper for a thorough bathing, Mrs Rawling seemingly having a weak spot for shaggy dogs that were selectively deaf to commands such as, "Don't roll in that!"

The day before, following attempts to conduct interviews in the village, Felicity had spent a good deal of time at her typewriter. Thereafter, she called in several stories to the Exeter news desk for inclusion in the morning edition.

One article provided a detailed, although not salacious, account of how Felicity herself had come upon Martin Granger's lifeless form on the beach. Another article presented a profile of the deceased artist. Felicity built the profile mainly from the information prepared for the exhibition's programme, including familial details, such as how Martin's mother had died from illness when he was still an infant, and how his father had followed a similar fate not long after Martin reached maturity. Martin's background was similar to Felicity's in that regard.

In a third article, which delicately side-stepped the question of precisely how Martin had met his end, Felicity discussed the potential dangers of Devon's clifftop paths and coast in general, although the piece was rather thin. Besides Martin's demise, the only fatal incidents in living memory — which Felicity gleaned from speaking to Ashdene's long-serving staff — were due either to inclement weather or to the war, when local boats had been engaged as mine sweepers.

The final article for the day announced that the art exhibition's opening had merely been delayed and not cancelled, as might have been expected. Felicity had included quotes from Isabella, who tearfully explained that abandoning the exhibition would have been extremely disrespectful to Martin's memory.

"Marty would want the village to continue to flourish as an inspiration to artists everywhere," Isabella had said while dabbing her eyes. "Even after this awful accident."

Felicity had nodded with understanding as she made notes in Pitman shorthand, allowing Isabella's use of 'accident' to go unchallenged. Yet what if it came to light that Martin's death hadn't been accidental? How appropriate would continuing with the exhibition look then?

She hadn't mentioned it to Isabella, as it risked upsetting her further, but Felicity was determined to learn more about the local smuggling activities. Was Captain Dunn involved? Or the unpleasant young man in the garish jumper? What about bare-footed, tangle-haired Grace Campbell? It was possible even Constable Thompson was complicit.

Having called in her articles, Felicity had attempted to telephone Alex, but the operator had reported a fault on the line. Felicity could handle the situation in Ottermouth by herself, of course. She'd reported on precarious situations before, but it would have helped to discuss her ideas with someone else. With Alex in particular, in fact.

That the call couldn't be connected was perhaps just as well. The entrance hall at Ashdene, where the telephone table was located and where any household member might overhear, had not been the right venue for discussing Felicity's suspicions about the local population.

The thick white-rendered chimneys and modest terraced garden of Seaview Lodge came into view as the path descended around the edge of the woodland. Felicity slowed to ensure her footing on the steep, muddy track. The Protheros had taken up residence at the cottage a year ago, and Felicity had an appointment — made by Isabella — with Harold for an interview. The plan was to ask him the questions Felicity couldn't put to Isabella in her emotional state.

Having been shown inside Seaview Lodge and furnished with a pot of tea by an efficient young maid, Felicity was positioned for her audience with Harold on a modest velvet sofa in what might have been a sitting room. The room was, however, so crammed with paintings, etchings, sculptures, and all manner of artworks, it was difficult to tell quite where one was. Thin strains of classical music carried down from a gramophone upstairs, where Elizabeth was apparently practising her calligraphy. A light breeze scented with salt and grass came in through an open window.

Harold stood among the chaos in a brown three-piece suit, the jacket unbuttoned, his pince-nez balanced on the end of his nose. He had a hand on his hip and a finger tapping his lips as his gaze darted between two seascapes that were so similar that one could flip a coin to decide which was better.

Felicity sat poised with her notebook on her knee. "Could you explain the thinking behind the decision to go ahead with the exhibition, Mr Prothero?"

Interviewing Harold was proving a challenge. In light of Martin's passing, changes were being made to the selection of art for the exhibition, and with much to do, and Harold was thoroughly distracted.

"Our readers will want to hear the explanation in your words, Mr Prothero," added Felicity.

The art dealer tore his gaze away from the two paintings, his round cheeks flushed. "Of course, your ladyship, of course." He went to the corner of the room and rearranged a selection of watercolours to reveal a wingback chair, into which he dropped his heavy form. "Forgive me for being so distracted. You now have my full attention."

There was a pause. Felicity repeated her question regarding the decision to continue with the exhibition.

"Oh, yes. Of course." Harold tucked his pince-nez into his top pocket. "The explanation is quite simple, really. I was contacted yesterday by the Granger family's solicitor. The family is rather sprawling and not very close. Second and third cousins spread across the Empire. In any case, the solicitor has made it clear the family are…" Harold's brow wrinkled. "The family are keen to have the Grangers' works put out into the world. So that a greater number of people may enjoy them."

Felicity nodded as she took notes. Harold had phrased it delicately, but it sounded as though Martin's relatives had no interest in art and wanted to make as much money as possible, as quickly as possible. Harold's explanation for continuing with the exhibition was quite different from Isabella's, yet his reasoning was more solid, albeit more mercenary. Perhaps the family were even keen to sell what artworks they could before too much probing was done into Martin's passing.

Felicity paused her note-taking. "Are we talking about both Martin's and his father's works?"

Harold churched his fingers before his lips. "Martin was extremely keen to share his father's art with the world. His father was prolific and left him a significant collection when he passed. Martin also enjoyed sharing his own works, of course."

Harold was politely saying Martin enjoyed making money

from selling paintings. The comfortable sumptuousness of Halcyon Cottage attested to this.

"The exhibition had been planned to focus more on Eustace Granger," continued the art dealer, "but it now seems fitting to give both father and son equal representation."

Felicity followed Harold's gaze to a row of oil paintings propped up against the unlit fireplace. The scenes were, by now, familiar. There were men working on deck, women busy with tasks ashore, and boats being tossed about on waves. The images all looked rather alike. If there was more than one artist represented in the collection, Felicity couldn't tell.

"To what extent do the father and son's painting styles differ?" she asked.

Harold stood up, fished his pince-nez from his pocket, and approached the row of paintings. "It's true their subjects are very much alike, and both father and son worked mainly in oils." He leaned towards an image of a fishing vessel in rough weather, waves frothing over the deck. "I suppose at a glance they may look similar, but Eustace's work carries confidence and energy. Martin's, on the other hand—" Harold gestured towards a painting of children at play outside a row of cottages "—is more naïve. More innocent." The art dealer stood up straight, tucking away his glasses and smiling a little awkwardly at Felicity. "Was there anything else, your ladyship?"

Harold spoke as if the interview were almost over, yet Felicity had barely started. Being stonewalled by the fishing folk was one thing. Being pressured to hurry by one of the people who stood to benefit from the paper's coverage of the exhibition was something Felicity wouldn't tolerate.

"What was your reaction when you heard about Mr Granger's demise?" she asked, ignoring the invitation to conclude her questioning.

Harold drew in a deep breath. "Surprise. Shock. Sadness." He shook his head. "What else might one feel?"

"And what do you believe happened to him?"

Harold's chin drew back sharply. "The police have said it's an accident, have they not?"

"Do you agree with this assessment?" Felicity couldn't rely on speculation for her articles, but neither could she tiptoe around issues in need of investigation.

Harold frowned, his hands behind his back. "Why wouldn't I? Why wouldn't anyone?"

A telephone rang shrilly in a neighbouring room.

"You warned your daughter off speaking to the customs officer," pressed Felicity, returning to the topic she'd broached with the art dealer at Isabella's soirée. "May I ask why?"

Harold continued to frown. "That's quite a different matter, your ladyship." He lowered himself back into his chair, acknowledging that Felicity would decide when she was finished with her questions. "Not that it made any difference. My Lizzie will do as she pleases."

"Still, I should like to understand why you were keen for Miss Prothero not to speak to Officer Marshall."

"Your ladyship, please. You must understand, this whole matter of… Of…"

Felicity placed her pencil flat on her notebook. She raised her eyebrows. "Smuggling?"

The art dealer paused, looking pained, then nodded. "It's in the very fabric of this village. The heritage of this whole area is built upon it. It's the natural order of things. I'm fully clear of it, you understand, but one can't come into a community like Ottermouth and re-educate the population to your liking. Especially not when you're benefitting from that same community." He turned his gaze to the myriad paintings depicting the fishermen's way of life.

Felicity's pencil remained flat on her notebook. "I understand you to be clear of it, Mr Prothero, but has there been any crossover between the artists and the smuggling in your experience?"

Harold's mouth gaped. "Lady Felicity—"

There was a light tap on the door to the room. Nigel leaned through the doorway, a green bow tie at his neck. "Mr Prothero? Mrs Basingstoke has arrived at Newton Abbot. She's telephoning to speak to you urgently. It's about the Whitburn she's hoping to buy. She says she's not coming any further along those 'ghastly country lanes' unless there's a Whitburn waiting for her."

Harold looked at Felicity, his eyes filled with something like relief. "I'm awfully sorry, your ladyship. Might we continue at some later date?"

Felicity wasn't fully satisfied with what she'd gleaned from the art dealer, but an impasse had been reached. "Naturally," she said. "There are other people to whom I need to speak."

As Harold exited the room, Nigel remained with Felicity as she prepared herself to depart.

Felicity stood up from the sofa and straightened her cloche. "Did you know Mr Granger well, Mr Davies?"

Nigel gave a curt shake of his head. "Never get too close to clients on either side of the deal. That's my motto. Which is just as well." He sighed. "There's simply so much to do before we open tomorrow."

Felicity straightened. "Tomorrow?"

Nigel frowned. "The exhibition will open tomorrow, your ladyship. Didn't Mr Prothero tell you?"

It left precious little time before Felicity would be swept up in reporting on the opening, and there was so much else to look into. She couldn't waste a moment.

Chapter Eleven

To Felicity's dismay, she wasn't the only journalist in Ottermouth who'd thought to speak with the Honourable Miss Audrey Lawson.

Two men in trilby hats and overcoats, one with a notebook and the other with a camera, were returning along Halcyon Cottage's neat brick path as Felicity approached via the woodland track.

"No one's home," one said as they passed Felicity at the garden gate.

"Either that or she's hiding from us," said the other.

"Can't hide forever, though, can she?" The two men laughed as they followed the path towards the artists' cottages.

Felicity's heart sank as she looked up at the house's fresh, neat frontage, with its arch-topped windows and doors. No wonder Audrey was hiding if she was being pursued like quarry by those seeking comment. But Audrey surely had the firmest notion of what had happened to Martin. She'd left Isabella's soirée with him. Had she been the last person to see him alive?

With the wooden gate still standing open, Felicity made her way towards Halcyon Cottage's front door. On a nearby boot scraper, she removed the build-up of red mud from her lace-ups

— perhaps needlessly, if she wasn't to be invited inside — and knocked lightly on the door.

After a brief pause, she knocked again, a little louder this time.

"Miss Lawson?" Felicity called. "It's Lady Felicity Quick. We met a couple of nights ago. I write for the Western Daily News, but there's no need to use your name in the paper unless you want that." She paused. The wind hissed through the trees. "You must be terribly shaken by all that's happened. Still, I should like very much to hear your side of things, if I may?"

Felicity waited. Distant waves crashed against rocks. Was anyone even there to hear what she'd said?

"Miss Lawson?"

It was no use. Audrey wasn't speaking to the press. She was perhaps even no longer in Ottermouth.

Felicity started back along the brick path.

Click-clack.

She turned. Halcyon Cottage's front door slowly opened.

The house's interior was expensively appointed but cosy and richly textured as arts-and-crafts homes usually were. Sketches in charcoal and pencil adorned the walls of the sitting room, baring the hallmarks of Eustace and Martin Granger's talents. There were gaps on the wall where paintings might once have hung before transportation to the exhibition. Several of the remaining sketches featured a captivating young woman with thick, wavy hair.

Seated on a carved oak chair with sage-green and mustard-yellow pillows, Felicity sipped on an exquisite Ceylon from a quaint little china cup, her notebook still firmly in the pocket of her tweed skirt.

Audrey sat opposite in the centre of a chaise longue upholstered in the same green-and-yellow brocade. The teapot from which she had poured with shaking hands sat on a small, round table between them. On the mantelpiece, a clock with dark wooden casing and an off-white face kept a gentle rhythm. An enormous bouquet of decaying lilacs scented the room with a sickly sweetness.

Audrey's faint smile was hollow, her hands clenched in the lap of her mint-green silk dress, the scooped neckline of which revealed prominent collar bones. She was perhaps thirty, with lines at the corners of her mouth and her white-blonde hair frizzed beyond the confines of its chignon. Compared to the rich earthy tones of the furnishings surrounding her, Audrey looked faded, even ghostly.

"We met up in London." There was a slight tremble in her voice. "My father's an art collector. Martin convinced me to come down here. I didn't much care for it at first, but I've grown used to the place. I'm not sure I'll be able to stay on without him, though."

Felicity nodded. She still wasn't sure what had prompted Audrey to open the door to her. Perhaps there was no one else in Ottermouth in whom she could confide? Felicity wouldn't rock the boat by drawing attention to the issue. Audrey was willing to speak to her. That was what mattered.

"Losing Mr Granger must have come as an enormous shock, Miss Lawson."

Audrey nodded, pressing her lips together to ward off another bout of weeping.

"Were you there when it happened?" Felicity's tone was sympathetic.

Audrey released her lips. She tipped her head. "When what happened?"

"When Mr Granger... When he... You know." Felicity couldn't risk pushing Audrey too hard.

"My goodness," she said, eyes widening. "I'm sorry. Of course." She knotted her fingers. "After we left Ashdene, we came back here."

Felicity raised an eyebrow, doing her best to restrain her reaction. So, Martin hadn't tumbled from the cliffs on his way home. There was more to it than Constable Thompson had wanted her to believe.

Audrey went on. "Then he went out to meet a friend."

"In the middle of the night?" Felicity controlled her surprise. "Was that a normal occurrence?"

Audrey nodded distractedly, as though leafing through recollections. "He always took a lantern. He was always careful."

"Might you know who Mr Granger went to meet?"

Tucking a wisp of white-blonde hair behind her ear, Audrey hesitated before shaking her head.

"Do you know where he was going?" Felicity spoke gently, but she was eager to know. Was there still a chance Martin had fallen from the cliffs? Part of her hoped it really was that simple. "Might he have headed back towards Ashdene?"

Audrey shrugged. "Sometimes he'd go across the rocks, or take a boat out." Tears were welling in the corner of her eyes. "He kissed me on the head, said goodbye, and that was the last I saw of him."

Felicity rose quickly from her seat and offered Audrey a handkerchief. She'd pressed her interviewee too hard and regretted having done so. Not only because powerful emotions risked closing the conversation down altogether, but because suffering the loss of someone dear was already so much to bear. As a reporter, Felicity felt her duty was to improve matters, not make them worse.

Audrey dabbed her eyes. "I'm sorry," she said, blinking at Felicity, who was crouched at her side.

"There's no need to apologise." Felicity put a hand on Audrey's. Her skin was cool and clammy. "Is there anyone else you can go to here in Ottermouth? What about Mrs Mountvernon? Or Mr Prothero? It's best not to be alone at a time like this."

Audrey sniffed. "Without Martin, I'm on my own. I've no friends here at all."

"Mr Granger's friends aren't your friends?"

Audrey pressed her lips together, then shook her head. "He kept us all quite separate." She gave a shaky sigh. "I should just get myself back up to London. Like the officer said."

"Constable Thompson?"

Audrey's brow furrowed. "I thought he said his name was Marshall? I don't remember a Thompson."

That Constable Thompson hadn't yet interviewed the last person seen with Martin beggared belief. Securing an audience with Audrey hadn't been straightforward, however. How had Officer Marshall managed it? Charisma was certainly not among the man's strengths.

"Officer Marshall works for His Majesty's Customs and Excise," said Felicity. "May I ask how he came to advise you to return to London?"

Audrey looked down at the handkerchief, which she squeezed hard in her lap. "It's my fault. It's all my fault." Tears rolled over her cheeks.

"How is it your fault, Miss Lawson?" The woman's behaviour was giving Felicity cause for concern. "You weren't there when Mr Granger met his end, were you?"

Audrey fixed Felicity with a stare, her eyes glistening. "I let him go. I could have asked him to stop."

Felicity didn't want to pressure Audrey. "Stop what?" she urged softly. She had to know.

Audrey sniffed. She blinked, and a tear rolled down her hollow cheek. "To stop seeing other women."

Chapter Twelve

An unexpected downpour sent Felicity to seek shelter under a large oak among the artists' cottages in the woods above the village. She issued a stiff reminder to herself to be more diligent about checking the forecast and bringing an umbrella as needed. There were copy deadlines to hit and having to wait for the rain to cease didn't help.

Audrey had become too emotional to continue her discussion with Felicity. It was sad and unsettling to see a woman blame herself for a man's infidelity. Not that Audrey and Martin had been married. Not that being unwed gave a man *carte blanche* to do whatever he liked.

Audrey insisted she didn't know who Martin's other women were. She was surprised at Felicity's interest in the specifics. Felicity had perhaps done too good a job of convincing Audrey she'd knocked at Halcyon Cottage's door out of concern alone. News of the exhibition opening the next day had also been a surprise for Audrey, and Felicity rather regretted dropping it into the conversation on the assumption she knew.

Having upset her enough, Felicity hadn't raised the topic of smuggling with Audrey. It was, however, perhaps significant that Officer Marshall had somehow spoken to her. In leaving Halcyon

Cottage, Felicity urged Audrey to seek the company of those who cared for her — an instruction that seemed to confuse the waif-like woman — but to ensure alignment with Constable Thompson before leaving the village, to avoid any misunderstanding.

Indeed, Felicity planned to seek alignment with the constable herself and had been on her way to find the policeman. Were there any breakthroughs in the case? Was Constable Thompson's position still fixed on Martin's demise being accidental? Felicity had discovered the body just the day before. Developments in the investigation could happen rapidly. But then the rain had started.

As large drops rolled off the oak's leaves and plopped onto her felt hat, Felicity pulled out her notebook. She couldn't allow a moment of her time to go to waste. In fluid shorthand, she wrote:

For the WDN:
Exhibition opening tomorrow. Father and son remembered together.
Cause of death: still under investigation. Check with Thompson for latest.
Fishing activities central to the art. Quotes from fishermen and their families?
Comments from artists and art collectors.

Felicity winced at the last line. She didn't relish the thought of delving back into the opinions and chatter of the art collectors, but it would have to be done at some point. For Isabella's sake, if nothing else.

A raindrop sploshed onto her notebook as she turned the page. Felicity continued writing.

For further research:
Smuggling — of what? By whom?
Martin Granger involved? Who else?
Death accidental? Still possible.
Who did Martin go to meet? And where?

'Other women'?

The shower stopped as suddenly as it had arrived. Felicity cut her note-taking short as she set off down the path towards Constable Thompson's cottage, which was in the heart of the village, squeezed between matching white-washed dwellings on a terrace overlooking the harbour. There were a great number of leads to follow. Could a lover's tiff have had anything to do with Martin's demise? It wasn't an area into which Felicity had much insight. Staying on the right side of the local authorities, however, was generally never a bad idea.

As Felicity rapped on the policeman's door, she observed how the rain had done nothing to suppress activities on the harbour. Work continued aboard the Maggie's wooden deck, where Captain Dunn and his crew remained busy with maintenance and repairs. The women were outside their cottages, washing laundry in large wooden tubs and putting items through a mangle. A solemn-faced Nigel Davies stood by the big gallery doors speaking to a pair of out-of-towners — presumably art collectors — who also looked incredibly grave. The other journalists Felicity had already come across were slinking about, attempting to interview local people and visitors alike.

Growing impatient, Felicity knocked on Constable Thompson's door again. There continued to be no response.

"Cici!"

Felicity turned.

"Yoo-hoo!" Dressed in a daring pair of trousers, a striped sailor-style top, and a red neckerchief, Isabella approached from the direction of Ashdene. On her head she wore a wide-brimmed straw hat upon which a pair of sunglasses had been optimistically perched. The American art collector, James Halliday, and Ashdene's butler, Mr Chivers, who was carrying a picnic basket, accompanied Isabella. The party was completed by a junior footman toting armfuls of umbrellas, and an expensively dressed middle-aged couple Felicity didn't recognise.

Felicity stepped away from the policeman's doorstep, and Isabella greeted her with a kiss on each cheek, her mood much improved from the day before. "Will you come with us?" she asked. "For a cruise along the coast? James wanted us to use his yacht, but I'm insisting we take Xantho."

Felicity looked from Isabella to her entourage. These were the art enthusiasts Isabella was counting on to make her vision for Ottermouth a reality. Now was absolutely not the time to ask Isabella if she knew anything about Martin's 'other women'.

"We've got oysters and champagne," continued Isabella.

"And umbrellas," chuckled James.

"You might also like to speak to Mr and Mrs Vance for the paper." Isabella gestured towards the sumptuously dressed couple, who stepped forward eagerly. "Mr Vance has an enormous collection of seascapes. Perhaps the largest in England. Certainly the most well curated."

Mr Vance frowned playfully. "You're too kind, Mrs Mountvernon."

"Mrs Basingstoke will join us as well," added Isabella. "Oh, do say you'll come with us."

Felicity wore her politest smile. The prevailing mood was one of there not having been a suspicious death in Ottermouth. "Yes," said Felicity, playing along. "I'd love to speak to Mr and Mrs Vance for the Western Daily News." It wouldn't be time wasted. The art scene still needed to be profiled, and some serious questions regarding reactions to Martin's passing had to be asked.

"I can't stay out for long though, I'm afraid," added Felicity as they set off towards the harbour, Isabella wrapping her arm through Felicity's. "There are deadlines to which I need to work."

"You are absolutely work-obsessed, Cici." Isabella smiled. Her perfume was powdery and sweet. "I've never known anyone like it. You should live a little."

Felicity returned Isabella's smile, but it was strained. She knew Isabella meant no offence and was perhaps even genuinely concerned that Felicity was too focused on her job. But Felicity had been the one to discover Martin's body. She hadn't yet forgotten the sight and doubted she ever would. How could she not take matters in Ottermouth seriously?

Still, she'd made a commitment to Jasper. "I don't have very good sea legs, I'm afraid," Felicity said with genuine apology. She couldn't dampen Isabella's mood.

As Felicity, Isabella, and the rest of the yachting party came to the harbour's edge, they were passed by the crew of the Maggie, who were heading in the inn's direction. None of the fishermen looked at Felicity, Isabella, or their companions. Only Captain Dunn gave Felicity a suspicious glance.

"Awfully atmospheric, isn't it?" whispered Mrs Vance to her husband, as though the activity on the harbourside were part of an open-air spectacle.

"Here we are, darlings," announced Isabella as the party arrived at the water's edge. "Jimmy's yacht might be a spot bigger, but I believe we'll be comfortable enough on my little boat."

Xantho indeed wasn't the largest yacht in Ottermouth's harbour — an experienced sailor might handle her by himself — but she was extremely luxurious, with a gleaming dark blue hull and polished wood and metalwork adorning the warm teak deck. A soaring wooden mast created imposing height. Even with her canvas sails furled, Xantho's graceful lines had clearly been designed for speed, although the cushioned benches behind the wheelhouse were built more for relaxation.

The butler and footman went onto the yacht first, bringing the supplies aboard and arranging a gang plank. Sunshine broke through the grey clouds as Felicity waited on the harbourside with the boating party. She engaged in appropriate conversation whenever required, but she couldn't chase the thought from her mind. Had Martin been out on the water the night he met his demise? Was that how he ended up lifeless on the shore? It was a great pity Constable Thompson had not been available. Felicity would make another attempt later to locate him.

Then something caught Felicity's eye. It was so striking the smile upheld only by politeness fell from her face.

"Please, do excuse me," she said to Isabella, James Halliday and the Vances already having boarded Xantho.

Isabella lifted the large brim of her straw hat. "You're coming back, aren't you, Cici?" she asked as Felicity moved swiftly away, too distracted to respond.

Chapter Thirteen

Felicity walked purposefully towards the women at work in front of the fishermen's cottages. Her target was the girl with thick, reddish-brown hair and sea-green eyes who'd cast a look full of curiosity at Felicity the day before. The curiosity was now Felicity's.

With the girl's wavy hair now loose across her shoulders, the likeness was as clear as day. She was the girl in the painting in the hall at Ashdene. She was the girl in the sketches at Halcyon Cottage. They weren't scenes of daily work captured aboard boats or outside the cottages. The girl must have posed for Martin Granger. She must have known him.

With the deck of the Maggie empty, might Felicity be able to connect with the women? She had to try.

As Felicity approached, the green-eyed girl looked up from a bucket of soapy water in which both her hands were plunged, the suds escaping onto the cobbles below.

"Good day," hailed Felicity perhaps too enthusiastically, for her greeting had the opposite effect she'd hoped for.

The girl looked down at her bucket, her pale cheeks flushing.

The grey-bunned woman who'd directed Felicity to the Maggie the day before left her work at a nearby washing line and was quickly at the girl's side. She whispered something to her, and with an obsequious nod, the girl disappeared into a nearby cottage.

Felicity could have kicked herself. While desperate to get to the truth, she knew better than to go charging up to a potential interviewee. A more delicate touch was needed. Especially in Ottermouth.

The older woman swept a strand of hair from her forehead and put her fists on her aproned hips. "If you have business with our Thora, you speak to her father." The sea-green eyes that met Felicity's were the same as the girl's.

"My sincerest apologies," said Felicity. "I meant no offence with my approach. Perhaps I'm mistaken, but I thought I recognised Miss Thora from a painting. I was wondering if she might tell me something about the artist."

The woman scowled. "You'll need to speak to my husband before you speak to our daughter."

So, this was the girl's mother. "Mrs Dunn?" ventured Felicity.

There was a pause before the woman reluctantly nodded. "Margaret Dunn, your ladyship."

Felicity had introduced herself the day before, although she hadn't received the woman's name in return. While the atmosphere wasn't entirely welcoming, and she was clearly not allowed access to Thora, Felicity hadn't exactly been sent on her way. Not yet. Might Margaret be more willing to talk while the deck of the Maggie was still empty?

"I'm very pleased to make your acquaintance, Mrs Dunn. Again, I can only apologise for my boldness in approaching your daughter." Felicity considered her next move carefully. "I assure you that the readers of the Western Daily News are very much like yourself. They're honest, hard-working people who wish to understand the world and its goings-on better, particularly on a local level." Felicity spoke evenly and without a hint of desperation. Internally, however, she prayed quite desperately for someone from the fishing community to open up to her. If they didn't, then the Western Daily News wouldn't maintain its lead over the competition for long.

"I've no wish to see my name or that of my family in the papers, thank you very much." Margaret Dunn turned towards her washing line.

"That's quite understandable." Felicity spoke rapidly and reassuringly, determined not to lose grip on this thinnest of threads. "There's no need to mention any name. And there's no need for specifics. I'm sure our readers would like to understand the relationship between the artists and the local people. From the perspective of the locals."

Margaret hesitated. She had opinions. Everyone did. But would she share hers with Felicity?

Her sea-green eyes darted along the harbourside. "We don't want any trouble. We want things to return to how they always were." Turning her back on Felicity, Margaret busied herself with the hanging out of clothes.

The opportunity was gone.

Felicity's stomach clenched. Margaret had been scared away from making further comment, and what had scared her was stalking along the harbour, heading directly for Felicity.

Chapter Fourteen

Officer Marshall of His Majesty's Customs and Excise smirked as he strode along the harbourside, the brass buttons of his dark blue uniform glinting in the sunshine.

"Ladies," he said, coming to a stop beside Felicity, his hands on his hips as he watched the fishing women disappear into their cottages, like rabbits fleeing from a hawk circling overhead. As Margaret disappeared inside, she flashed Felicity a cold, hard look that said, *I shouldn't have spoken to you*. Regrettably, there was no immediate solution to alter that perception.

The customs officer chuckled. "Really, such a warm welcome is unnecessary. I know none of you will speak to me. I'm here for Lady Felicity."

Felicity raised her eyebrows, both surprised and curious. "I understood you'd been banished from Ottermouth, Officer Marshall."

He frowned mockingly. "Constable Thompson can hold an opinion on how I ought to conduct myself, but Customs and Excise doesn't take its instructions from the local constabulary. I can moor my vessel in Ottermouth's harbour if my work calls for it." Officer Marshall folded his arms over his broad chest. His height made him rather imposing. "You're happy enough to speak to me, though, aren't you, your ladyship?"

A cool breeze whipped a curl onto Felicity's cheek, which she swept back under her cloche. "I couldn't possibly say without knowing the topic." She spoke loudly, hoping Margaret would hear before she slammed the blue-painted cottage door behind her.

The game was a tricky one. Felicity wanted to be trustworthy in the eyes of the local fishing community, as there was surely much they could tell her, but maintaining Officer Marshall's favour was also important. Quotes from the authorities were excellent fodder for the paper, and the customs man had raised early doubts about the manner of Martin's passing.

Officer Marshall sighed, as though exasperated by a wayward child. "I understand what you're trying to achieve here, but trust me. It won't work. These folk don't talk to outsiders, uniformed or not. You're wasting your time."

Felicity offered a perfunctory smile. Ahead of Officer Marshall arriving on the scene, she'd sensed she was getting somewhere. "What was it you wanted to speak to me about, Officer Marshall? Any news on the autopsy you said you'd insist upon?"

The customs officer narrowed his eyes. "As a matter of fact, I've a proposition for you, your ladyship."

If anyone was still listening from within the cottages, it wasn't ideal. "I will hear what you have to say, but I make no promises. Shall we take a stroll?"

Brash and heavy-handed though he was, Officer Marshall wasn't slow on the uptake. "Let's do just that," he said, and he started towards the sea wall, moving away from the cottages. Felicity followed.

They walked slowly, the customs officer maintaining a respectable distance from Felicity. Outside the harbour, steely blue waves chopped and churned as far as the horizon, where grey clouds gathered. No doubt there'd be another shower or two before the day was out.

Officer Marshall tugged on the peak of his cap as the wind picked up. "A man is dead, your ladyship. You know that better than anyone, having come across the unfortunate fellow yourself."

Felicity nodded her acknowledgement, keeping her manner businesslike. Officer Marshall wasn't the sort to whom one opened up emotionally.

"Mark my words," he continued, "there's foul play involved, but the local police won't have it. We'll have the autopsy report soon enough, and I'm confident they'll confirm my suspicions."

Felicity withdrew her notebook from her skirt pocket. "May I ask what your suspicions are exactly?"

The customs officer held up a hand. "If you please, your ladyship." He cast a disapproving look towards the notebook. "The whole situation here is a powder keg, and it could go off any moment. Let's keep this just between you and me for now."

Reluctantly, Felicity returned her notebook to her pocket. "Very well, but then I trust you will allow me to speak frankly?"

They were nearing the end of the sea wall and the harbour's entrance. Only the gulls wheeling about in the air above could overhear them.

Officer Marshall came to a stop, arms folded. "Please do."

"Is there a link between Mr Granger's death and smuggling?"

The customs officer looked down at Felicity with something like pity. "When you say 'smuggling', your ladyship, what exactly do you mean?"

Felicity blinked. "Well." Wasn't it obvious? When Elizabeth Prothero had hissed the word in the woods, Felicity had known what she'd meant. Hadn't she? "I can't say I've investigated the topic in Ottermouth specifically."

The customs officer smiled. "If you're imagining brandy, laces, and tobacco, your ladyship, think again."

A flush of embarrassment crept into Felicity's cheeks. That was exactly what she'd been thinking.

"Matters have become much more serious than that," continued Officer Marshall.

Felicity swallowed. "Serious in what way?"

The customs officer hesitated. He eyed Felicity warily. "Can I trust you, your ladyship?"

"Why yes, of course. Why ever not?" Did Officer Marshall imagine she might be in league with the smugglers?

"Can be hard to tell, that's all. But you agree we should work together?" Officer Marshall tightened the cross of his arms and scrutinised Felicity with utmost seriousness. "If we work together, I can tell you everything."

Felicity went to speak but snapped her mouth shut. Her stomach sank. The true intentions of Officer Marshall were now transparent. He'd correctly identified that information was most precious to Felicity, and he'd put it just out of her reach. The condition of 'working together' served the customs officer and his goals, but what would it mean for Felicity? It would likely destroy her chances of anyone from the fishing community opening up to her.

It was also deeply unpleasant to be manipulated in such a manner.

"Well," she began. Despite her misgivings, Felicity was reluctant to sever communication with the customs officer entirely. Like everyone else in Ottermouth, Officer Marshall possessed knowledge he was as yet unwilling to disclose.

What was the correct reply to his invitation to collaborate?

Felicity didn't have to think for long. The perfect solution had appeared at the harbour's entrance.

Chapter Fifteen

With her grey hair blowing about her shoulders in the wind, Grace Campbell sat in the prow of a small wooden rowing boat that was moving swiftly into the harbour. At the oars was a man in faded overalls with a long silver beard, whom Felicity had seen on the water before.

Their arrival was Felicity's way out.

"I'm awfully sorry." Felicity addressed Officer Marshall with a polite, vaguely apologetic tone. "There's someone with whom I need to speak."

"I rarely take no as the final answer, your ladyship," called out the customs officer as Felicity hurried back along the harbour wall. No doubt this wouldn't be her last encounter with Officer Marshall, but Felicity would be ready for his manipulative ways next time.

The rowing boat moored beside a set of seaweed-strewn steps in the harbour wall. When Felicity reached them, Grace was climbing out of the little boat, her skirts tucked up to allow her bare feet to find purchase on the slippery stone of the steps, a crate of black, shining mussels in her arms. Having tied the rowing boat to a nearby mooring ring, the bearded man joined

Grace in carrying another crate packed with glistening shellfish up the steps.

"Hello again, Mrs Campbell." Felicity's tone was bright and purposeful as Grace and her companion climbed the steps. If the customs officer was still watching, Felicity would appear to have business with Grace. In reality, Felicity was searching her mind for viable lines of questioning, none of which looked promising. Though friendly in manner, Grace had already announced she, like the rest of Ottermouth's fishing community, wouldn't furnish Felicity with information.

Grace smiled warmly but blinked with disbelief to see Felicity waiting for her at the top of the steps. "Good day to you, your ladyship. Interested in a purchase of fresh mussels? Joe and I collected them not an hour ago. And you already know I've nothing to say to the papers."

Felicity saw an opening. "Oh, I don't believe I've yet had the pleasure of meeting Mr..." She trailed off expectantly, ready to meet the bearded man's gaze with a charming smile.

Reaching the top of the stone steps, Joe glanced briefly at Felicity, then at Grace. He had deep lines at the corners of his eyes above his dense, silver beard. With a thud, he put his crate down beside Grace's feet, the shells of the mussels clacking together. He gave Grace another glare, then turned and went back down the steps without a word.

With a knitted brow, Felicity watched Joe climb into the rowing boat, undo its mooring, and take up the oars. Were she not so desperate for information, she might have laughed. How impossible it was to communicate with anyone was verging on comical.

"Did I say something wrong?" Felicity asked Grace.

The older woman sighed, lowering her crate of mussels to the ground and folding her arms as she watched Joe skim across the water. "You did nothing wrong, your ladyship. That's just what Joe's like. I'm lucky he still speaks to me. Not all the time, mind you. He has his moments. But he's about the only one I can depend on."

The rowing boat quickly disappeared through the harbour's mouth.

"Is he a fisherman?" enquired Felicity.

Grace continued to gaze after the little boat. "He's the lighthouse keeper, your ladyship."

Felicity pondered the revelation. Ottermouth's lighthouse keeper was surely someone to interview. If any boat left the harbour the night Martin met his end, the lighthouse keeper would have noticed, would he not?

Grace sighed and hoisted her crate. "I suppose I'll have to come back for that one." She nodded towards the crate of mussels Joe had deposited at the top of the steps.

"Might I help you?" Felicity glanced down at her jacket and skirt, considering whether the moss-green tweed could withstand the saltwater and the sliminess of any seaweed still clinging to the shells. The crates were awkward to carry, but they didn't appear to be heavy. Would ruining a decent outfit be worth the possibility of earning Grace's trust?

Grace smiled wistfully, the lines on her weathered cheeks deepening. "Don't worry yourself, your ladyship. I'm used to managing on my own. My husband died many years ago."

Felicity frowned, genuinely saddened. "I'm very sorry to hear that."

"Fishing's a risky job. The sea's a dangerous place." Grace rested the crate of mussels on the front of her hips. "Working with Customs and Excise now, are you, your ladyship?"

The question surprised Felicity. "Of course not," she said, perhaps too quickly. "I work for a newspaper, Mrs Campbell. It's my duty to gather the facts, and to do that, I must speak to everyone."

The crew of the Maggie were approaching along the harbour wall, returning from their break at the Dolphin. It was a welcome distraction.

"Good day, gentlemen." Felicity stood aside. She expected someone to offer Grace help with her crates. Instead, the men walked by without even looking at Grace or Felicity. The only person to shoot them a glance was Lawrence Whitburn, who was melded into the group as though a fisherman himself. The look he gave Felicity carried a hint of contempt.

The men having passed, Grace chuckled. "You can speak to whoever you like, your ladyship. Whether they speak to you is a different matter."

Seagulls squawked overhead, as if joining in with Grace's laughter. Felicity's cheeks burned. She wasn't a particularly proud person, but being frustrated at every attempt to connect with the locals, being unable to carry out even a simple interview — it was beginning to sting.

"The men didn't acknowledge you either, Mrs Campbell," she said.

Grace continued to smile. "I've never really fit in properly, your ladyship."

"Were you not born and raised here?"

"I was."

Felicity hesitated. It wasn't anything for the newspaper. It also had nothing to do with Martin's passing, but Felicity needed something to satisfy her own desire to understand matters. "I realise it's none of my business, but may I ask what happened?"

Grace pursed her lips. She shook her head.

There weren't grounds for further prying, but Felicity remained curious. She couldn't imagine being shunned by one's own community. "If you don't fit in, may I ask what keeps you in Ottermouth?"

"Family, your ladyship." Grace's green eyes flashed. "My sister. My niece."

How had Felicity not noticed before? Grace's wild hair and bare feet were so unlike Margaret's aproned primness, but the eye colour was unmistakable. "Is Mrs Margaret Dunn your sister? Which would make Miss Thora Dunn your niece?" Felicity's mood brightened. Another avenue for questioning was opening up.

Grace smiled sadly. "This crate is beginning to feel rather heavy, your ladyship."

"Of course, yes. I quite understand. May I just ask one more thing?" Before Felicity could formulate a question about Thora's association with Martin, a voice rang out across the harbour.

"Cici! I say, Cici!"

Isabella was waving frantically from beside Xantho's gangway. Grace took advantage of the distraction to depart with the first of her mussel crates.

With a deflated sigh, Felicity waved back at Isabella. Chasing after Grace wouldn't help gain the woman's trust, and there was no putting it off any further. A trip on Isabella's yacht was inevitable. Mrs Basingstoke, whoever she was, had likely arrived and probably needed interviewing along with the Vances.

As Felicity rounded the harbour, Isabella continued waving. Felicity smiled stiffly. *I'm on my way*, thought Felicity somewhat impatiently. Then she saw why Isabella was waving so frantically. Her stomach dropped.

Chapter Sixteen

Constable Thompson stood alone on Xantho's teak deck with his helmet tucked under his arm. At the harbour's edge, Isabella, her guests, and her staff watched anxiously as the local constable lifted coils of rope with his truncheon and leaned to look between winches. Above a table upon which oysters had been abandoned mid-shucking, the policeman paused and sniffed, the ends of his mouth tugging downwards under his grey moustache.

Isabella flew to Felicity as she arrived beside the yacht, the wide brim of Isabella's straw hat almost colliding with Felicity's cloche as she clasped her hands in hers.

"I'm so incredibly glad you're here. There seems to have been some kind of mix up." Isabella's wide, frightened eyes darted towards the policeman, then towards her confused-looking guests. Leaning towards Felicity, Isabella lowered her voice. "Constable Thompson has chosen now of all moments to search Xantho. He has no respect for what Harold and I are trying to achieve here. The man's a stubborn old ox that simply won't listen." She put a hand to her chest, eyes fluttering. "And after everything that's happened, I'm not sure how much more I can take."

Felicity's commitment to Jasper moved swiftly to the forefront of her mind. "I shall do what I can."

Leaving Isabella in the watchful care of her butler, Felicity approached Xantho's gangway. "Constable Thompson," she called out. "It seems you've ejected Mrs Mountvernon and her guests from her yacht. Mrs Mountvernon informs me you're searching the vessel. May I ask why?"

The policeman didn't look up from his work. "I'll be going below deck now, Mrs Mountvernon." The constable glanced briefly at Isabella, not asking permission but informing her and ignoring Felicity completely.

"Oh, dear. Oh, heavens." Isabella put a hand on her butler's shoulder to steady herself. "I'm feeling rather queer."

"Constable Thompson." Felicity raised her voice in a forthright manner. It wasn't her normal style, but she had to try. "I say, Constable Thompson."

The policeman looked wearily in Felicity's direction. "What is it, your ladyship?"

"May I ask what your business is aboard Mrs Mountvernon's yacht?"

The policeman frowned at Felicity as though she were a few sandwiches short of a picnic. "I'm searching it, your ladyship. For evidence. I believe you're familiar with police procedure. You've meddled in enough of our constabulary's cases."

The jibe carried a mild sting, which Felicity ignored. "Evidence of what, Constable Thompson?"

The policeman sighed. "Evidence connected to the death of Mr Martin Granger, your ladyship."

"Oh, goodness." Isabella fanned herself. Mrs Vance clung to her husband, their confusion becoming concern.

"This surely can't be happening, can it?" enquired James Halliday, his worried gaze darting between Felicity, Isabella, and the policeman.

But it was. It was happening.

Felicity couldn't just stand by and watch. "Constable Thompson. You told me Mr Granger's demise was accidental."

The policeman rocked back on his heels. "Situation's changed. Didn't your friend Officer Marshall tell you that?"

He's anything but my friend, thought Felicity, but she withheld the urge to make comment. She wouldn't be derailed. "Changed in what way?"

"Autopsy report's come back. They had a good look at Mr Granger. Turns out it wasn't drowning what did for him. It was a blow to the head."

A chill swept through Felicity.

Mrs Vance gasped.

"My goodness." Isabella tottered. The butler maintained his support of his mistress while the footman shored her up on the other side.

"A blow to the head from impact on the rocks, you mean?" Felicity had been wary of Constable Thompson's insistence Martin's end had been an accident. But she didn't actually want it to have been murder.

The constable shook his head slowly, a rather inappropriate glint of enjoyment in his eye. "It was a blow to the head from a cleanly lined implement. Something man-made, your ladyship. Not a rock."

Her shock subsiding only slightly, Felicity reached for her notebook. She had to get this down for the newspaper. "You no longer believe Mr Granger's passing to have been accidental, Constable Thompson?"

The policeman narrowed his eyes at Felicity. "We're looking into the matter, your ladyship."

"But why search my yacht?" Isabella was now standing without the support of her staff, her despair giving way to indignation.

Constable Thompson approached the gangway, his shiny black boots falling heavily on the smooth wooden deck, his helmet still clasped under his arm. "Mr Granger was bumped on the head before he fell in the water. Given where his body was found, there's the possibility he was on a boat at the time."

Felicity remembered Audrey's testimony. The evidence was stacking up, and this fresh development would make headlines. She would have to call in an article as quickly as possible.

The policeman continued. "Your yacht had its gangway down, Mrs Mountvernon, so I thought I might as well start here."

"I don't object to the search, Constable Thompson," said Isabella, placing her hands on her hips. "I've nothing to hide, but why now? Can you not start with some other vessel?"

"There's no time to lose, Mrs Mountvernon," said the policeman. "The inquest's the day after next. The jury must have all the evidence to make the right decision, and I need to search all the boats in the harbour."

What the constable was saying changed everything. Keeping her astonishment in check, Felicity continued to capture it all in her notebook.

The policeman huffed. "Now. As I said, I'll be going below deck for a look around."

"But Constable Thompson, my guests are already upset—" Isabella threw a hand towards James Halliday and the Vances "—and Mrs Basingstoke's due at any moment."

The policeman frowned. Was he supposed to know who Mrs Basingstoke was? Felicity also felt disbelief at Isabella's attitude. Isabella and Martin had been friends, and Ottermouth's art scene had practically regarded him as royalty. Did Isabella not want the police to investigate? Did she not wish to know what really happened to Martin?

"Constable Thompson!"

Footsteps clattered along the cobbles of the harbourside. It was the girl Felicity recognised from the painting, her cheeks pink and her green eyes wide.

The constable hurried across Xantho's gangway. "Miss Dunn. What is it?"

Isabella's shoulders collapsed with relief as the policeman stepped ashore. "Thank goodness," she sighed.

Her breath coming quickly, Thora pointed over the water. "He's boarding Pa's boat. He's searching the Maggie."

Across the harbour, under a sombre sky, a group of men were engaged in a rather intense debate aboard the trawler. At the centre of the rabble was Officer Marshall, his peaked cap and broad shoulders towering above most of the fishermen. The women had left their cottages to congregate on the harbour wall beside the vessel. The tension was evident, even from a distance. A physical altercation seemed imminent.

"That filthy rascal." His eyes burning with sudden rage, Constable Thompson set his helmet atop his head, fastened the chin strap under his jaw, and went striding towards the Maggie.

The Vances remained wide eyed with surprise at all they'd witnessed. James Halliday stepped forward. "Is it over, Bella?"

Thora trailed after the constable, but before reaching the Maggie, she disappeared down an alley leading away from the harbour.

Isabella let out an enormous sigh. "Yes, Jimmy. I do believe it is. And we have Cici to thank."

Felicity's attention snapped back to the yachting party. "Me?"

"If you hadn't intervened, I don't quite know what I'd have done." Isabella adjusted her straw hat as sploshes of rain began darkening the harbourside cobbles and the wood of Xantho's deck. "And, look! There's Mrs Basingstoke."

Trundling towards the harbour was a woman in her seventies adorned with gold jewellery and with a bright white chignon tucked under a feathered hat. The enthusiastic wave she gave the yachting party seemed to lift everyone's spirits. Isabella dashed forward to greet her.

"You'll join us for a trip out to sea, won't you, your ladyship?" enquired James Halliday as the butler and footman set about positioning awnings and umbrellas across Xantho's deck. "You

Brits are more than used to the rain, as I understand it," he added with a smile.

"I'm afraid I shan't." Felicity's reply was polite yet firm. The situation had become rather more serious. Considering the autopsy results relayed by Constable Thompson, continuing with the boat trip was incongruous, but that wasn't why Felicity turned down the invitation. There were other urgent matters to which she must attend, including one glaring priority.

Chapter Seventeen

Pip and Beetle were extremely pleased to see Felicity when she arrived at Ashdene, her moss-green tweeds quite wet from the rain that had turned torrential at the house's gates. But there wasn't time to play with the dogs or even change clothes.

Promising the eager hounds a long walk later, Felicity went up to her room and sat at her typewriter. The piece she wrote led with the revelation that Martin Granger's death had been from a blow to the head by a man-made object, not from a fall from the cliffs as previously suspected. Felicity also included mention of the vessel searches being carried out both by the local police and Customs and Excise. For although Felicity hadn't stayed to watch, that was what the ruckus aboard the Maggie was about.

After calling the article into the paper's Exeter newsdesk for urgent publication, Felicity returned upstairs to write a piece about the plans to open the art exhibition the following day, but her mind kept drifting. Audrey Lawson had said it wasn't uncommon for Martin to take a boat out at night. He might have tripped, hit his head, and fallen overboard. It was still a possibility Martin's passing was an accident.

But what were the chances he'd been on his own?

Felicity watched as rain pelted the guest room's windows.

Someone in Ottermouth — maybe more than one person — knew more than they were letting on. Yet everywhere Felicity turned, she met with obstacles. People who wouldn't speak to her, or who would only do so under specific conditions. Those who seemed happy to talk were perhaps not telling the whole story.

Felicity refocused her attention on the article about the exhibition. After she called it in, she would attempt a telephone call to Alex. A tête-à-tête with her friend was long overdue. Speaking to him about the goings-on in Ottermouth would help her get her thoughts in order.

The promise of a discussion with Alex having spurred her on, Felicity was wrapping up her second call to the newsdesk when Isabella and James Halliday arrived in Ashdene's entrance hall. They were laughing and close, having shared an umbrella, a rather damp butler and footman in their wake.

Felicity stood up from the telephone table to greet them.

"Splendidly awful weather out there, Cici." Isabella was in high spirits. "I'm happy to say that Constable Thompson didn't come back, but there was no chance of sailing out. Still, the picnic on deck cheered everyone up. The Vances and Mrs Basingstoke fancied a bit of local colour, so they've gone to the inn. Did you get your stories written up? Might now be an opportune moment for an interview with James?"

"Bella, really. The focus shouldn't be on me." James appeared rather cool on the surface, but a sparkle in his gaze gave away his interest in being interviewed for the paper.

"Nonsense, Jimmy." Isabella waved a hand. "What do you say, Cici?"

Felicity forced a smile. The telephone call with Alex would have to wait.

Felicity, Isabella, and James moved to Ashdene's salon for the interview, which was long and meandering. Isabella had changed out of her Riviera outfit into a long, slinky number and held a cigarette in an elegant holder, the smoke wafting out over the terrace. She watched James with rapt attention. Dark clouds clung to the horizon beyond the treetops of the garden, making the sea a cold, steely shade of grey.

James Halliday wasn't a vain or unpleasant man, but as he spoke about his business achievements, his interest in art, and his travels over the world, Felicity suppressed an urge to fidget. While she had been tasked with profiling Ottermouth's art scene, she ought really to have been down in the village, working on having people open up to her, learning everything she could about Martin Granger. Or at least she ought to be on the telephone, developing ideas with a fellow reporter.

"Did you know the Grangers at all well, Mr Halliday?" enquired Felicity hopefully.

James shook his head. "I'm sorry to say I became interested in Eustace's works only after his passing. And Martin, well. Thanks to Isabella, I met the fellow once or twice, but we weren't close." He sighed sadly. "Such talents. Both taken too soon."

In the end, it was Pip and Beetle that rescued Felicity, Isabella having no objection to their presence in the salon, and neither of them having given up on the promise of the long walk. Pip was the first to whine. Then Beetle joined in and rested his chin on Felicity's lap, pleading eyes shining through shaggy fur.

"It's no longer raining, and I'm more than happy to take both dogs," insisted Felicity when Isabella protested at the fuss. It was a useful excuse to escape the interview with James without causing offence, the conversation having found its way onto profit-making through strategic sales of certain works of art, which was not a topic of interest for readers of the Western Daily News. A brisk walk would also allow Felicity to gather her thoughts and decide what to do next.

As Pip and Beetle stood with wet noses pressed against Ashdene's front door, Felicity collected an umbrella from the stand — for her tweeds had had time to dry, and she wouldn't be caught out again — and turned to bid farewell to Isabella and James. Beside them, on the wall of the entrance hall, was the painting of a lone girl on the beach, her hair caught in the wind.

"This girl is local, is she not?" asked Felicity of Isabella and James. "She lives in the fishermen's cottages on the harbour, if I'm not mistaken. We saw her a little earlier, when she came to fetch Constable Thompson." *And then disappeared down an alleyway*, recalled Felicity, but that was a separate matter.

Pip whined. Was there to be further delay to the dogs' walk?

James' smile was both knowing and kind. "I'm afraid that's not possible, your ladyship. This work is by Eustace, not Martin." He pointed towards the signature in the canvas' corner. "Their work is similar in some respects, but this can't be the young woman we saw earlier today. She was likely not even born when this painting was completed." Again, James gestured to the painting's signature, beside which was a date.

Felicity leaned forward and squinted at it. "Thank you for clarifying the matter, Mr Halliday. I must learn to look more carefully."

Again, Pip whined, Beetle joining in.

"Jim knows such an awful lot about paintings," said Isabella admiringly. "He's more than a collector. He's a true connoisseur."

James smiled modestly. "I wouldn't go that far, Bella."

At last released into the open air, the dogs barked all along the garden path. Following behind them, Felicity's thoughts churned.

From the date on the canvas, which was decades ago, Thora indeed couldn't have been the model. Yet the painted figure had looked awfully familiar. Was it merely a coincidence?

A completely different but just as puzzling matter was the smuggling. A secretive, illicit atmosphere permeated Ottermouth. Felicity had come close to discovering more in her discussion with Officer Marshall, but were there other routes she could take?

And those weren't the only issues to consider. The suggestion of Martin's 'other women' and the rivalry between Martin and Lawrence Whitburn might also be significant.

What reasons might there be for someone to do away with Martin? Were there grudges held against the deceased artist about which Felicity was so far oblivious?

Felicity hadn't needed to talk to Alex for the path ahead to become clear. A walk in the fresh air had done the trick. She would return to the village and strive to have people open up and be honest with her. There was simply no other way to move forward. The information was there. She just had to get at it.

"Pip! Beetle!" Felicity called as the wind blew grey clouds overhead. It was time to return to the house, but through canine enthusiasm and Felicity's inattention, the two dogs had barrelled off along the track leading down to the cove where Felicity had discovered Martin's lifeless form.

Felicity called the dogs again, but the wind whipped away her words as Pip and Beetle continued towards the beach, yapping and caught up in their games together. Felicity wasn't eager to return to the shadowy cove, but as the barking intensified, she hastened forwards. Looking down the cliff, she saw immediately there was nothing else for it. She would have to go down to the beach. It was an opportunity that couldn't be missed.

Chapter Eighteen

The tide was much lower than it had been the morning Felicity found Martin Granger. The pebbled beach now stretched out to a low formation of rocks that extended beyond the furthest point of the cliffs. A rich, briny smell blew in as the waves shushed rhythmically against the shingle.

Standing far out on the rocks was a lone figure with a fishing rod. His mop of unkempt sandy hair made him immediately recognisable, even half-tucked under a cap in the same faded blue twill as his jacket and trousers. This was Col, the young crew member of the Maggie who'd drawn a knife at the Dolphin Inn.

Away from Captain Dunn and the rest of the men, might Col speak to Felicity? Would it be a wise decision to approach him?

But there was an even more pressing matter.

Pip and Beetle — the larger Briard much faster than the little Yorkie — had gone flying towards Col, splashing through rock pools, barking their hearts out. While the barks were from excitement rather than aggression, someone unaccustomed to dogs could misinterpret the enthusiasm.

Extremely keen to avoid any kind of misunderstanding, Felicity dashed across the beach, calling the dogs' names.

Col flinched but stood his ground in heavy leather boots as

the two dogs reached him. They didn't get too close, but nor did they cease their barking. Even with tails wagging, it was an invitation to play delivered with rather more gusto than appropriate for a first encounter.

"Pip, Beetle! Please!"

As she stepped onto the rocks, Felicity's Oxfords slid on seaweed and her foot dipped unexpectedly into a limpet-encrusted pool of ice-cold water.

Still, she pressed forward. "Will you please cease your barking? The gentleman has no interest in playing with either of you."

Col's eyes were a little wide. He was perhaps frightened of dogs while doing his best not to appear so.

Arriving on the scene, Felicity caught Beetle by his collar. The Briard whimpered, admitting defeat, and sat beside Felicity on a large rock, his tail still wagging. With his friend out of the game, Pip retreated from the fisherman, although he continued to growl and occasionally yap.

"My apologies," Felicity said to Col. She glared with disapproval at the Yorkie, although the dogs' presence bolstered her confidence in approaching the man. "They mean no harm."

The young man shrugged his shoulders and adjusted his grip on his fishing rod. "No harm done, your ladyship."

"Aha." Felicity smiled. "So, you know who I am?" Determined to burrow into Ottermouth's secrets, she would seize any opportunity for discussion tossed her way.

Col nodded. "You're the reporter. Lady… Lady…"

"Lady Felicity Quick," finished Felicity, still smiling. "And you are?"

There was a pause as the young man looked out to sea. He perhaps hoped the Maggie might sail around the promontory that hid the village from view and save him from the encounter. "Colin Reynolds, your ladyship." He touched the peak of his cap in a polite gesture, his other hand remaining on his fishing pole.

The end of the fishing line drifted in the wind in a spot of what looked like rather shallow water.

"Pleased to meet you, Mr Reynolds." Felicity had to raise her voice above Pip's growls, Beetle's whimpers, and the wind blustering in from the sea. "May I ask what you're fishing for?"

Colin looked confused for a moment. He glanced at the line trailing in the water. "Mackerel." The man's gaze darted nervously to the dogs.

"How fascinating." Felicity looked around for a way to distract Pip and Beetle, who were clearly making the young fisherman uneasy.

A chunk of slimy seaweed on a large stick-like appendage lay on a nearby rock. Picking up the stick — which felt oddly rough in her palm — Felicity released Beetle's collar, whistled to get both Pip's and the Briard's attention, then hefted the seaweed stick into the air. It span before landing a good distance away on the shingle, both dogs running off excitedly after it. Felicity brushed her hands.

Colin smiled a little. A titled lady hefting a wet slimy plant up the beach was perhaps a rather odd sight. The young fisherman had a charming face, his cheeks ruddy from time outdoors. He appeared too young to have fought in the war.

"Do you fish here often by yourself?" enquired Felicity.

The smile left Colin's face. He knew better than to let his guard down for too long. "I fish all along the coast, whenever the mood suits me, your ladyship."

"Is fishing aboard the Maggie not enough for you?"

The man was quiet for a moment. The tide hissed over the shingle. "It's for my supper, your ladyship."

Good-natured growls came from further up the beach. Pip and Beetle each had a hold on the seaweed stick and ran with it in tandem, occasionally stopping for a brief tug-o'-war.

"Mackerel for supper, how delicious," said Felicity, though the young man had no bucket with him. "I must admit, Mr Reynolds, I'm happy to be speaking to you. I was hoping to collect some comments from the local people for the newspaper."

Again, Colin cast a concerned gaze out to sea. He also looked towards the path along which Felicity had accessed the beach. He was considering escape, but Felicity had him rather cornered. Was his real purpose for being on the beach the catching of mackerel for his supper? Felicity recalled the package Elizabeth Prothero had found. And the 'package' she'd found herself on that very beach.

Felicity swallowed. She also remembered the knife shining in Colin's hand at the inn. What had the altercation been about? She had to proceed carefully.

"Might you be able to tell me what the feelings of the fishing community are towards the artists of Ottermouth?" It was the most innocuous yet still relevant of questions she could muster. "I can anonymise your comments, of course."

Colin's brow lowered suddenly. Had Felicity put a foot wrong?

Fwap!

The two dogs, both still holding the ragged, slimy seaweed stick in slobbery jaws, slammed into the back of Felicity's legs, causing her knees to buckle slightly. "Goodness," she said with breathless surprise.

Pip released the stick and barked commandingly. *Throw it again!*

Felicity leaned down, ready to oblige, although Beetle was less keen to let go, and the situation became a struggle, Felicity's feet slipping on the rocks.

Colin saw his chance. Winding in his line, he moved swiftly over the rocks and towards the cliff path. "I have to go."

With an almighty tug, Felicity freed the seaweed stick from Beetle's jaws and threw it across the rocks, almost reaching the sea. Both dogs went flying after it.

"Your community was of great interest to the recently deceased artist, was it not?" Felicity would not give up on the only fisherman who'd said more than a handful of words to her. She attempted to follow Colin, but crossing the rocks was slow work. "Not just the fishing, but also the life ashore?"

Colin shot Felicity a hard glance as he reached the shingle. His eyes were suddenly hot with anger, as they had been at the inn, his knuckles white on the fishing rod clutched at his side. He said nothing in response.

Inwardly, Felicity chastised herself. She ought not to have been so pushy. She should have built trust, established a rapport.

"My sincerest apologies if I've caused offence, Mr Reynolds." Felicity lagged severely behind as the young fisherman crunched away across the pebbled beach. "If you change your mind about talking to me…" She trailed off, her voice drowned by the waves and the sea breeze.

Even if Colin could still hear her, he was no longer listening. He joined a pathway through the rough undergrowth of the cliffs that Felicity hadn't even noticed as leading down to the beach. Moving in the village's direction, he disappeared into the thick vegetation covering the promontory.

Another chance had been dashed.

Felicity sighed, deflated, as Pip and Beetle reappeared before her, ears pricked and tails wagging eagerly. The seaweed stick was now in two parts. Pip dropped his section and barked.

Felicity inspected the back of her tweed skirt. There was seaweed slime and slobber where the two dogs had crashed into her. One of her shoes was also sopping wet. Before doing anything else, Felicity would have to go back to Ashdene and change.

She continued to mull over her defeat as she scrambled across the rocks and followed the dogs up the beach, throwing sticks for them along the way. But by the time Felicity reached the path back up towards Ashdene, her despair had left her. Speaking to people from the fishing community on their own was a better approach. Although she'd learned almost nothing from Colin Reynolds, he had spoken to her. There was at least one other person Felicity might easily corner.

The dogs had rushed ahead towards the gate to Ashdene's gardens, barking with abandon, no doubt impatient for a bath and a plate of sausages from Isabella's doting housekeeper. Drawing closer to where Pip and Beetle had come to a stop, Felicity sensed a different tone to their barks. All sense of play had gone.

Then someone stepped out onto the path.

Chapter Nineteen

Elizabeth Prothero had been waiting by the tall clipped laurel hedging that extended from the gate at the bottom of Ashdene's garden. Emerging onto the path before Felicity, Elizabeth folded her arms across her plain, burgundy-velvet dress. Her pretty face showed displeasure, but she appeared unaffected by the barking.

"Good day to you, Lady Felicity. I was informed I'd find you walking the dogs." Elizabeth looked down at the Yorkie and Briard with stiff disapproval as they continued to yap and growl.

Amid attempts to convince Pip and Beetle to cease their noise, Felicity responded. "You came to Ashdene especially to speak to me, Miss Prothero? Are preparations for the exhibition not keeping you busy enough?"

"I'm not my father's employee." The upright young woman tightened the fold of her arms. "I told you what I know. I was hoping you'd tell me what you've been able to find out on the matter."

Felicity arched an eyebrow. At what point had she given Elizabeth the impression they had an agreement? Also, while Elizabeth had been the first to dare to mention the matter of smuggling to Felicity, she hadn't shared further details or any proof. She hadn't even looked inside the package she'd found before handing it over to Customs and Excise.

"I'm a reporter for the Western Daily News, Miss Prothero, as you well know. Anything I find out and can share, I share with our readers first. Should you wish to purchase a copy—"

"I'm not talking about matters for the paper, your ladyship. From what I know of how you work, your investigation will go deeper than that."

Felicity stopped herself from displaying surprise at the young woman's tone. When Elizabeth asked Felicity to walk with her in the woods by Halcyon Cottage and suggested that she look into Ottermouth's smuggling activities, Elizabeth had sounded desperate, even pleading. Now she spoke as though she paid Felicity's wages.

Even if Felicity felt inclined to share with Elizabeth, it was a moot point. Despite interactions with many people, she was no closer to the truth about smuggling or any connection to what had happened to Martin Granger.

The wind rustled the laurel bushes as the dogs sniffed the surrounding vegetation. Pip gave Elizabeth's black one-strap shoes a serious nose-led inspection.

"You mentioned smuggling to me, Miss Prothero," said Felicity coolly, "but you didn't give me any details upon which to base my investigations." Felicity recalled the embarrassment she'd felt when Officer Marshall had challenged Felicity to define what she understood by the word.

Elizabeth responded with an air of frustration. "I told you I don't have details. I expect you to fill them in."

It was almost painful. The only person in Ottermouth desperate to speak to Felicity had essentially nothing to say.

On another day, in another situation, Felicity might have taken pity on the girl. With the mistakes made while speaking to the young fisherman still fresh in Felicity's mind, and with a pressing need to move on with her investigation, Felicity's desire to be accommodating had already worn thin.

"Miss Prothero, forgive me for speaking bluntly, but I've not been engaged by you to investigate. I'm engaged by the paper to report, and I have deadlines to make. So unless you have something to share that will help my reporting, I shall have to wish you a good day."

Elizabeth brought a hand to her chest, her forthrightness suddenly gone. "My apologies, your ladyship. It's just… Did you, by any chance, speak to Officer Marshall?"

The two dogs were now sniffing around Ashdene's garden gate. It wouldn't be long before they started whining.

"I did," said Felicity. Their interaction on the harbour wall hadn't been pleasant, but the outcome could have been worse. "There wasn't much he would tell me."

Elizabeth snatched at wisps of her light brown hair as they danced in the wind. "He did exactly the same to me, you know. When I reported that package, I expected him to do something about it. Instead, he turned the whole thing around, tried to tell me it was my duty to help him. There was some kind of ruse he was working on to trap the smugglers. He wouldn't even tell me what was in the package, yet he expected me to act as bait. The nerve of it."

Felicity felt a pang of regret at becoming short with Elizabeth. Officer Marshall was quite a piece of work. "Let's attempt to look at matters in a different light," she began. "Do you believe that national law, originating in the seats of power in London, can be at odds with what is right for a local community?"

Elizabeth drew back her chin. "Whatever do you mean?" Her sense of right and wrong was perhaps less nuanced than Felicity's had become during her time working for the newspaper.

Felicity continued carefully. "What I mean to say, Miss Prothero, is that while Officer Marshall may take his job incredibly seriously, there are worse evils than unpaid taxes."

"But that's not it." Elizabeth's dark brown eyes were ablaze with sudden passion. "It's not just that. It's worse. Much worse."

The assertion echoed what the customs officer had said.

"Worse? In what way?"

Elizabeth shook her head impatiently. "Trust me, I just know it's worse."

Felicity was quiet for a moment. The dogs were whining to go back inside, but Felicity wouldn't be hurried. Elizabeth was perhaps simply parroting what she'd heard from the customs officer and knew nothing more about the smuggling than Felicity did. A different tack was required.

"You're well acquainted with Mr Lawrence Whitburn, are you not?" A build-up of evidence had led Felicity to this hypothesis. From Elizabeth's defence of the artist's refusal to sell his work, despite it going against her own father's interests, to the way Felicity had seen them looking at each other in the woods.

"Not especially well acquainted." The colour that appeared in Elizabeth's cheeks implied otherwise.

"Might you be able to arrange an interview with him for me?" continued Felicity. "I had a short encounter with Mr Whitburn soon after the discovery of Mr Granger, and Mr Whitburn seemed rather agitated. He's deeply embedded in the fishing community, isn't he? I'm sure our readers would appreciate hearing his point of view."

Elizabeth's forehead wrinkled. "Lawrence had nothing to do with Mr Granger's accident, you know."

Felicity blinked. "I never imagined he did," she said, her curiosity about the man intensifying. "May I ask what makes you so sure?" It was perhaps coarse to even think it, but might Elizabeth be Lawrence's alibi for the night Martin met his end?

Elizabeth hesitated. She wrung her slender fingers together. "I shall do my best to speak to Mr Whitburn on your behalf and will come back to you on the matter." Brushing past Felicity, Elizabeth started along the path. "Please excuse me, your ladyship. I must be getting back."

Felicity watched Elizabeth hurry along the track back into Ottermouth. Shaking her head, she opened the gate at the bottom of Ashdene's gardens. Pip and Beetle flew like rockets towards the big house. At her own pace, Felicity followed.

Whichever way Felicity turned, she bumped into a dead end, leaving her guessing about the missing details. In Elizabeth's case, the guessing was easy. The girl had a special interest in Lawrence Whitburn, and the feeling was perhaps mutual.

The deduction, however, didn't bring Felicity closer to unravelling the deadly secrets at the heart of Ottermouth.

She would go up to her room and change out of her dirty tweeds. It was then time for a completely fresh approach. And it would involve quite a climb.

Chapter Twenty

In a russet-brown wool skirt and jacket matched with a brown bicorn hat trimmed with mustard ribbon, Felicity departed Ashdene without dogs and without an umbrella, the skies over Ottermouth having mostly cleared. Climbing the steep path that circumnavigated the village, Felicity paused for a moment as her destination came into view on the headland, but only for a moment. She'd wasted quite enough time already.

Besides greeting Pip and Beetle with a soft brush and fresh towels, Ashdene's housekeeper had urged Felicity to sit down for a sandwich. It was past noon, and Felicity had not eaten since breakfast. Felicity had been reluctant, but the brown bread's warmth, the cheddar's mature tang, and the sweet richness of the pickle caused her to opt for a second round.

It was during the second helping at the big oak table at the centre of Ashdene's cellar kitchen that the butler came with news of a telephone call that had been received. A gentleman had asked to speak to Felicity, but the line was bad and the connection broke off, so it hadn't been possible to gather further information from the caller.

Now, looking down on the spur of rugged land upon which Ottermouth's lighthouse stood, the salty wind ruffling the curls at her cheeks, Felicity reflected on her selfishness. She'd been glad the call hadn't connected, for it had no doubt been her brother. It wasn't just content for the newspaper that Jasper cared about. He was protective of Isabella, the widow of his dear friend.

Felicity had little advancement to report in either respect. Yes, Constable Thompson's search of Xantho had been interrupted, but that Isabella's yacht was being investigated in the first place would be a cause of deep concern for Felicity's brother.

Felicity did now, however, know how to break the stalemate in her investigations. She was on her way to speak to Joe, the lighthouse keeper, whom she'd met briefly via Grace Campbell. Felicity couldn't force Joe to answer her questions, but by going to the lighthouse to find him, she was surely limiting his opportunities to escape her.

The section of the path that led from the hills above Ottermouth towards the lighthouse was less well-used than the route between the village and Ashdene. Steep and crumbling, it was also less well-maintained. At a fork in the path offering two options for the next leg of her journey — a scramble over rocks at sea level or another section of the same crumbly path that was perhaps even steeper — Felicity chose the flattest option, even if it involved sliding about on seaweed and the risk wetting one's feet in a rock pool.

She only regretted her choice when, on the other side of a large, smooth boulder, she came upon Billy Seddon. He was seated on a jumble of pinkish-grey rocks as though sitting on a throne, a well-tailored waistcoat snug over a crisp, white shirt. The smell of his cigarette mingled with the odour of decaying seaweed to create an unpleasant cocktail. Out on the water, a little way beyond the rocks, a sleek wooden runabout was anchored, its varnished hull sparkling in the sunshine.

"Good day to you, your ladyship. And what a fine day it is for a scramble over the rocks." Billy smiled at her.

"Good day, Mr Seddon." Felicity smiled good-naturedly and spoke politely, but his presence gave her an uneasy feeling.

As she continued picking her way along the shoreline, Felicity could feel Billy watching her, and the sensation was far from pleasant. Despite Billy's willingness to speak to her, Felicity had no desire to engage in conversation with him. Were she a male journalist instead of a female one, the situation might be different. Hopefully, the exchange of greetings was the end of the encounter with him.

Unfortunately, it wasn't.

"It's all right," he called out. "I'm used to it. Not keen to befriend a fellow who's incomplete, I suppose, your ladyship? You make a sacrifice for King and country, and that's the thanks you get."

Felicity stopped and turned towards Billy. How had she not noticed it till now? Lying back on his rocky throne, he held his cigarette in one leisurely hand. Resting in his lap, where his other hand ought to have been, was a leather cuff with a hook attached to it.

"Oh," said Felicity, feeling ashamed of her behaviour. "I didn't realise."

"Quite handsome, otherwise, aren't I?" Billy winked.

Any sympathy Felicity felt for his disfigurement immediately evaporated. Unable to abide arrogant, inappropriate behaviour from anyone, she continued her uncomfortable journey over the rocks, her jaw taut with frustration.

"Biggest regret of my life, signing up for the war," continued Billy as though Felicity wasn't ignoring him. "If I'd known I'd never fish again, I wouldn't have volunteered myself, but they'd have got me in the end, anyway."

Felicity cast a reluctant glance in Billy's direction. Considering the sacrifices made by the men who had gone to war, it was difficult to maintain complete disregard for him. Fishing hadn't been a protected profession, which explained why the Maggie's current crew appeared to be too old or too young to have been conscripted. It was perhaps also why the Maggie seemed to be the only trawler left in the village. A number of men would certainly have been lost.

Nonetheless, Felicity almost instantly regretted turning her gaze towards Billy.

"Go for a ride with me, will you? Just the two of us. That's my boat out there," he added, nodding towards the runabout bobbing on the water. "What do you say?"

"Thank you, Mr Seddon, but no," said Felicity firmly, hurrying as much as she could over the slippery rocks. Alex was a war veteran. He'd suffered injury as well. Her brother Jasper had also fought. Neither of them ever used their experiences to garner sympathy. But then neither of them had had their livelihoods stolen from them by the conflict.

"Powerful little number, she is, your ladyship. Excitement guaranteed." Billy chuckled. "It'll be quite the thrill ride, I promise you."

Felicity kept her focus on the rocks ahead, but something tugged at her. Was she being too dismissive? Could she not bear the discomfort for the greater good? Billy seemed more ready than anyone to open up to her. Might Felicity be able to push through his audacious flirting and discover something truly relevant to her investigations?

Billy pulled on his cigarette as he continued to watch Felicity. "She's moored right there. I'll bring you out, of course, your ladyship. No need to get your dainty feet wet."

The offer to carry Felicity through the water was so highly inappropriate, it didn't deserve serious consideration, let alone a response. The little boat bobbing on the waves beyond the shore indeed looked capable of high speeds. It also looked brand new. How did an injured war veteran no longer capable of making money from his profession afford such a vessel?

Despite having no desire to get any closer to Billy, Felicity's curiosity had been piqued.

She managed a smile in his direction. "That's awfully kind of you to invite me, Mr Seddon. Perhaps another time." While she couldn't yet stomach his company, Billy might still prove useful. For now, an end to Felicity's awkward progress across the rocks was almost within reach.

"I'll be at the harbour this evening if you change your mind, your ladyship. I'd be happy to motor you over to Brixham or Torquay. Buy you a packet of fish and chips." Billy's smile hinted at mockery. "I know you write for them, but I don't suppose you've eaten out of newspaper before, have you, your ladyship?"

At last, Felicity stepped off the rocks and onto the sloping path that wound gently up the side of the headland towards the lighthouse. It was a mystery why Billy believed insulting Felicity would make his offer more attractive to her. Coincidentally, she had eaten fish and chips out of newspaper for the first time just recently, when she and Alex met by Exeter's canals for one of their confabs. But that was none of Billy's business.

"I shall think about it, Mr Seddon," called Felicity as she briskly ascended the headland path.

"I'll be waiting." Billy's response was accompanied by a wave of his cigarette. Thankfully, he was quickly obscured by the tangle of long grass and brambles that smothered the edge of the trail up the cliff.

Although the incline was gentle, the path up the headland was long, and Felicity soon felt it in her legs. Even before her grim discovery at the cove, even before arriving in Ottermouth, Felicity had known her visit to Ottermouth would be hard work. There was what Jasper had asked of her, and there was her instinct to always delve deeper. Yet it had been inconceivable that she would face quite so much adversity.

Hard work was what Felicity wanted, though, wasn't it? She'd yearned for the challenge of serious journalism for so long, and the beautiful yet hostile environment in Ottermouth was among her biggest challenges so far. If she wanted an easy life, she could accompany Isabella and talk to art collectors or go to the gallery and watch Harold and Nigel deliberate over repositioning paintings.

Exactly what Felicity hoped to discover by speaking to the lighthouse keeper — if indeed he'd speak to her — wasn't fully clear, even for Felicity. There was, however, one question she had to ask.

Halfway up the side of the headland, the path plateaued. Felicity paused, breathing hard, and took in the view. Fluffy white clouds rolled in fast over the sparkling blue water as the wind rustled the stubby grasses and shrubs that covered the headland. In the distance, the sharp gables of Ashdene peeked out above the house's lush gardens. In the village below, the harbour was abuzz. More gleaming yachts had arrived, and colourful bunting fluttered from the glossy green walls of the gallery.

Billy Seddon was back in view on his rocky throne on the shoreline below. Again, he waved up at Felicity with his intact hand, but she pretended not to notice and recommenced her ascent. Despite the double round of sandwiches, the energy in her legs was flagging, and she was only halfway up the headland. There was, however, no turning back.

As the path looped back on itself to continue its climb, the vegetation cloaking the rock face grew thin. Beyond the spindly arms of brambles and trailing ivy, an arched doorway had been carved into the solid stone of the promontory. The doorway was framed with large, chisel-marked blocks of pale grey granite. A date carved into the keystone read *1802*. A damp breeze whistled through the opening.

Brushing back fronds of vegetation, Felicity put a hand on the cool granite of the door frame. Within, everything was black, except for another doorway in the distance through which daylight shone. The tunnel seemed to slope upward.

Considering the date and the robustness of the construction, the tunnel was likely part of works carried out along the coast when Britain feared invasion during the Napoleonic era. Was this an easier route to the lighthouse than the steep path?

Had Felicity not left Pip in the devoted care of the housekeeper at Ashdene, she wouldn't have had the time to reflect on whether to take the tunnel. The little Yorkie would have gone charging into the darkness, leaving Felicity no choice but to follow.

Still, what did Felicity have to lose? She had the freedom to double back if it turned out to be the wrong direction.

The interior of the tunnel was damp and cool. Smooth granite slabs underfoot quickly gave way to less even footing, which felt very much like compacted earth. Water could be heard dripping steadily. It wasn't somewhere Felicity wanted to linger, but the daylight of the open doorway up ahead was an easy beacon to follow, and as Felicity advanced, the view through the doorway widened. There was blue sky, pale grey clouds, granite walls, and whitewashed buildings. Yes, she could see the gleaming apparatus of the lighthouse. Felicity was on the right track. She was almost there.

The view disappeared, the light from the doorway suddenly blocked by a silhouette.

Someone was waiting for her at the other end of the tunnel.

Chapter Twenty-One

Felicity halted her advance along the tunnel. The sound of water dripping continued as the silhouette lingered in the doorway ahead.

"You shouldn't be in here."

The man's voice boomed down the tunnel. Was it the lighthouse keeper, Joe? His features were in shadow.

"My apologies," called Felicity, her voice echoing in the darkness. "I saw no sign barring entry. I can return the way I came."

Felicity's apology was met with nothing but the sound of dripping water. The silhouette persisted in the doorway.

"I was hoping to visit the lighthouse. Indeed, I was hoping to speak to the lighthouse keeper." Felicity added a hint of hopeful expectancy to her voice. "I'm a reporter. For the Western Daily News."

There was a pause before the man's silhouette disappeared from the doorway. Daylight reentered the tunnel. The water continued to drip.

Was it an invitation?

Felicity straightened and proceeded towards the blue sky and the whitewashed buildings at the other end of the tunnel. She'd wanted a different approach. There was no point turning back now.

Emerging from the doorway, a strong wind gusted, pulling at Felicity's hat, which she clutched just in time, her curls whipping across her face. She'd reached the headland where the lighthouse was located. The view of the coast beyond the coves of Ottermouth was dramatic. The sky's expanse seemed bigger than ever.

There was only a single, crooked tree hardly taller than Felicity. The grass underfoot was stubbly, with clumps of blue spring quill and pulmonaria nodding rapidly in the wind. The nearby buildings were also squat and tough, as though crouched defensively against the wind hitting the headland. Even the lighthouse lacked height. Accommodated in a short, cylindrical tower under a riveted dome, its lamp and inner workings were clear to see under sparkling, curved glass. But a tall tower wasn't needed. The promontory was high enough for the lighthouse to be visible to ships for many miles.

"Your ladyship."

Felicity turned.

Having stepped away from the tunnel's entrance, the man still stood to one side of the doorway, his back to the rocky outcrop through which the tunnel ran, his hands pushed into the pockets of faded blue overalls. His grey beard was long enough to move with the wind, the peak of his battered cap pulled low on his forehead.

It was Joe, the lighthouse keeper and Grace Campbell's oarsman. And he knew who Felicity was.

"The tunnel's dangerous." He took a step forward but didn't come close. "You shouldn't be in there."

"Oh," said Felicity, pressing her hat onto her head. The wind on the headland was fierce. "I wasn't aware. I'm not from around here, you see. And I didn't notice any sign."

"I know you're not from around here." Joe eyed Felicity with suspicion. His manner was far from welcoming, but in the context of Felicity's previous encounters in Ottermouth, the mere act of him engaging in conversation with her was a triumph.

"My apologies, Mr…" Felicity trailed off hopefully.

"Ferris," said the man sternly. He had a Westcountry accent but didn't sound Devonian. Bristol, perhaps? "Joseph Ferris."

Every moment spent in discussion, even if it was just formalities and platitudes, was an achievement. There was one thing Felicity was eager to ask, but she would proceed cautiously. She'd learned from the mistakes made in Ottermouth so far. "Very pleased to make your acquaintance, Mr Ferris. As I mentioned, I work for the Western Daily News. Might you be willing to speak with me? Your name need not appear." Unattributed quotes were not Felicity's preferred approach, but Ottermouth was an exception.

Joe glared at Felicity from under the peak of his cap. It wasn't a warm welcome, but he was at least giving Felicity's approach serious consideration, which, again, was a minor victory.

He turned, his beard catching in the wind, and set off towards the lighthouse. "Come on." He issued the command as though Felicity were a dog or a lost child, but she wasn't offended. Her stomach rose with excitement. The lighthouse keeper would talk.

Felicity had taken the stocky single-storey building connected to the lighthouse as being associated with the workings of the powerful lamp. In opening the door, Joe had revealed a tiny dwelling, a single room that was a sitting room, kitchen, and bedroom, all rolled into one. Although neatly arranged, it was full to the brim with the utensils of daily life. Felicity was invited to take the only seat, a plain wooden stool by the cast-iron stove. Joe sat on a narrow bed with a thick tartan blanket.

No refreshments were offered, but the little dwelling was at least out of the wind. A wicker basket with a green-and-white checked cloth covering its contents stood on the kitchen worktop.

Above, a small window offered a view of the sea. Dried herbs hanging in bunches sweetened the air.

Building up slowly, but not so slowly as to waste time, Felicity began with the questions she was expected to ask.

"Did you know Mr Granger?"

Joe sat stiffly on his little bed, hands gripping the edge of the mattress, his cap on the blanket next to him. He shook his head.

"Have you been the lighthouse keeper here for very long, Mr Ferris?" she asked, her pencil poised on her notebook.

"Nearly twenty years, give or take."

"I assume Mr Granger's sad passing is not the first you've witnessed in that time."

The lighthouse keeper took an uneasy breath. "His wasn't the first body to wash up on our shores, no."

With a little further coaxing, Joe recounted the story of a trading vessel that dashed against the rocks in a terrible storm before the war. Three crew members lost their lives. There had also once been an accident on the coastal path where a local farmhand went over the edge, chasing after a wayward sheep. While he was badly injured, the vegetation broke his fall, and he survived.

"There's the odd pleasure yacht that gets into trouble." Joe's grip on the mattress eased. "Down to inexperience mostly, and mainly during daylight. The lifeboatmen from Brixham have been out here once or twice in the past year alone."

Felicity wrote everything in her notebook. "Are there many incidents at night?" She didn't look up from the page as she spoke. She would keep her eagerness in check, but the opportunity to ask her question was approaching.

"I've been the attendant at this lighthouse since it came into operation. Would have been many more accidents if it weren't for this old girl." He nodded towards a small door in the wall beside the stove, beyond which lay the great lamps.

Felicity was eager to pounce, but she continued to circle around the topic. "Is it much work, looking after the lighthouse?"

Joe shrugged. "I turn it on in the evening. Do a bit of maintenance. Keep an eye on things. It's not complicated."

"Does it involve being awake at night?"

Again, a shrug. "Sometimes."

"Is there much activity on the water after dark?" Felicity was closing in.

A slight tension returned to Joe's shoulders. "Not much."

The time was right for the question Felicity was desperate to ask, the question that had driven her to seek the lighthouse keeper. "Did you see anyone out at sea the night Mr Granger met his end?" She was proud of the coolness of her tone.

Joe's eyebrows drew together. "That's a matter for the police, your ladyship."

It wasn't over yet.

Felicity lay her pencil flat on her notebook. "The police have announced the cause of Mr Granger's demise to have been a head injury from a smooth, man-made object. One hypothesis is that the injury occurred while Mr Granger was on the water aboard a vessel."

The wind rattled the little window above the kitchen worktop. The lighthouse keeper maintained Felicity's gaze but didn't speak.

"You found him, didn't you, your ladyship?"

The question caught Felicity off-guard. She'd almost put what she'd seen at the cove out of her mind.

She straightened on the little wooden stool. "Our readers will want to know how such a thing might happen." She cleared her throat a little. "Having discovered the body, as you rightly point out, I am, myself, quite keen to understand what happened to Mr Granger."

Joe nodded thoughtfully. "There are many hazards aboard a boat, your ladyship. A swinging boom has sent many a careless sailor overboard."

"Did you see any vessel leave Ottermouth harbour on the night in question, Mr Ferris?"

A smile appeared under the lighthouse keeper's silver beard.

"No one sees anything in Ottermouth, your ladyship. You know that by now."

Felicity wouldn't give up. "Might you know why Customs and Excise have a persistent presence in the village?"

Joe sighed. "That officer fellow came up here the other day. Asked rather similar questions as to what you're asking me now, your ladyship. I told him the same as what I've told you. I saw nothing."

Felicity's hope for a breakthrough was waning. Was it a fair assumption that those who refused to speak about smuggling were those directly involved? She was on the brink of confronting the lighthouse keeper with the hypothesis when she remembered she was in the man's home. He'd had the decency to allow her into his dwelling and to answer her questions. Felicity had no right to take out her frustrations on Joe. She would have to review her approach. A different method was once again needed, although Felicity was running out of ideas.

She nodded with understanding. "You've paint on your overalls, Mr Ferris. Are you involved in Ottermouth's art scene?"

Joe frowned as he looked down at his somewhat tattered overalls. "I only maintain the buildings up here around the lighthouse." He swiped at the marks.

"You've been in Ottermouth a long time, Mr Ferris. Did you perhaps know Mr Granger's father?" Felicity readied her pencil. It was the kind of colour and context the newspaper's readers would appreciate. It also fed into her original reason for being in Ottermouth, which was to spotlight the community's artistic achievements.

Joe tugged on his beard, still frowning. "I want nothing to do with that side of things." His tone was suddenly a growl.

"Oh," Felicity said with surprise. Her next question would have been a request for Joe's reaction to the exhibition going ahead. Instead, she sat in silence, not wanting to upset the man further.

The wind rattled the little window.

"I've work to do, your ladyship." Reaching for his cap, the lighthouse keeper stood up from his bed. "If you'll excuse me."

Avoiding whatever danger lurked in the Napoleonic-era tunnel, the longer route back to Ottermouth was rather tough going. At first, the pathway was clearly worn between the stubbled grass. Crossing bedrock, it disappeared, leaving one to scramble about on granite striations, peering towards the side of the promontory in the hope of rejoining the trail on the other side of the headland.

As Felicity's Oxfords lost purchase for the umpteenth time, her ankle almost twisting as her foot wedged between the rocks, she wondered if the tunnel could really be more dangerous. Still, it would have done no good to return the way she'd come. Joe had warned her off using the tunnel, and Felicity was keen to remain in good graces.

But was that the right approach?

At the rate people were warming to her in Ottermouth, it would be years before any of the locals would speak to her properly. Even then, they probably wouldn't tell her anything about smuggling.

The stories Felicity had written so far had been met with satisfaction and appraisal from the newsdesk, with a lift in sales expected across the Southwest thanks to Felicity's exclusive Ottermouth articles. Isabella also seemed content with Felicity's coverage of matters. Having a relatively biddable journalist on hand to interview her art collector friends was certainly appreciated.

Yet Felicity felt a distinct lack of personal satisfaction. Trying to uncover anything about smuggling was like chasing a ghost. Could she have done more to drill down into the essence of the story? Might she have been bolder? What about being more tactful? Or was smuggling not anything important at all, and she was simply chasing after shadows?

Rejoining the path along the side of the headland and passing the entrance to the tunnel, Felicity took in the view of the village, the harbour, the secretive coves, and the pointed gables of Ashdene on its perch above it all. There was also Seaview Lodge nestled into the side of the woods and Halcyon Cottage hidden among the trees. Somewhere, down there, lay the answers. Felicity had come to Ottermouth to re-establish herself as a journalist. It was a journalist's job to dive ever deeper in search of the truth.

Wasn't it?

Or should Felicity be content to report on what was within her grasp and move on?

A sailing yacht cut across the blue-grey water. With its mast leaning and sails billowing, its hull skimming the white-tipped waves. Above, a lone, soaring gull let out a melancholy cry.

It wasn't at all logical, but Felicity wished she'd had the opportunity to speak to Alex. Not that she needed his instruction or even his advice. There was simply no one else she could talk to like she talked to him. She wanted to hear his news, too, of course. The passion he had for his work was contagious.

Her mind was made up. Felicity would return to Ashdene and dine with Isabella, then she would telephone her friend. After speaking to Alex, Felicity would know what to do.

To avoid the rocky beach where Billy Seddon still sat smoking, his motorboat bobbing on the tide, Felicity hiked along the steep, wooded path above the village. With the sun sinking slowly behind the hills, the dimness made the uneven track with its overhanging trees even more inhospitable. Felicity was perhaps hurrying a tad too much when her foot slipped on a loose rock. She skidded but remained upright, her heart banging hard. The rock she'd slipped on continued its tumble off the path, bouncing off the cliff far below.

"Ought to be more careful, your ladyship."

Startled, Felicity looked up.

Chapter Twenty-Two

Officer Marshall's akimbo stance communicated confidence and self-assurance, but his presence on the shadowy wooded path above Ottermouth wasn't comforting. The smug, superior expression on his clean-shaven face immediately put Felicity ill at ease.

She stood tall and lifted her chin. "Officer Marshall. Can I help you?" It was a rote statement delivered in an unhappy tone, but Felicity ought to have chosen her words more carefully.

"I hope so, your ladyship. I really do hope so."

The last time they'd spoken, Officer Marshall expressed an interest in recruiting Felicity in exchange for information. Was this encounter to be a repeat of the last?

At least half the village wasn't in earshot.

Still, there was a hardness to the custom officer's manner that didn't sit well with Felicity. Elizabeth Prothero had reported a similarly unpleasant experience in her dealings with the man. Did he specialise in manipulating young women, or did his efforts extend to all sorts?

The brass buttons on Officer Marshall's uniform gleamed in the dim light. "Have you given any further thought to our potential collaboration?"

Officer Marshall's goals aligned with the wishes of the crown. Indeed, he seemed to be the only person in Ottermouth dedicated to upholding the law to its fullest extent. Even the local constabulary wasn't fully on board in that regard. Yet despite this higher calling, Officer Marshall wasn't the sort of man to hold the welfare of the individual in high regard. As much as Felicity wanted to contribute to the greater good, she must also look out for herself.

Standing with her back to the wind, Felicity folded her arms. "Constable Thompson has said that Mr Granger's head wound wasn't caused by a fall down the cliffs."

Officer Marshall gave an amused huff. "I realise you're a clever one, your ladyship. You're barking up the wrong tree with that old lighthouse keeper, though. Been keeping tabs on him, of course. He's squeaky clean."

Felicity kept her cool. "Mr Granger was a different story, though. Was he not?"

Taking off his peaked hat and tucking it under his arm, Officer Marshall took a couple of slow steps towards Felicity. Tall and strong-jawed, the customs officer could be considered dashing. His blue gaze was intense and oddly captivating. His character, however, was severely lacking.

Felicity stood her ground, maintaining the lift of her chin.

"This path you're on, your ladyship. Do you know who made it?"

A frown passed over Felicity's brow. She glanced at the ground beneath her feet. "Who?"

Officer Marshall tapped his uniformed chest. "We did. His Majesty's Customs and Excise. We walked these paths for decades. For centuries. Patrolling the coast. Keeping our country safe."

Felicity remained unmoved. Normally, she loved enriching her understanding of Devon's past. But with a harsh sea wind gusting into her back and the customs officer's purpose still not declared, Felicity wasn't in the mood for a history lesson.

"Your point is, Officer Marshall?"

"In a hurry, are you?"

"I'm expected at Ashdene." While no one was exactly keeping tabs on Felicity, it seemed prudent to mention that she was far from at a loose end.

"My point, your ladyship, is that the battle for the safety of our country is still raging. It's all around us. You've seen it yourself." Officer Marshall gestured to where the harbour was visible through the trees. "You know there's something not right down there. The question is, are you ready to be part of the battle? Are you ready to do your bit?"

It was an obvious play for Felicity's sense of duty, and it failed.

"Officer Marshall. We appear to be going around in circles. I asked you earlier for details of what's happening here in Ottermouth, but you weren't forthcoming. I'm a journalist. I want information. Stories. Topics our readers care about. Revelations they can't read anywhere else. If you've nothing for me in that regard, then let us please cease wasting one another's time."

The customs officer tucked his chin. He looked hurt. "You've no interest in doing what's right for King and country?"

"I didn't say that."

Officer Marshall was cunning. The whole situation was extremely delicate. Felicity couldn't again be accused of defying the will of the authorities during a criminal investigation. Yet if she became known as an accomplice to Officer Marshall, all hope of getting anyone local to open up to her would be lost.

Felicity tightened the fold of her arms. "You told me matters were serious, Officer Marshall. Just how serious are they? You can't expect me to jump to your assistance just because you say you're doing the King's work. One must look before one leaps. At present, I have no inkling of where you're asking me to leap."

The wind hissed through the trees. The steep drop down the cliffs below was visible through their branches.

Officer Marshall chuckled. "You've more gumption about you than that gallery fellow's daughter, your ladyship." He tucked his hat under his other elbow. "If I tell you the details, then it's not for the paper. Not yet. When the evidence is there, you'll have the scoop. But for now, we've not enough to go on, not for a conviction, and if anything squeaks out before that, the rats will all rush back into their nests."

Felicity suppressed the urge to sigh with exasperation. "Please, Officer Marshall. Speak plainly."

The customs officer gave a brief, apologetic nod. Was Felicity's commanding tone having an effect?

"What we're dealing with here, your ladyship—" he leaned in and lowered his voice "—is the importation of illicit drugs."

Felicity's eyebrows shot up with surprise.

She'd lived a sheltered, privileged life, but she wasn't entirely naïve. She'd known abusers of such substances and seen first-hand the suffering for which they were responsible. But drugs in a village like Ottermouth?

"Cocaine, morphine," continued Officer Marshall, his tone deadly serious. "Likely others as well, brought in from Spain and Belgium and wherever else. It's not a question of unpaid taxes. These substances threaten the very fabric of our society, and it has to be stopped. I hope you agree with me on that point, at least, your ladyship?"

"Of course," said Felicity, yearning to reach for her notebook. "And I would be happy to write an article publicising the dangers of the trade and its failure just as soon as you have the evidence to secure the conviction." Would there be a way to frame such a story so that it wouldn't damage Ottermouth's artistic reputation? It was possible there might not be.

"Excellent." The customs officer's smile was devious. "So, you're willing to help gather the evidence?"

Felicity hesitated. Was it time to form an alliance?

Chapter Twenty-Three

Tea at Ashdene was a sprawling affair. Plate after plate of savouries and sweets — potted shrimp, warm cheese straws, gingerbread cake, and custard tartlets, to name just a few — were brought up to the salon. The terrace doors were, as usual, open, offering an escape for the pungent build-up of cigarette and pipe smoke plus expansive views of the sea beyond the garden's waving treetops.

Isabella was at the centre of it all in a long, purple-and-gold dress that shimmered when she moved, her warm brown hair loose around her shoulders. A gaggle of art collectors surrounded her, including the Vances, Mrs Basingstoke, and James Halliday, all enthralled by Isabella's gregarious nature, not to mention her collection of paintings. Even Felicity herself was an unintentional point of interest. Some of Isabella's guests were fascinated by her role as a reporter. Others seemed quite thrilled to be in the presence of the daughter of an earl.

Felicity smiled, sipped tea, and answered questions politely, all while turning over in her mind the impromptu meeting with Officer Marshall that had interrupted her journey back to Ashdene. Drugs in Ottermouth? It still didn't quite seem believable. The somewhat aged, well-to-do art buyers were no more addicted to dope than any of the hard-working fishermen.

Having spent a suitable amount of time among Isabella's guests to satisfy the hostess — not that Isabella was demanding of Felicity's time, but she wanted to remain faithful to the commitment she'd made to Jasper — Felicity excused herself from the gathering and went upstairs. The agreement she'd reached with Officer Marshall left no time to telephone Alex. Despite a strange tension in the pit of Felicity's stomach, the way forward was now clear. That was most important.

Felicity changed into her royal-blue woollen skirt and jacket, which would stave off the wind's chill while out on the water. As Felicity pulled on a snug-fitting cloche with a narrow brim, which wouldn't be ripped off by a sudden gust, Pip and Beetle watched her from the rug on the bedroom floor. Their tails wagged expectantly, but Felicity transferred the responsibility of taking the dogs for their evening run to Ashdene's dog-loving housekeeper, who seemed oddly excited by the novel idea of throwing seaweed sticks.

Ducking under low branches that overhung Ashdene's garden path, Felicity reminded herself of why she'd agreed to the customs officer's plan. It appeased Officer Marshall and served King and country. It would also work to the advantage of the Western Morning News if it turned out to be the scoop the customs officer was quite certain it would be. Best of all, there was nothing obvious about the activity that hinted at Felicity's collusion with the authorities.

Still, the tension in her stomach tightened further as she arrived at Ottermouth's harbour. Was it the prospect of going out on the water that made Felicity feel slightly queer? She'd not felt at all well on the ferry she'd taken to Ottermouth. Or was it the sight of Billy Seddon, lounging on a pile of crates with a cigarette balanced in his fingers, that gave her pause?

A glimmer of pleasant surprise showed in Billy's features as Felicity walked towards him, like a child presented with a birthday gift he wasn't expecting. Any trace of child-like innocence quickly disappeared, however. He stood up as Felicity approached, tugging on his waistcoat and flicking the remains of his cigarette into the water of the harbour with calculated self-assuredness. The hook where a hand once had been glinted. "I knew you'd come."

It took Herculean effort for Felicity to smile at Billy. "Good evening, Mr Seddon."

Officer Marshall had been searching the thicket above the shoreline and had overheard Felicity's encounter with the former fisherman. His plan was for Felicity to take Billy up on his offer of a boat tour along the coast that evening. Felicity would use the opportunity to look around Billy's vessel — which had so far always outrun the customs cutter — and perhaps even be shown some notable nooks and crannies along the coast.

"Why should I do this?" Felicity had asked the customs officer.

Officer Marshall had narrowed his eyes. "When it comes to the drugs trade in these parts, Seddon's the kingpin. There's no doubt about that. The only thing that's lacking is evidence."

As unpleasant as it was to have been spied upon by Officer Marshall, Felicity hadn't instantly dismissed his proposal. She'd been undercover before — although never for the newspaper — and what was there to lose? She might find nothing, and it would be simply a ride around the coast with a rather unsavoury character. Or she might find evidence of wrongdoing that would result in a triumphant story of Ottermouth being saved through the valiant collaboration between Customs and Excise and an intrepid local journalist.

The endeavour risked dashing Felicity's hopes of digging further into the fishing community, her position as a suspected snitch cemented as true. But Billy had been the one to offer the invitation, and Felicity couldn't wait forever for the story to unravel itself.

It was only now, standing before Billy on the harbourside, that

Felicity regretted her decision. Her stomach was in knots. Injured war veteran or not, Billy was not the sort of man a young woman should trust.

Billy grinned, his slick, dark hair glistening, the smell of tar and landed catches all around them. "Can't stay away, can you?"

"That's absolutely not the case, Mr Seddon," said Felicity firmly. She'd made her decision. There was no turning back. She'd navigated trickier situations, and if worst came to worst, she knew how to swim. "I'm interested in seeing something more of the coast. That's all."

"Might I join?"

The voice came from behind. Felicity's heart skipped a beat.

Felicity's colleague and friend, Alex Cooper, stood on the harbourside, his calm dark-blue eyes shining with interest as he looked between Felicity and Billy. Wearing an elegant grey suit under an unbelted tan overcoat, and with an amused half-smile on his clean-shaven face, Alex easily caught one's gaze against the messy chaos of the harbour, with its bollards wound with fraying ropes, piles of crab pots, and gulls fighting over fish tails.

"Alex. What are you doing here?" The words escaped Felicity's mouth unthinkingly. It sounded like she objected to his presence, but her feelings were quite the opposite.

"I'm very pleased to see you, too, Lady Felicity." Continuing to smile, Alex removed his homburg hat and held it to his chest. He nodded in Billy's direction. "Not encroaching on anything, am I?"

Felicity's cheeks glowed with embarrassment. She'd hoped no one in Ottermouth had heard the way Billy spoke to her, let alone Alex.

Billy's lip curled into a snarl at Alex. "Clear off, will you? This maid's mine for the evening. Find yourself another."

Felicity's cheeks grew pinker still as Alex raised his eyebrows.

Thankfully, he at least continued to look amused. "I'm not here to upset anyone's plans. I realise I've arrived here unannounced. However, I should like to hear from Lady Felicity herself about her intentions for the evening."

Felicity cleared her throat. "I can change my plans." *And despite how it might have sounded, I am happy to see you*, she wanted to add, but she would not discuss personal business in front of Billy. "Really, it's no problem at all."

"Now, hang on just a minute." Billy's demeanour was becoming hostile. "You just said you wanted to spend the evening with me."

"The gentleman has a point," said Alex calmly. "There's no need for plans to be changed on my account." He smiled at Felicity, this time without an ounce of amusement. "I'll be waiting for you, your ladyship, whatever you decide to do." Alex often used a polite form of address when they were in company. "I missed one meeting with you already. I shan't miss another."

Felicity returned her friend's smile. She trusted that Alex would wait for her, and she'd already weighed her options and come to her decision. Alex's arrival had helped ease the tension in her stomach, but if the plan was to work, Felicity must proceed alone. Billy clearly had trouble tolerating Alex's presence.

She redirected her attention to Billy. "Mr Seddon. You offered me a ride out in your boat along the coast. If that offer still stands, I should like to agree to it and strictly nothing more. I'm confident I've done nothing to encourage your understanding otherwise. And if you insist on using a disrespectful tone, then there shall be no boat trip at all."

Billy blinked, surprised by Felicity's forthrightness. "I meant no disrespect, my lady."

Gulls screeched and cawed overhead.

"Should there be room for a third, I would be happy to accompany you out on the water," suggested Alex, lifting his brow, revealing the scar on his forehead.

Billy cleared his throat. "Really, my lady, I didn't mean to offend. I'm but a lowly villager, and a disabled man at that." He waved his hook for Alex's benefit. "It would be an honour, Lady Felicity, to have you aboard my humble craft." He gave a bow, like a sarcastic jester in a Tudor play, extending his arm towards the sleek little motorboat that bobbed in the harbour. "Sadly, there's only room for one passenger."

Alex raised a hand to acknowledge Billy's assertion about his vessel's capacity. His gentle, open expression communicated that he was merely there if Felicity needed him. The familiar scent of meadows he always had about him somehow reinforced this.

Felicity gave Alex a firm nod. *Trust me*, was what she hoped to convey.

Alex replaced his hat on his head. "I'll take a stroll along the breakwater, your ladyship."

As Felicity followed Billy down the narrow stone steps leading to the water, something tugged inside her. Having just been reunited, was it right to leave Alex?

It had to be.

Felicity was on a mission for King and country, and if she came back ashore with a scoop, having Alex there would make the victory all the sweeter.

Chapter Twenty-Four

Felicity had little choice but to accept Billy's offer of help for stepping onto his boat from the slippery stone stairs built into the harbour wall. Thankfully, he held out his hook, which was preferable to the touch of his skin, his intact hand gripping the shining wooden gunwale of the little craft to steady his own position.

Soon they were motoring gently across the harbour, Felicity seated on a hard narrow bench behind where Billy stood at the helm. As they headed out onto the open sea, Alex waved from the harbour wall. Since arriving in Ottermouth, Felicity had wished for the opportunity to speak to him. Having been reunited, she was now off with a stranger suspected of drug smuggling, no less.

After so many obstacles in her investigations, had Felicity been too desperate for a breakthrough when she'd agreed to the boat ride with Billy? It was now far too late for a change in plan. Reminding herself that she at least knew how to swim only mildly eased the knot that had returned to her stomach. This journey needed to count for something very special indeed.

Alex's form grew smaller as Billy's boat motored further out to sea. Thankfully, the water was only slightly choppy, and Felicity felt no trace of the queerness she'd experienced on her initial boat ride out to Ottermouth. The briny wind was sharp and refreshing. The view towards the coast was quite spectacular.

"You all right back there?" Billy glanced over his shoulder but didn't give Felicity time to reply. "Let me show you what she can do." With a sudden roar of the engine, the boat pulled violently forward, a plume of white flying up from the stern.

As the vessel veered to the right, Felicity fell sideways in her seat. She pressed her cloche onto her head, her other hand grasping for purchase on the gunwale. The little motorboat wasn't designed for passengers. The bench upon which Felicity was seated functioned better as a shelf for stowing crates, although Billy's boat was far too highly polished for fishing work. Indeed, the deck was suspiciously spotless, but that was hardly evidence for Officer Marshall.

"Perhaps you might slow down, Mr Seddon," called Felicity over the roar of the engine. She had agreed with Officer Marshall that she would look around Billy's boat. It wouldn't be possible to take the narrow steps beside the helm to check below deck while travelling at such speeds. "I shouldn't like to get sea sick. Let's keep the voyage gentle, if you please."

Billy glanced over his shoulder and shrugged. The growl of the engine subsided to a rumble. "As you wish."

They were now so far from the harbour that the figures ashore were mere specks. The jagged, rocky coast was full of hollows and recesses. It was no wonder Customs and Excise faced difficulties gathering evidence. Some coves weren't even visible from the path above the cliff. Many seemed accessible only by water, and even then, only by small boats when the tide was right in.

Oddly, the boat's slower speed made Felicity's stomach roll. She took a deep, fortifying breath. "Were you acquainted with Mr Martin Granger?" she asked, reaching in her skirt pocket for her notebook. Her cover was her dedication to her job, her overt aim for the boat trip with Billy being the gathering of input for an article.

Billy threw a grin over his shoulder. "Come on now. Let's not play games. I know why you're on my boat."

Had Felicity been found out? They were so far away from land. She had to hope not. "You knew me to be a reporter when you invited me aboard your boat, Mr Seddon."

Billy chuckled. "I may have lost a hand, but my head's intact. I know you're working with that customs officer."

Felicity's stomach dropped like a rock. The shore continued to recede. "May I ask what gives you that impression, Mr Seddon?" Could she play it cool long enough for them to return to the harbour?

"Oh, just a wild guess." He flashed another grin at her as they continued to glide through the waves, the engine purring, the water casting the occasional salty spray across the deck.

Felicity gripped the gunwale tightly, her curls whipped by the wind. The ride was smooth, but her stomach churned. It had been a mistake to dismiss the instincts warning her against the trip with Billy. There would be no chance of surreptitiously searching the little boat. Felicity had made a grave miscalculation, and her priority now had to be her own safety.

"If you believe me to be a spy, Mr Seddon, why bring me out on your boat?" Could she convince Billy she was innocent?

The former fisherman's jaw was tight, his eyes fixed on the sea ahead. Copious pomade kept his dark, shining hair unmoved by the wind. "You wouldn't be the first that customs git has tried to recruit. And you won't be the last. He's out for me, all right." The boat accelerated, sending up spray as it turned. "But he won't get me. I'm too clever for that." Billy spun the steering wheel, sharply changing the vessel's course.

"Oh!" Felicity was nearly thrown from her seat.

Billy laughed. "Enjoying the ride?"

Was he trying to intimidate her? Billy clearly enjoyed making Felicity uncomfortable. She'd known that going into the situation. But with her cover blown, she was now alone out at sea with him for nothing. She'd walked away from Alex for nothing.

No. Not for nothing. Felicity was determined to make it count.

"Yes, the ride is rather thrilling." Her voice rose confidently above the engine's growl. "And what a lovely view of the coast. Tell me, Mr Seddon. What makes you so sure Officer Marshall won't catch you?"

Billy spun the steering wheel in the opposite direction. Water sprayed onto the deck. Felicity pressed herself hard into the corner of the wooden bench, resisting Billy's attempts to toss her about.

He threw a glance over his shoulder. "You don't lose your hand and your profession and end up where I am by chance, you know. There are war veterans begging on the streets. Not me. Oh no, not me."

"You indeed have smart clothes and a handsome boat." Felicity spoke as though unperturbed by the waves slamming against the hull. "What is it you do for work exactly, Mr Seddon?"

The engine roared and the boat lurched forward. Had Felicity gone too far? Her stomach swirled but not with fear. *Please, no*, she asked of herself. *I mustn't be sea sick again. Not now.*

"It is beautiful, isn't it?" Billy looked back at the coast, the runabout now practically flying over the water, bouncing and splashing across the crests of the waves. "So many secluded spots. So many possibilities. A lot can go on here and no one would ever know."

Was it another attempt at intimidation, or was it a twisted romantic suggestion? The latter notion made Felicity's stomach roll even harder.

She swallowed. "Like a murder, you mean, Mr Seddon?" It was a daring leap, but if he was trying to frighten her by throwing the boat about, she wanted him to know it wasn't working. "Do you know what happened to Mr Granger?" She was determined to bring something worthwhile back to shore. The trip had to count for something.

The acceleration eased slightly. Billy's forehead wrinkled with disappointment. "Is that what you think of me? I saw enough of that nasty business in the trenches. I've not hurt a living soul since then." His smile returned. It was less slick and more hopeful. "What say we go down the coast to Dartmouth? Fish and chips, like I promised. My treat."

Water sloshed at Felicity's ankles. She ignored it. "Was Mr Granger involved in your work, Mr Seddon? Did the two of you perhaps have a falling out?"

Billy frowned. "Oh, come on now. You're having a laugh, aren't you? Why would I…" He wiped his good hand over his mouth. "I mean, the fellow fell down the cliffs, didn't he? Drunk or something, wasn't he?"

Water continued to roll about the little deck, but wet feet were the least of Felicity's concerns. At last, Billy was engaging in the kind of discussion she actually wanted to have. "That was the initial assumption. The results of the autopsy indicate otherwise. The blow to his head came from a man-made object."

The motor died right down. Billy turned fully towards Felicity and leaned back against the helm, his arms folded. "Well." He let out a long, blustering exhale as the boat bobbed about on the waves. "Fancy that." If Billy had been involved in Martin Granger's death, he was a talented actor in imitating surprise. His eyes widened further. His gaze went from Felicity's feet to his own. "How long's that water been there?"

Felicity shook her head. "I can't say I've been keeping track. I'm not the captain of this vessel, Mr Seddon. You are."

"Curse it!" Billy leaned over the side of the boat, then disappeared below deck. There was splashing and clattering. More oaths were uttered. With no roar from the engine and without Billy on deck, the sloshing of the water and the gentle sea breeze were almost calming. Felicity blinked up at the wide blue sky.

But when Billy reappeared in the tiny stairway beside the helm, his shirt sleeves were soaked, and he looked as white as a ghost.

"There's a hole," he said. "We're sinking."

Chapter Twenty-Five

Billy swung into action in an uncharacteristically efficient manner. They couldn't motor towards the shore, as moving any further would only speed the ingress of water. While Felicity carried out instructions to bail — using her cloche hat, no less — Billy withdrew flares from a locked box, uttering oaths as his hook slipped on the latch, and sent up two in quick succession. The explosions happened with puffs of red smoke quite a distance above their heads. He then joined the bailing, using an oilskin bag brought from below deck and fashioned into a scoop, and looked anxiously towards Ottermouth for a sign that someone had seen his distress signal.

Felicity considered swimming for shore. It would be a last resort, only to be carried out if the little boat went fully under. She would have to take off her shoes and perhaps even strip to her undergarments to prevent being weighted down. They weren't too far from the coast. It was, however, hard to gauge the strength of any currents lying below the water's choppy surface.

Yet as potentially dangerous as the hole in the boat was, Felicity felt oddly peaceful. She was more at ease in Billy's presence now that he was quietly concentrated on bailing, though the rolling motion of the waves still threatened to turn her stomach queer.

"Is there a danger no one will reach us before we sink?" Felicity asked, keen to distract herself.

"We won't sink," growled Billy, barely looking at her.

Though the end of the day was fast approaching, the shadows of the hills long across the sea, Felicity was inclined to believe him. First, because she had no intention of drowning that day — or any day — and second, because Ottermouth's harbour was never quiet enough for no one to have noticed the flares. And there were more in the box.

"What caused the hole, Mr Seddon?" asked Felicity, the thick felt of her cloche doing an excellent job of holding water.

"Keep bailing." His teeth gritted, Billy glanced towards the shore. A vessel was leaving Ottermouth's harbour.

Felicity could bail while talking. "Checking a boat for holes before boarding should be standard procedure. Or am I mistaken?"

Billy growled an oath, the oilskin scoop slipping in his grasp.

"You still didn't tell me what you do for a living, Mr Seddon."

More oaths, some quite vulgar, filled the air. The boat that had left the harbour could now be recognised. The customs cutter was heading towards them, its sharp helm slicing through the waves.

Although less nimble than Billy's runabout, the cutter was a powerful vessel and was quickly upon them.

"Lady Felicity." Officer Marshall smiled with surprised satisfaction and offered a hand, allowing Felicity to make her way up the bobbing metal gangway that had been extended from the cutter to the little motorboat. The deliverance of Billy and his vessel was perhaps more than the customs officer had expected from Felicity.

In all honesty, it was more than Felicity had expected from herself. It was quite the result.

"Good evening, Officer Marshall." Felicity never imagined she would ever be pleased to see the customs officer, but she was glad to step off the sinking vessel and keen to return to shore. She looked forward to rejoining Alex.

"Mr Seddon." Officer Marshall continued smiling, thoroughly amused by the predicament faced by the one-handed man as he stormed along the gangway.

The smart little runabout disappeared half under the water as it was dragged back into the harbour by the larger vessel. It was a step too far to imagine the customs officer had anything to do with the hole in Billy's boat. At least, Felicity hoped it was. Officer Marshall had surely not deliberately endangered her life.

Billy scowled angrily from the aft deck as he watched his ruined boat, his wet shirt sleeves clinging to his forearms. He was as tight-lipped with Officer Marshall as he had been with Felicity and continued to insist he had no idea what caused the hole.

"Your boat will be impounded, Mr Seddon," called the customs officer from the helm as he guided the cutter through the harbour entrance.

Felicity watched the shore's approach from the starboard gunwale, her stomach at last settling as they drew closer to the village. Felicity's feet were exceedingly damp. She clutched her ruined cloche under her arm, her auburn curls dancing in the cool evening breeze.

In the context of everything that had happened, it was a rather silly thought, but Felicity couldn't fight a sense of regret that she wouldn't be able to change into a less bedraggled outfit before seeing Alex again. At least he wouldn't give her a telling-off like her brother might. While the trip with Billy had carried risks, Felicity couldn't have known it would end in nearly drowning. And the ultimate result might yet be positive.

"There's no running from me now, Mr Seddon," continued Officer Marshall. "I'll be searching that boat of yours inside and out."

Averting his gaze from his ruined runabout, Billy's expression turned into a sly smile. "Search her all you like. You won't find anything. Especially not now she's had a thorough soaking."

As the cutter eased towards its mooring, Billy sprang from the boat before it came to a stop and bounded along the harbourside.

Officer Marshall said an oath or two. "I'll be reporting you for unsafe sailing to the coastguard," he bellowed as he dropped the cutter's fenders into place, unable to be distracted from protecting his vessel from colliding with the harbour wall.

"I'll have a new boat in no time," called Billy, fishing his cigarettes out of his trouser pocket with his hook as he hurried along the harbourside. "You'll be welcome for another ride, Lady Felicity, but only if you're no one's spy."

Felicity might have responded by calling back that she wasn't anyone's spy, but the accusation wasn't entirely misplaced. Thankfully, no one except Alex was near enough to hear.

With his homburg hat pressed firmly on his head, and his unbelted overcoat flapping in the wind, Alex made his way briskly towards the cutter. He lowered his eyebrows at Felicity as she waited on the deck, but there wasn't a hint of remonstration in his gaze. His expression communicated concern.

Officer Marshall established the gangway between the cutter and the harbour wall. "So, your ladyship, what did you find out?"

Felicity drew back her chin. That the customs man had no interest in her welfare shouldn't have been a surprise. "Mr Seddon's boat is now in your possession. Have I not done my part for King and country?"

Officer Marshall folded his arms, not yet ready to offer Felicity help in stepping onto the gangway. A yacht had just entered the harbour, sending waves and making the gangway rather unsteady.

The customs man smiled condescendingly. "Slippery fellow, isn't he, that Mr Seddon? Did you find out anything through questioning him, or was he immune to your feminine charms?"

"Officer Marshall, I should like to go ashore." Felicity spoke firmly, annoyed by the talk of using 'feminine charms'. "Now, if you please."

"Lady Felicity?" Alex placed one foot on the gangway and, removing his hat, extended a hand in Felicity's direction.

Without hesitation, she took it. "Thank you, Mr Cooper." She leaned into the firmness of his grasp and swept onto the harbourside with ease.

Alex released his grip as soon as Felicity had both feet on solid ground. "You're most welcome, your ladyship."

"Good luck searching Mr Seddon's boat," called Felicity to the customs officer as she and Alex set off side by side along the harbour, passing Billy's runabout, which was almost fully submerged. She didn't look back at the customs officer. Felicity would need to cool off considerably before seeking an update on his investigation. The man was extremely vexing.

"Are you all right?" Alex's thick eyebrows were drawn low.

"My feet are rather wet, and my hat is quite ruined, but I'm all right. Rather glad to be away from that Billy Seddon fellow, not to mention that deeply unpleasant customs officer."

With a smile, Alex replaced his hat and shook his head.

"You can laugh," said Felicity. "But please don't say it."

Alex's smile disappeared. "Say what?"

Felicity sighed. "I know I can be a reckless fool. You don't need to tell me. I should never have gone out on the water with such a character."

The lines on Alex's forehead deepened further, his scar apparent. "Why would I even think that?"

Felicity gazed at him for a moment as they continued along the harbour wall. He was sincere. When was he ever not? "What's funny, then?"

Her friend's smile returned. "Your reaction. You might have drowned. They don't come much cooler than you, Cici."

It was a compliment that almost made her blush.

Luckily, Alex was keen to move the conversation forward. "I've read every report you've written about this place. Yet I clearly don't know the half of it, do I?"

Felicity's stomach squeezed, something like the queerness she'd felt out on the water threatening to return. "I should have warned you. I tried telephoning. Matters here are complicated. Should you wish to leave, I would quite understand."

Alex huffed. "What, and miss another Lady Felicity adventure? Never."

A weight lifted from her shoulders. "I'm glad to hear you say that."

Alex came to a stop before a pile of tattered crab pots. Putting his hands in the pockets of his overcoat, he cast a gaze over the harbour and its surroundings. "When can you fill me in on everything I've missed?"

"There's a secluded bench with a wonderful view up on the coastal path. How about we head up there and I tell you everything right—"

"Oh, Cici! Cici!"

"—now." Felicity's voice trailed off.

Isabella, in a flowing gown with long sleeves and trails of beads around her neck, hurried along the harbourside faster than Felicity had ever seen her move. "Cici, how miraculous that you're here. You're always in the right place at the right time. Listen, there's something I simply must tell you." Her eyes landed on Alex. She looked him up and down, her expression softening. "My goodness. Who is this handsome young fellow? I don't believe we've been introduced."

Alex lifted his hat. "Alexander Cooper. Reporter for the Western Daily News. I'm a colleague of Lady Felicity's."

"Are you staying with us up at Ashdene?" Isabella clapped her hands together. "Oh, do say you will."

There came a clearing of a man's throat. "Mrs Mountvernon?" Constable Thompson had followed Isabella along the harbourside. The silver buttons on his policeman's jacket shone dully in the evening light as he came to a stop slightly behind her.

Isabella glanced at the policeman. "Yes. Of course. Cici, darling. Listen." She clasped Felicity's elbow and drew in close, turning their backs to Alex and the constable. Her perfume was heavy and musky. "Please, don't tell Jasper. I don't want him worrying. You know what he's like, and this is nothing for the papers, you understand. This isn't something we want reaching the artists or the collectors." She laughed. "Or anyone at all, really. Do you promise?"

It was difficult for Felicity to commit without knowing the details. "What is it?"

Isabella sighed. "I'm to be brought to Torquay. To the police station there."

Felicity shivered. "Whatever for?"

"For questioning, nothing more. Look, Cici. Really. You absolutely mustn't tell Jasper. Please swear it."

"Mrs Mountvernon." The policeman approached. "I can't have the chaps from Torquay wait much longer for you. I'm afraid you'll have to come along now."

Isabella's eyes widened with desperation. "Constable, really. Give me the space to at least explain to my dear friend what's going on."

Alex raised his eyebrows questioningly.

Felicity was touched Isabella considered her a dear friend, but they had met merely days ago, and she wasn't sure she could comply with Isabella's request for secrecy. Jasper would never forgive her.

The constable twitched his grey moustache. "The explanation is rather simple." He narrowed his eyes at Felicity. "A pair of heavy brass binoculars was found aboard Mrs Mountvernon's yacht. They were caught in a rolled-up sail."

Felicity looked from the policeman to Isabella. "Brass binoculars?"

The policeman's eyebrows rippled slightly. "The binoculars have blood on them, your ladyship."

Felicity felt her face grow pale. Alex gave her a grave look. She was glad she hadn't promised to keep matters secret, but Felicity didn't relish the idea of informing Jasper about the unsettling development.

Isabella brought a hand to her throat. "But I didn't even know Marty was out on Xantho. And I certainly didn't do away with him. I didn't do anything at all."

"You can tell that to the detectives." The constable spoke calmly, rocking on his heels with his hands behind his back. "Come along now, Mrs Mountvernon."

Isabella slapped the back of her hand to her forehead. "Oh, but wait — the exhibition! It opens tomorrow. I must speak to Mr Prothero. I simply must."

The policeman stepped in front of Isabella, preventing her from fleeing towards the converted boat shed, its gay-looking bunting fluttering in the wind in a manner that felt, at that moment, highly inappropriate.

"Mrs Mountvernon." The policeman was becoming impatient. "This is a serious matter. I'm not sure you grasp that. Mr Granger's death is looking like murder, and it appears the deed happened aboard your yacht. Anything you have to say in your defence should be shared with the detectives without delay. We need a statement from you for the inquest."

Isabella's bottom lip quivered. She agreed to make no more fuss.

Felicity's stomach swirled with worry as she and Alex watched her accompany the policeman towards the road that led out of the village. There were no art collectors in the vicinity to see the proceedings, although they'd hear the news, eventually. The fishing folk in the harbour glanced discreetly at Isabella and the policeman, pretending to ignore the scene.

Alex took off his hat and held it to his chest, his slicked, dark-blond hair catching a little in the wind. "There's rather a lot I need to catch up on, isn't there?"

Felicity grimaced. "Yes. Perhaps rather too much."

Chapter Twenty-Six

Rain pattered gently onto the roof of the little mint-green tea house in Ashdene's garden. Within the wooden structure, which was open on one side, was a set of chairs in curled metalwork and furnished with thick chintz pillows. The chairs were gathered around a small table bearing a full complement of mid-morning refreshments. An elegant china teapot containing a steaming Darjeeling was accompanied by a top-up pot of hot water and a dainty jug of milk. On the tiered tea stand were slices of honey-roast ham between fingers of soft white bread, colourful jam tarts with exquisitely scalloped edges, and shortbread biscuits flecked with burned caramel.

Outside the tea house, a bright green lawn sloped towards a bank of the thick jungle-like planting that typified the valleyed garden. Blocked from view by expansive Azalea shrubs and gigantic fern fronds trickled a thin stream, leading down to the sea. On the grass, Pip and Beetle tumbled together, oblivious to the onset of rain, perhaps even looking forward to the bath Ashdene's housekeeper would no doubt give them. The two dogs were so obsessed with one another that Pip had barely given Alex's shoes their customary sniffing upon his arrival at Ashdene.

Isabella was still in her room, having returned from Torquay rather late the night before. Felicity hadn't seen her. She understood from the housekeeper that despite being extremely tired and weak, Isabella had expressed a singular concern — that Alex must be made to feel welcome at Ashdene. While Felicity was touched by Isabella's regard for her friend, it confirmed what Constable Thompson had said the evening before on the harbourside. Even with the discovery of the binoculars aboard her yacht, Isabella had yet to grasp the gravity of the situation.

With Isabella still in her room, Felicity and Alex were alone in the tea house. Alex was in the chair opposite Felicity on the other side of the table, steam rising from the cup and saucer in his hand, his long legs in his elegantly tailored grey suit trousers crossed at the knee. Felicity was dressed in her moss-green woollen suit with the generous pleat at the back of the skirt. She'd opted for her brown bicorn hat for better coverage from the rain. With her Oxfords still drying out following the ill-fated boat trip the day before, she had on a pair of low-heeled brown T-strap shoes.

As they sipped their tea, the trickle of the stream, the rain on the tea house roof, and the dogs' playful growls were the only sounds. While their silence was comfortable, there was a tension to it. To the best of her abilities, Felicity had told Alex everything. In doing so, it had become apparent to both of them that there was a great deal Felicity didn't know. In addition, a pressing question dangled above them.

What ought to be done next?

"When I read you were the one to discover the poor chap on the beach—" Alex watched as a breeze shook a shower of raindrops from the thick vegetation. His jaw was tight. "I considered rushing directly over here."

Felicity blinked at Alex. He kept his gaze on the trees, his expression deadly serious. "You were still busy with the Tamar Bank case, were you not?" Alex had already apologised enough for missing the meeting they'd planned at the Dolphin.

"I found out from Jasper where you were staying and tried

telephoning. The first call didn't go through. The second time, the connection got cut off." He looked at Felicity with a self-conscious smile. "I'll be honest. I wanted to know you were all right. I didn't want to come running if you didn't need me, but then…" He winced.

Felicity smiled. "You came anyway. And I'm glad you did." It was remarkable to think how far their relationship had come since their initial encounter in Lower Diddleton almost a year ago.

Confidence returned to Alex's expression in the form of a smile. "I ought not to have hesitated. I see that now. This is a big story. It makes sense to have two of us on the case."

Felicity sipped her tea. "I came to Ottermouth to report on something so simple and really quite dull. A collection of paintings in an old boat shed. Now, look at the situation. A man is dead, and it's likely murder. There's a suspected drug-smuggling operation, with the fact that no one will speak essentially confirming it. Not to mention yesterday's near-sinking." Felicity looked across the table at Alex. "I'd wished for more excitement. But not for all this."

Alex had picked up a shortbread biscuit. He paused, frowning. "Excitement rather has a habit of seeking you out, though, doesn't it?" He took a bite from the biscuit.

"I'd hoped to concentrate on my work. I told Jasper I'd support Isabella." Felicity sighed. "The binoculars on her boat and the fact she was questioned by the police — it will need to be written up. We should have written it up already, even." Felicity noticed she was grasping her cup and saucer rather hard.

Finishing his biscuit, Alex leaned forward. "What's your take on it?"

Felicity allowed her grip on her teacup to relax. "I've done my best to find the right angle for presenting Ottermouth and its art scene in a good light. I worry it's rather muddied my view of things."

Alex looked thoughtful. "Your brother's a very good friend of mine, as you know. However, I would say he's compromised your position."

Felicity lifted her eyebrows. As his sibling, Felicity was accustomed to finding fault with Jasper. She was less used to others being openly critical of the Earl of Denbury.

"Jasper is a fantastic newspaperman," continued Alex, "but he spends more time with advertisers these days than he does in interviews. He does an excellent job keeping the newspaper ticking along as a business, but as reporters, we have a duty to our readers and to the truth."

Alex was absolutely right, of course. While Felicity had never lost sight of her role as a journalist in Ottermouth, she hadn't prioritised it adequately. She'd come to the village to reestablish herself as a reporter. Could she still fulfil that aspiration?

Felicity sipped her tea and thought for a moment. "Jasper needs to hear about the binoculars. And I shall have to write it up. I know Isabella won't like it, but if we get it in the News first, that takes rather a lot of puff out of the other papers' sails."

Alex observed Felicity carefully. "What's your view on Isabella? Might she be involved? One of Martin's 'other women', perhaps?"

Felicity frowned. "I would prefer to think not," she said with little reflection, but is that what Alex meant about her position being compromised? Felicity recalled how Isabella clung to James Halliday and the attention she gave 'handsome, young' Alex. Was there an angle Felicity had overlooked?

Her frown deepened. "I mean, I sincerely hope Isabella's not involved."

Alex nodded slowly, his gaze shifting to the rain trickling off the tea house roof. "I met Isabella for the first time yesterday. I didn't know Major Mountvernon at all. Rather above my grade. The only reason I met your brother is because of the newspaper he started out of Ypres." The corner of Alex's mouth hooked up slightly in a sad sort of smile. His gaze bounced to Felicity. "I've heard about the major, though. Rather a brave fellow, by all accounts."

"I'm not sure how well Jasper actually knows Isabella, but Major Mountvernon was certainly a dear friend of his. I hope that counts for something. Isabella seems so awfully nice."

"We've known awfully nice people before who've turned out to… You know."

Felicity didn't need reminding. "I know." She gazed out across the grass, where the continuing rain had done nothing to dampen the dogs' enthusiasm for play.

Alex folded his arms over his chest, his dark blue eyes calm but serious. "What about the hole in that boat you went out on?"

"I'll have to tell Jasper about that as well." Felicity sighed. "To say he won't be pleased is an understatement. At least it's another story for the paper."

"Do you think it was sabotage?"

Felicity set her teacup on its saucer in her lap. "I don't suppose it's terribly common for an expensive and well-maintained runabout to suddenly develop a hole in its hull. If Mr Seddon had damaged it while motoring about the place, I imagine he'd have noticed. He seemed rather surprised by the damage. He also didn't want to talk about it."

"Say it was sabotage. Who was the target? Seddon or you?"

Felicity swallowed a sip of tea rather awkwardly. "Me? Why would I be the target?"

Alex shrugged. "Why, indeed?"

Recovering from her surprise at the suggestion, Felicity considered the possibility. "The only person who knew ahead of time that I would be on that boat was Officer Marshall, and why would he want to sink it? He wishes to prosecute Mr Seddon, not do away with him."

Alex was quiet for a moment. "Have you made any enemies since arriving here?"

Of course not, Felicity wanted to say, and if she'd been reporting from any other village in Devon, that might have been her response.

Ottermouth was, however, different.

"Not enemies, exactly, but it feels like there's a growing number of people who won't even talk to me. I don't quite know what they must think."

The chintz-cushioned chair creaked as Alex leaned back. "When I was still on Fleet Street, I covered the odd gangland story. Never pleasant business, of course. Kidnappings and murders and the like. But from a reporting perspective, getting blood out of a stone would have been easier. Some people are raised not to trust the police or journalists. Any symbol of authority or social order is suspect. But there can be ways of getting around things." He tilted his head a little. "Shall I give it a try with the fishermen?"

Felicity paused. If it were any other journalist, any other man, telling her he could probably do her job better than she could, Felicity wouldn't have stood for it. But Alex was a friend. He wasn't remotely interested in highlighting Felicity's inadequacies. He cared deeply about reporting, and that he was a more experienced journalist was simply a fact. In addition, whenever they worked together, they were a rather formidable team.

She nodded. "Please. I wish I could say it was just the fishermen. It's also their wives and children. I've had exchanges, but they've told me practically nothing. There's also an artist who spends a great deal of time with them. Something of a rival of Mr Granger's. It might be interesting to talk to him if you can pin him down."

"That Whitburn fellow you mentioned?"

"That's him."

Alex's brow creased. "Aren't the artists all keen to be made famous?"

Felicity set her cup and saucer on the table. "Not everyone sees compatibility between artistic endeavour and commercial activity. Mr Whitburn refused to sell his work at the exhibition. Yet the whole art world remains aflutter about him."

Alex reached into his jacket and adjusted his notebook. It was where he always kept it, in the inside pocket. "I shall do my best. There's no guarantee I'll get any further than you did, but there's no harm trying."

Felicity sat up straighter. It made perfect sense for the Western Daily News to have two journalists in Ottermouth. The story grew more complicated by the day. "If you're going for the fishermen, I'll go for the art crowd. The exhibition was supposed to open today. Considering Mr Granger's passing is now likely to have been murder, and with the murderer not yet being apprehended, I wonder if there's still appetite to run with the exhibition."

The dogs had tired themselves out and lay beside the tea house table, panting and casting the occasional hopeful glance towards the remaining sandwiches and tarts.

Alex frowned. "The inquest is rather soon, isn't it?"

"Tomorrow, or so I've heard."

He looked thoughtful. "It might be delayed, you know, given the finding on Isabella's boat. The police will need time to gather further statements and evidence. I suppose they'll bring in extra manpower, too. I imagine the local constable's out of his depth."

Felicity raised an eyebrow. "I wouldn't underestimate Constable Thompson. He has quite a hold on the place. He certainly has an excellent relationship with the fishermen, and there's absolutely no love lost between him and Officer Marshall."

Alex smoothed his dark blond hair back from his forehead. He smiled. "I think I'm going to enjoy getting to work here."

Felicity reciprocated the smile, though an anxiousness grew within her. There could be no putting it off. "I know who I should speak to first."

Chapter Twenty-Seven

After delivering two exhausted and rather damp dogs to the doting Mrs Rawling, who was actually excited to give the mischievous pair a bath, Felicity attempted to reach Jasper via telephone. Relieved to find him unavailable, she left a message with his secretary, although Felicity's unease wasn't dispelled completely.

With Alex having departed for the village, Felicity ascended Ashdene's main staircase alone. Rain tapped at the tall, elegant windows overlooking the stairs. The surrounding walls were lined with a great number of works of art, many of which had the local area as their subject.

Was Felicity at last beginning to recognise the artists' different styles?

Lawrence Whitburn's paintings were the most arresting, so full of energy and life. Eustace Granger's creations were calmer and less aggressive, although still very realistic. Martin's works were like his father's but with more romance and exaggerated emotion. His brushwork was not as delicate as Eustace's.

Arriving at the door to Isabella's room, Felicity took a fortifying breath and knocked softly. There came no response, but Felicity couldn't walk away. She knocked again. It wouldn't be pleasant, but it had to be done. It was Felicity's duty as a journalist.

There came a groan. "Oh, what is it now?"

The door creaked as Felicity gently pushed it open.

The long, tasselled curtains were not fully drawn back, allowing only a slither of grey light into the bedroom. Framed artworks adorned the walls, sumptuous rugs lay underfoot, and furniture collected from across the world had been scattered tastefully throughout the space. At the centre of the room was a beautifully carved four-poster bed draped with layers of gauzy fabric.

A gasp came from under the covers. "Cici." Isabella scrambled to sit up in bed. "You should have said it was you. I'm so sorry. Please, do take a seat. I can only apologise that I didn't come down for breakfast."

As Felicity approached the four-poster, Isabella plumped a thick bank of pillows at the top of the bed, her long brown hair splaying across her shoulders. She wore an ivory night gown with long lace-trimmed sleeves. Her eyes were ringed with red. She looked a good deal older than the day before.

"Is Mr Cooper comfortable? Oh, I'm being such a terrible hostess. Please, Cici." Isabella pushed herself into the pillows and tapped the counterpane. "Sit with me."

Felicity obliged, perching on the edge of the mattress.

On the side table, among piles of books, a brush, an ashtray, and various other haphazardly strewn personal items, was a framed photograph of a high-ranking military officer. He appeared a good deal older than Isabella, even as Felicity saw her now. He was a bear of a man, with a bushy moustache and broad, powerful shoulders.

Felicity had seen no other images of the man around the house, but to keep a photograph by one's bedside was extremely intimate.

"Is that Major Mountvernon?"

Isabella followed Felicity's gaze. She nodded. "I was a much better person when Timothy was still around. He used to hold me together. When he… When they told me he…" She sniffed. "I shattered in every direction. It was years ago now, of course, but it still feels like I received the news just yesterday. I'm still reeling from it." She looked at Felicity. "He was my rock. My absolute rock. Oh, I'm such a mess without him."

It was a striking combination, the strength and orderliness of the military man and Isabella's gentle, chaotic amiability. The two might well have held one another in balance.

Felicity put a hand on Isabella's. "I'm sure you meant the world to him, too."

Isabella returned her gaze to Felicity. "Art saved me. It really did. Coming here to Ottermouth, discovering the work of Martin and his father. Of Lawrence and all the others. Promoting their art gave me a sense of purpose and meaning. Oh, it's not about the money. You must know that. I don't care if Harold loses every penny I've sunk into that exhibition. Have you ever been completely transported by a painting? So captivated you forget the world around you?"

Felicity wasn't sure she had. She squeezed Isabella's hand, eager to continue listening.

"That's why this exhibition means so much to me." Isabella shifted to sit up straighter, leaning away from the pillows, her hair cascading down her back. "Art has the power to heal. To inspire. To change lives."

Felicity smiled sadly. Everything in Ottermouth was going so terribly wrong. Everything Isabella had worked towards was being undone.

"Will the exhibition still open today?" Felicity had to fulfil her role as a reporter, but her approach with Major Mountvernon's widow would be gentle.

Isabella blinked. "Why would it not?"

Felicity stiffened. Isabella could surely not still be in denial. "A man has been murdered. And not just any man. An artist whose work was to be at the centre of the exhibition." She hesitated. "A man you considered a friend."

Isabella's forehead wrinkled slightly, then cleared. "Cici, listen. What I said to you yesterday. At the harbour. I wasn't in my right mind. Of course, you'll need to tell Jasper what's happened. He has a right to know."

Felicity saw no need to mention that she hadn't awaited Isabella's permission for this.

"And if you need to write things up for the paper, then you should do that. I won't stand in the way of your job." Isabella leaned forward. She gripped Felicity's hand. "But you'll be kind, won't you?"

"Of course." Felicity offered her reassurance without hesitation. At least she didn't have to convince Isabella of the need to set the story straight in the Western Daily News before other, more scandalous papers came prowling. "That's why I'm here. Would you be willing to speak to me now?"

"An interview, you mean?"

"If you feel you have the strength for it."

Isabella bit her lip. She nodded.

Taking her notebook and pencil from her skirt pocket, Felicity coaxed Isabella through a set of rather straightforward questions. She asked about her experience at the police station in Torquay, whether the binoculars found on Xantho belonged to Isabella — they did — and what Isabella understood the next steps in the investigations to be.

After these milder questions, Felicity asked, "Were you with Mr Granger on Xantho the night he met his end?"

Isabella frowned. "Of course not. I saw him for the last time at the soirée. I didn't leave Ashdene that night. The entire household can attest to this."

"Have you any idea how Mr Granger came to be on your yacht?"

"Tim used to say I was generous to a fault." Isabella's smile was laced with sorrow. "If anyone asks, I always allow them to take Xantho out. There are also times when I'm not asked. Even then, I rarely object. This would have been one of those times."

"Was Mr Granger in the habit of using your yacht without asking?"

After a brief hesitation, Isabella nodded.

"At night?"

Another pause. Biting her lip, Isabella nodded.

"Might you know why? And with whom?" Felicity's questions were now hard-hitting, but she must do her job. And do it well.

Isabella sighed. "Darling, listen. I don't expect you to believe me. The detectives in Torquay certainly wouldn't. But I simply never asked him. That's the community we have here in Ottermouth. Had here," she corrected, the lines on her forehead deepening. "We never got overly bothered with other people's business. There are not the same constraints as in normal society. Artists need their freedom."

Felicity reflected as she took down Isabella's words. At first glance, Ottermouth seemed so quaint, almost idyllic. It was, however, anything but a normal village.

Isabella sniffed. She sat up straighter. "The police will come here today. They want to speak to my staff. I said go ahead. Everyone will confirm I was here all night."

Felicity laid her pencil down on her notebook, but she wasn't done with her questions. "To your knowledge, did anyone wish harm on Mr Granger?"

Isabella squinted at Felicity. "Martin was well-liked. He was friends with everyone."

Felicity immediately knew that not to be true. "Was he friends with Mr Whitburn?"

Isabella gave a petulant frown. "They were rivals in some ways, yes. But to murder a fellow artist? No. Not in Ottermouth. Not here. I say, what time is it? I ought really to get dressed. I need to be there for the opening."

Could the exhibition really go ahead? It wasn't Felicity's role to interfere. The thought of Alex down in Ottermouth digging for details among the fishing community bolstered her resolve. She had a duty to expose everything she could.

Felicity folded away her notebook and pencil and stared squarely at Isabella. “Have you told me everything I ought to know?”

Isabella shook her head in bewilderment. She slid towards the other side of the mattress. “I’ve answered all your questions, haven’t I?”

She had, but there were questions as yet unasked. Felicity had to push deeper.

“I heard Mr Granger had liaisons with more than one woman. Might that have been a reason for his taking your yacht?”

Isabella chuckled as she threw open the counterpane. “As I told you, artists need their freedom. I’ve never pried into such things.”

Felicity was losing her interviewee. She quickly changed tack. “Was Mr Granger involved in the smuggling of drugs?”

Isabella stopped, half out of bed. “What kind of question is this?” Her tone was deadly serious.

“Officer Marshall has confirmed that substances such as cocaine are being brought into the village.”

Isabella frowned, then stood up. She went to the curtains and roughly pulled them open, flooding the room with grey light. “Have you seen anyone plagued by such a dependency in the village?”

The question tapped into Felicity’s own doubts. She’d seen no evidence herself and had only Officer Marshall’s word for it. Felicity wasn’t at all at home in reporting on such issues or even discussing them. Yet she had to keep going.

“If Mr Granger were involved in such activities, then might that explain his borrowing of your yacht at night time?”

Isabella went to a wardrobe outside which a set of clothes hung. She tugged on the collar of the blouse and sighed with exasperation. “Cici, darling. I’m sure I don’t know what you’re talking about.”

Felicity stood up from the four-poster and approached Isabella. She wouldn't give up. "I know you're innocent in all this," she said, counting on Isabella's association with her brother to bear this assumption out, "but the police don't see it that way. They see a man who met a violent end on your yacht."

After a pause, Isabella looked from the outfit to Felicity. "What I'm about to tell you is not for the newspaper. Do we agree on that?"

Felicity nodded, doing her best not to appear too eager. Would this be the breakthrough she'd wanted all along?

Isabella folded her arms over her nightdress. "I purchased drugs from Martin. On occasion. Only cocaine, and never very much."

A flutter of excitement danced within Felicity. She did her best to control her facial expression. At last, there was a link between the deceased artist and the illegal activity in the village, and it had been under her nose the whole time.

"Not for myself, you understand," continued Isabella. "I'd never use that rubbish, but for my parties. For the art collectors visiting from London. It's very much expected these days, you know." Isabella took in a shaky breath. "That's something you absolutely mustn't tell Jasper. My goodness, he'd probably never speak to me again."

"I won't," confirmed Felicity. While she could no longer protect Isabella from her investigations into Ottermouth's darker side, a journalist had a duty to protect her sources. "If I find evidence elsewhere, however, then Mr Granger's connection to the drug trade will need to be revealed in the paper." The readers of the Western Daily News deserved the truth, and the newspaper had a right to the scoop.

Isabella stared blankly at Felicity for a few moments. She perhaps regretted her disclosure, but it was too late. A crucial piece of the puzzle had been revealed. "Leave me now, would you, darling? I really must get myself ready. There's so much to do ahead of the opening."

Felicity had no objection to Isabella's request. She rapidly descended the main stairs, the sun breaking through the clouds and casting pillars of light through the tall windows. A picture of the actual situation was at last beginning to emerge. And for further clarity, Felicity knew exactly where to go next.

Chapter Twenty-Eight

The rain resumed as Felicity neared Halcyon Cottage, heavy drops plopping onto the umbrella she'd borrowed from Ashdene's hallway. Pip and his new best friend, Beetle, had been snoring before a roaring fire in the drawing room when she'd left. Felicity was happy to have Pip with her, but she no longer felt compelled to take him wherever she went. The little Yorkie was enjoying the company of Isabella's dog, and Ashdene's housekeeper devoted more attention to the canines than Felicity could spare.

As the wind hissed through the tall trees, Felicity knocked on Halcyon Cottage's arch-topped front door. She had been rather gentle with Audrey Lawson the first time around. Felicity wouldn't be rude or rough in questioning Audrey a second time, but she had a clear goal. Further confirmation of Martin's involvement in the drugs trade was needed. The word of one person who wouldn't be named wasn't enough to report on it, and Felicity would need to be careful not to put Isabella in the spotlight for having made the link.

Undaunted, she knocked at the arch-topped front door a second time. She shivered as she waited, the rain blowing into her umbrella. It made perfect sense, didn't it? A shadowy transaction gone wrong, carried out aboard a borrowed yacht under the cover of darkness, in which a man lost his life.

"You're too late."

Felicity turned. Lawrence Whitburn stood just beyond the cottage's garden gate. His hands were in the pockets of his shabby corduroy trousers, his paint-flecked cable-knit jumper and dark wavy hair growing wet in the rain.

"Audrey's cleared out," he said.

Felicity started along the path. The rain bouncing off the paving stones. "Did you see Miss Lawson leave, Mr Whitburn?"

Lawrence frowned with mock affront. "Do you not trust me?"

Not quite, thought Felicity, and the feeling was no doubt mutual. "Might you know where she's gone?"

"Back to whatever rats' nest she crawled from in London, I expect."

Felicity's heart sank. Who else could provide her with the evidence she needed? It made little sense to question Lawrence. When it came to his views on Martin, the rival artist couldn't be considered a reliable witness.

"Thank you for informing me, Mr Whitburn," said Felicity, concealing her disappointment. "I'm sorry it meant you getting caught up in this awful weather."

The artist folded his arms over his dampening jumper. "You're mistaken, your ladyship. Audrey isn't the reason I came to speak to you."

Felicity halted on the paved pathway. "Oh?" She wasn't keen on the manner in which Lawrence had positioned himself in front of the only exit from the cottage garden.

Lawrence lowered his brow. "I'm here to tell you to stay away from Elizabeth."

Felicity frowned in confusion. The art dealer's daughter had accosted Felicity twice. She couldn't recall approaching the girl herself. "I'm not sure I follow, Mr Whitburn."

Lawrence huffed with amusement. "I can't make my meaning

any plainer. And with all due respect, you're far from stupid, your ladyship."

Felicity straightened under her umbrella. She sincerely wished Lawrence would step away from Halcyon Cottage's garden gate. "May I enquire what your relationship to Miss Prothero is, exactly, Mr Whitburn?"

"You may," said the artist, "but you shan't get an answer from me."

"You rather take after your friends aboard the Maggie in that respect." Felicity stopped herself from going any further. If Lawrence was involved in the smuggling, it wasn't wise to make such an accusation while alone with the man, and he wouldn't talk to Felicity about it in any case.

But what might that mean for Lawrence's bond with Elizabeth? Felicity had imagined a romantic connection between them, but if the artist was involved in smuggling, then that made little sense.

Felicity altered her strategy. "Miss Prothero has approached me herself more than once. I thought she and I were on good terms. Can you tell me why I ought to stay away from her?"

And what might be the consequences if I didn't?

Felicity kept this question to herself. She was still trapped on the garden path. Nevertheless, she was nearing the end of her tether with being told what she may or may not investigate.

Rain ran down Lawrence's face. "For Elizabeth's sake. That's all." The artist turned and walked away from the gate.

Despite the relief at Lawrence's departure, Felicity's cheeks burned warm. Her hands tightened on the umbrella's handle as she passed through the garden gate and rejoined the woodland path. Telling a journalist to mind her own business was like putting a match to dry tinder.

Rain splashed into the clefts between the harbourside cobbles. Water trickled from furled sails onto dark, wet decks. A heady, briny scent washed in from the sea. The gallery and Seaview Lodge were equally likely locations where one might find Elizabeth. The converted boat shed being closer and easier to access in less-than-rugged T-strap shoes, Felicity had plumped for the gallery.

She wasn't in the habit of being obstinate or contrary, but if Elizabeth wished for Felicity to stay away, then she wanted to hear it from Elizabeth herself.

"Felicity!" Her name rang out among the bundled nets, racks of oars, and general clutter of the harbour.

Alex hastened along the water's edge, rain dripping from the brim of his homburg hat.

Felicity insisted he join her under her umbrella, which was broad enough to accommodate two. They were a stone's throw from the gallery, the bunting wet and slapping against the old boat shed, but the interruption to Felicity's quest was welcome. Alex, like Felicity, probably had news to share.

"If you've no objection." Ducking under the umbrella, he shook the excess rain from his hat and smoothed his hair before returning the hat to his head. "Shall I?" Gently, he took the umbrella from Felicity. The drips from his overcoat hit the tops of Felicity's feet. Somehow, she didn't mind.

"Any news?" he asked

"As a matter of fact, yes." Felicity raised her voice above the sound of the rain. "But are you done with your interviews? I don't want to drag you away if you're onto something."

Alex sighed deeply. They were close enough for Felicity to feel the warmth of his breath. "No luck with the fishing tribe. The women wouldn't even look at me. I'll give the chaps another try later, but it's as you said. They're a closed community. I spoke to the authorities, however."

"And?" Alex was very used to dealing with the police and

other officials, who — despite society's many advances in recent years — still usually responded better to men.

"The customs officer said the fellow who took you out on the water yesterday has vanished without a trace. Not that he could have done anything with him. They found nothing on the little motorboat. Or what was left of it."

Felicity nodded. Billy's disappearance wasn't much of a blow. He'd clearly had no intention of revealing his secrets to the papers. "Did Officer Marshall say anything about the cause of the boat's sinking?"

"It was sabotage all right." Alex's scarred brow rippled with suppressed concern. "A rather neat little hole cut into the bilge. By rights, the boat should have gone under much sooner. The vessel had been customised to reach high speeds, and the unusual shape of the hull slowed the ingress."

The rain gusted onto the back of Felicity's woollen skirt. "Any leads on who might have done it?"

"Marshall suspects it could be another smuggler. They're often at odds with one another. He didn't seem too concerned, though. Said it was a matter for the police, not for Customs and Excise. So, I spoke to the local constable."

"Constable Thompson?" Alex had got an awful lot done in a short amount of time.

"That's the one." Alex tightened his grip on the umbrella as the wind blew. "He didn't seem that bothered by the sabotage, either. I reminded him you were on the boat. That you might have drowned. Thompson said he'd report the matter to the coastguard and refused to say anything further. Unbelievable, isn't it?" Alex was on the verge of becoming indignant.

Felicity was less interested in justice for the sabotage of Billy's boat. "Isabella admitted she purchased drugs from Martin."

Alex's dark blue eyes sparked with interest. "Now, that's more like it. Wait, don't tell me. She doesn't want you to print it?"

"Exactly."

Again, the wind blew the rain against Felicity's back. Alex repositioned himself to shelter her from the brunt of the gusts.

"I need to find a corroborating source," continued Felicity. "Preferably someone willing to be quoted in the paper."

Alex stroked his jaw and nodded, his gaze wandering across the rainy harbour. "Do we think the dead man was a smuggler?"

"It's too early to be certain, but Martin had the right connections for selling the goods onwards. I went to find his—" Felicity struggled for the right word "—his companion just now at his residence here in the village. Apparently, the Honourable Miss Audrey Lawson has left Ottermouth. I ran into the delightful Mr Lawrence Whitburn, who informed me. He also told me to stay away from Elizabeth Prothero."

Alex smiled. "So, you're on your way to find Elizabeth?"

It was only mildly embarrassing that Alex found Felicity so predictable. She gave a firm nod. "Absolutely."

"Shall we go together?"

"Let's." A crackle of excitement passed through Felicity. Working as a team made all the difference. No longer would Felicity be frustrated at every turn. Her investigations in Ottermouth were at last going somewhere.

Felicity went to slip her hand through Alex's arm. In a deft move, he slid the handle into her grasp and exited the umbrella's shelter, trotting ahead through the rain towards the gallery's entrance.

Felicity frowned, but there was no time to ponder Alex's gentle withdrawal.

The gallery's doors stood open. Raised voices carried from within, and the tone wasn't exactly friendly.

Chapter Twenty-Nine

Considering that the exhibition was, according to Isabella, opening as planned that afternoon, the gallery was in a surprising state of disarray. There were gaps where artworks had once hung. Multiple paintings attributable to Martin Granger and his father — as far as Felicity could recognise them — were both hanging and lying about the place. Lawrence Whitburn's works appeared to have been removed entirely.

On a table in the centre of the room, trays of empty glasses stood awaiting visitors. The rain drummed on the windows in the roof, filling the space with a soft, maudlin rumble.

In the open doorway, the wind thankfully blowing the rain away from the entrance, Felicity folded her umbrella while Alex shook his hat. As expected, Harold Prothero and his assistant, Nigel Davies, were present, both in neat suits with bow ties, which were green and blue, respectively.

As Felicity had hoped, Elizabeth was also there, standing meekly beside her father in a long grey dress. Audrey Lawson was present, too. She wore the same pale green silk dress as the day before with a brown wrap-style coat thrown over the top, her bright blonde hair caught in a messy twist at the back of her head. Beside her slender ankles stood a bulging leather valise.

As Felicity put her umbrella in the stand and Alex hung his coat and sopping hat on the rack, no one seemed to notice their arrival. The tremendous row taking place beside the forlorn-looking drinks table held everyone's attention.

"But Mr Prothero, you're not listening to me. I need the money." Audrey's tone was commanding yet desperate.

"The decision is about more than just your personal financial situation, Miss Lawson."

It wasn't Harold in disagreement with Martin's companion, but Nigel, his arms folded, his thin, dark eyebrows lifted in a remonstrating manner. "Mr Prothero's business relies on his excellent reputation. Mr Granger's death is now to be considered murder. Who's to say the killer isn't still among us? What if there's another death? What if someone is murdered at the exhibition? The risks to Mr Prothero's reputation are too many to mention. We should at least wait until after the inquest to plan a new date for the opening. I mean, what if Mr Granger was involved in something untoward?"

Felicity advanced slowly from the doorway, Alex following her lead. It wasn't right to listen in unannounced, but Felicity didn't want to interrupt proceedings. Nigel was speaking the most sense she'd heard since arriving in Ottermouth.

Audrey gasped, affronted. "Are you going to allow your assistant to speak to me like that, Mr Prothero? Do you not want my custom?"

The art dealer's mouth opened, his brow furrowed, but Nigel beat him to it.

"Please, Miss Lawson," continued the assistant, arms still folded, "you have a single preparatory watercolour for sale in the exhibition. I'm quite certain Mr Prothero would be happy for you to take your custom wherever you pleased."

Harold glanced with only mild disapproval at Nigel. He appeared tired, with dark circles under his eyes. "Now, now, Mr Davies. I think we owe it to Miss Lawson to—" He broke off, eyebrows lifting. "Ah, Lady Felicity. How nice of you to join us. Quite the worst possible weather, isn't it?"

Still standing beside her father, Elizabeth only glanced at Felicity and barely looked up when Alex stepped forward for a round of handshakes. Did Elizabeth, as Lawrence had indicated, wish for Felicity to keep her distance? If so, why?

Audrey's hollow smile dropped as soon as the introductions were over. "Mr Prothero, you were about to respond to Mr Davies. Will the exhibition go ahead as planned? Will you be selling my piece?" Audrey had also undergone a change since Felicity saw her last. No longer was she timid and withdrawn.

Audrey's question was, however, extremely relevant and rather pressing. Was the exhibition going ahead?

Harold seemed intent on ignoring it. "How is Mrs Mountvernon?" he enquired of Felicity, wincing.

Felicity's tone was grim. "I suppose you've all heard about the discovery aboard Mrs Mountvernon's yacht."

The art dealer nodded gravely. Elizabeth kept her gaze on the floor. Nigel maintained an air of disapproval, arms folded and eyebrows raised. Audrey sighed with impatience. Alex watched carefully, no doubt taking the measure of each of them.

Between Audrey and Elizabeth, Felicity was actually keenest to speak to Audrey. First, however, clarity on an important point was indeed needed.

"Will the exhibition open today as planned?" Felicity looked from Audrey to Harold as the rain continued to drum on the old boat shed's roof.

Harold sighed deeply and adjusted his jacket where it stretched over his rotund form. "The opening has been delayed once already. And the circumstances that led to poor Mr Granger's, ah…" He took off his pince-nez and went to work on the lenses with a handkerchief drawn from his pocket. "Something that has been shown time and again, throughout the history of art—"

Nigel rolled his eyes. He'd heard Harold give this speech before, perhaps more than once.

"—is that a man's private life, while inextricable from his artistic output in some ways, does not determine the longevity or appreciation of his work." Harold replaced his pince-nez on his nose. "Particularly not after his death."

"So the exhibition opens today?" enquired Alex, who had a marked preference for straight talking.

Harold nodded. "It does."

Audrey seemed buoyed by the pronouncement. Nigel put his fingers to his brow and shook his head but offered no further arguments. Felicity wore a polite smile. It didn't matter whether she considered opening the exhibition appropriate. What mattered was her reporting.

"Father has invested so very much," added Elizabeth quietly, glancing only briefly at Felicity. It was as if Felicity frightened her. What had caused this change in the girl?

Harold put a hand on his daughter's shoulder. "It's not just about me, Lizzie. The whole village stands to gain from the raising of Ottermouth's profile, artistically speaking."

Alex turned to Felicity, an eyebrow raised. She knew exactly what his look meant. *You pick, and I'll take the other one.*

Felicity gave her friend a subtle nod. "I don't wish to interrupt anything," she said, addressing the room, "but I was hoping to have a word with Miss Lawson."

"Of course, of course." Harold flapped a hand. "We'll not stand in the way of your reporting, your ladyship. We've work to do ourselves, haven't we? Mr Davies? Lizzie?"

Felicity looked to Audrey, but the blonde-haired woman's gaze had shifted towards the gallery's big double-doors, which still stood open. A figure hovered at the edge of the doorway, rain dripping off an oversized hat, a thick weatherproof coat hanging past her knees.

Even with the over-sized clothing, the silhouette was reminiscent of the figure in the painting in Ashdene's hallway.

It was Thora Dunn.

Audrey blinked nervously. "Please, excuse me for a moment." Her heels tapped across the gallery floor as she headed towards the doors.

Felicity and Alex exchanged glances. What could Audrey and Thora possibly have to say to one another?

As Harold, Nigel, and Elizabeth returned their attention to the preparations in the gallery — which was another touch of oddness, as Elizabeth hadn't seemed particularly hands-on with her father's work before — and the rain continued to batter the gallery roof, Audrey's and Thora's conversation in the doorway couldn't be overheard. It ended abruptly, however, with Thora running off, out into the rain.

Felicity turned wide-eyed to Alex.

"Go," he hissed. "I'll stay here and get what I can."

Her heart pounded. Felicity indeed wanted to give chase. Snatching her umbrella from the stand, she passed a confused-looking Audrey and ventured out into the rain.

Thora moved at quite a pace, but Felicity kept up, trailing not far behind as the rain bounced off the cobbles and splashed her ankles.

It seemed Thora was heading for the fishermen's cottages. Felicity had been rebuffed by the fishing community before, but she wouldn't be turned away so easily now. It was time for answers.

Chapter Thirty

Perhaps aware that Felicity was following her, Thora took a circuitous route towards the fishing cottages. Or at least, that's what Felicity thought. After winding along alleyways with gurgling gutters that overspilled onto her umbrella, Felicity arrived at the row of blue- and white-painted fishermen's cottages to find no trace of anyone out in the rain.

Had Thora intentionally shaken Felicity off?

The chase had been in vain, but Felicity wasn't in the least deterred. She started back towards the gallery, where she would reunite with Alex. She had questions not only for Audrey and—

"Your ladyship?"

Felicity stopped.

The outline was so similar — voluminous wet-weather clothing hanging from a slender frame — Felicity mistook the figure for Thora. Only it wasn't the daughter. It was the mother.

Margaret Dunn stood a short distance away from Felicity, rain dripping from the sagging brim of her hat, a woven bowl full of winkles in her hand. She appeared to be on her way back to the cottages.

"The Maggie's getting ready to go to Brixham, your ladyship.

For spare parts. My husband and his men are too busy to speak with anyone today."

It was more than Felicity expected the fisherman's wife to say to her.

"Thank you for informing me, Mrs Dunn." Felicity did her best to play along and sound disappointed, even though it wasn't the fishermen she'd been hoping to see. "That's a pity."

Felicity had to be careful. She mustn't repeat the mistakes made with the young fisherman on the beach and scare Margaret off from talking further. Felicity also knew nothing about the relationship between mother and daughter, except what she'd witnessed. Margaret was protective of her child. Perhaps Thora wasn't supposed to mix with the people at the gallery? If Felicity got Thora in trouble with her mother, it could jeopardise any chance of speaking to the girl.

At the end of the row of cottages, a door opened. Grace Campbell, the member of the fishing community from whom Felicity had so far heard the most, stepped onto the cobbles in front of her little house. She had a thick woollen blanket draped over her head and shoulders, protecting her from the rain. She stared enquiringly at Felicity and Margaret.

Margaret threw a worried glance at the woman Felicity knew to be her sister. It was hard to say which was the older of the two.

"Won't you come inside, your ladyship?" said Margaret. "At least till the rain stops."

Felicity almost fell over with surprise at the invitation. "Why, yes. Thank you. How incredibly kind." Alex would have to handle matters at the gallery alone.

Stooping was necessary when entering through the blue-painted door of Margaret's cottage, but the ceiling inside was high enough for Felicity to stand straight. A coal fire burning in a blackened hearth gave the space a welcome warmth and the air an earthy, smoky scent. The floor's rather rough stonework had been rubbed smooth by years of activity. There was a little table, a stove, several chairs — the furniture all of uncomplicated design in darkly stained wood — and room for not much else. The rain tapped against the squat window, its glass thick and mottled.

If Margaret and her family were involved in smuggling, the interior of their cottage provided no hint of it.

After removing her coat and hat to reveal a plain brown dress and her hair swept in an unfussy bun, Margaret lit a pair of oil lamps at either end of the mantelpiece.

"Please, your ladyship." Margaret gestured for Felicity to sit.

"Thank you, Mrs Dunn." Felicity had an abundance of questions for Margaret, but she couldn't hurry matters.

Margaret kept her back to Felicity as she busied herself putting a kettle of water on to boil. "We were all very sorry about what happened to you out on the water, your ladyship."

Had sympathy motivated Margaret to invite Felicity into her home? That Felicity had — mistakenly, as she now saw it — agreed to work with the customs officer would by now be known to the fishing people. News travelled fast in tight communities. Surely Felicity's collaboration with the authorities would outweigh any empathy for her?

"It's not your fault, Mrs Dunn. I'm quite recovered and completely unharmed." She considered withdrawing her notebook from her skirt pocket. *Not yet.*

Without looking at Felicity, Margaret set cups, saucers, and a jug of milk on the little table. The earthenware was rough and the rims of the teacups rather thick, but they were more likely to survive a drop onto the rough stone floor than the china pieces used at Bradley Court.

Still waiting for the kettle to boil, Margaret remained standing. Behind the deep lines in her face and her scraped back hair, she was possibly younger than she looked.

"This is not for the papers, your ladyship," she began.

"Of course not," said Felicity, her decision to leave her notebook in her pocket vindicated.

Margaret's sea-green eyes flashed. "I would just like you to know that we're sorry for what happened to you. It wasn't the intention for you to be caught up in it all."

Felicity blinked. Was she hearing things correctly? Did Margaret just apologise?

The kettle whistled. The fisherman's wife turned quickly to remove it from the boil.

Felicity spoke carefully. "Forgive my ignorance, Mrs Dunn, but are you apologising because you were in some way involved in sabotaging Mr Seddon's boat?"

"No." Margaret shot a glance at Felicity. "But we know who it was, and the matter's being dealt with."

Felicity raised her eyebrows. "I don't suppose you'd be willing to tell me who it was?"

Margaret poured steaming water into a bulbous teapot of the same rough earthenware as the cups. "No, your ladyship."

"Might you be able to say something about the motivation behind the sabotage?" Felicity was perhaps going a little far, but Margaret seemed more uncomfortable about what had happened to Felicity aboard Billy's boat than about her asking questions.

Margaret put the teapot and a tea caddy on the little table and seated herself opposite Felicity. "It wasn't the intention for the boat to sink with people aboard." Margaret's mouth was pursed as she spooned twists of black tea leaves into the pot. "It wasn't the intention to cause anyone harm." She replaced the teapot's lid and fleetingly met Felicity's gaze. "That's all I can tell you, your ladyship."

Felicity nodded. "Thank you, Mrs Dunn." To ensure her precarious relationship with Margaret remained in good standing, there would be no more questions on the topic, even though Felicity's mind whirred with possibilities about who the saboteur might be.

There was an awkward silence as they waited for the tea to

steep. Margaret kept her hands in her lap and her eyes on the table. Although the atmosphere wasn't easy, she seemed in no hurry to get rid of Felicity.

Felicity used the time the tea needed to reflect before speaking. The approach towards the questions she really wanted to ask had to be gradual. "The fishing community here in Ottermouth is quite self-reliant, isn't it?"

Margaret frowned a little, as if she didn't understand.

"That you have even your own ways of meting out justice, for example," clarified Felicity, without explicitly circling back on the sabotage, even though she yearned to understand more.

Picking up a tea strainer, Margaret began pouring. "Out at sea, you can't call for help. You can't wait for someone else to come and fix your problems for you."

Felicity lifted the cup of tea Margaret had poured for her. Tasting the brew, which was rich and quite delicious, she couldn't help wondering about its provenance. She'd tasted much worse tea at finer establishments than the harbourside cottage. Had the correct taxes been paid upon the leaves in Margaret's caddy? Ought Felicity even to be drinking it?

She kept her focus on her job. "I was hoping to gather comment from your community regarding the passing of Mr Martin Granger. Our readers would very much like to know the local people's views on the matter."

Although she'd poured a cup of tea for herself, Margaret wasn't drinking it. She pulled at the cuff of her dress and said nothing. Perhaps she regretted inviting Felicity into her home.

Felicity adjusted her expression to communicate both sorrow and concern. "The police now say it's murder."

"It wasn't us." Margaret's jaw tightened. "We shan't mourn the man, but his death has nothing to do with us."

"My apologies, Mrs Dunn." Did Margaret's response come from a need to protect her clan, or was it the genuine truth? She'd been tight-lipped, but Margaret didn't strike Felicity as dishonest. "I don't mean to upset you with this kind of talk. It's just that a passing like Mr Granger's is an unusual occurrence in a quiet village such as Ottermouth, is it not?"

Margaret took a little sip of tea. "It is unusual, yes."

Felicity waited. She wouldn't push her.

Margaret took another sip. "Nothing but trouble, those artists."

While this was precisely the sort of comment the newspaper needed, Felicity left her notebook in her pocket. It wasn't worth the risk. Keeping Margaret talking was more important. How else would Felicity truly comprehend what was happening in the village? "What makes you say that?"

Margaret's cup and saucer clattered onto the table. The question was unwelcome.

Fearful the fisherman's wife might clam up completely, Felicity offered an alternative path. "You've a daughter, haven't you, Mrs Dunn?" Might Felicity be able to find out more about Thora without getting the girl in trouble?

Margaret nodded. "Had a son, too." Her voice wavered. "Lost him in the war."

"My sincerest condolences." It was a common story, but that didn't make it any less heartbreaking.

"Stanley was a good lad. Thora looked up to him, and he doted on his little sister. When he didn't come back…" Pain flickered across Margaret's face. She blinked hard. "We all miss him. But she can be such a silly girl."

Excitement rose within Felicity. Was Margaret alluding to Thora associating with the art crowd? "Your daughter's very young though, isn't she?" Matters could not be rushed.

"She's eighteen."

Felicity had imagined Thora to be younger.

Margaret met Felicity's gaze. "Not much younger than you, I expect, your ladyship. But she hasn't half your sense."

Internally, Felicity winced at Margaret's criticism of her daughter. "I imagined Thora to be a bright girl."

Margaret lowered her gaze, perhaps regretting what she'd

said. Felicity had witnessed Margaret being protective of Thora. It was to Margaret's mothering instinct that Felicity would appeal.

"Do you know where Thora is now?" Felicity knew she was pushing, but she was doing so as gently as possible. "Might it help if I were to speak to her?"

Margaret pressed her lips together and shook her head. "I wish I knew where she went. And perhaps you might talk some sense into her, your ladyship. She's a good girl at heart, but her father and I can't get through to her."

"What is it that worries you?" Felicity remembered her surprise at seeing Thora speaking to Audrey. If Martin was involved in trafficking drugs, and Audrey was too, had Thora been dragged in? Is that what Margaret meant when she said the artists were 'nothing but trouble'?

But Felicity already knew that kind of information wouldn't come from Margaret or anyone in the fishing community.

The fisherman's wife stood up from the table. She turned her back to Felicity, as though busying herself with the stove. Surreptitiously, she wiped her eyes. "There's work to be done before the men get back from Brixham." The window of opportunity to speak with Margaret had suddenly closed. "If you'll excuse me, your ladyship."

The cobblestones of the harbourside were still slick and shining, but the downpour had passed. Only a mist of fine rain wafted through the air, the masts of the vessels in the harbour bobbing gently on the tide.

Felicity took in a deep, salty breath. Should she go looking for Thora? Not only were there questions to ask, but might Felicity be able to help the girl? Margaret hadn't given Felicity much to go on.

Or did it make more sense to return to the gallery? There

were questions for Audrey not only about Martin but also about Thora. Might Alex already have the answers?

Peeuuw-wheep!

A shrill whistle broke the air.

Grace Campbell was standing outside her cottage, her blanket draped around her shoulders. She was beckoning to Felicity.

Not feeling especially charmed to have been summoned as one might call to a dog, Felicity nevertheless approached. "Am I to understand you wish to speak with me, Mrs Campbell?"

"I can tell you where you might find Thora, if that's of any interest to you."

Felicity drew back her chin. "How did you know I wished to speak with her?"

A mirthless smile creased Grace's weather-worn features. "I know a lot of things. Do you want to find her or not?"

Felicity nodded. In Ottermouth, one took what one was offered. She listened carefully as Grace provided instructions.

Before dashing off, Felicity had to ask. "Why are you helping me?"

Grace sighed. "I'm not helping you, your ladyship. My sister's barely spoken to me in twenty years, and she brought up her daughter to regard me with disdain. But Maggie's right to be worried. My niece may be in trouble."

Chapter Thirty-One

The path Grace had described to Felicity was narrow, rocky, and overgrown, barely noticeable to the untrained eye. It wove from the harbourside, past the back of buildings and along a generous cliff-side ledge. It was also exceedingly steep.

Using her folded umbrella to push aside brambles, and with a steadying hand on the cliff face, Felicity quickly became out of puff. She paused her ascent. Below, the sea was greenish grey, the horizon blurred by fine, misty rain. Another yacht was arriving in Ottermouth's harbour, presumably a collector keen to get their hands on a piece or two from the exhibition. A trilby-wearing reporter accompanied by a photographer emerged from the inn and headed for the gallery. Nothing of the coast was visible beyond the lighthouse.

Was it right to chase after Thora? Should Felicity be back at the gallery, working in tandem with Alex, focused entirely on her reporting? That might have been the logical way ahead.

But if Felicity could help Thora out of whatever predicament she was in, didn't she have a duty to do so? The bonds in the fishing community, no matter how troubled, were strong. It wasn't clear what Grace had done to deserve being ostracised, but the love for one's kin could be powerful.

Holding the sopping bracken out of the way with her folded umbrella, Felicity continued along the narrow, overgrown path. If talking to Thora resulted in a clearer picture of the goings-on in Ottermouth, then so much the better. Yet somehow, that was no longer Felicity's priority.

The path dipped downwards in quite a treacherous manner. Felicity used her umbrella as a walking cane, although her heart still jumped whenever her shoe slipped on the wet rocks. At last, the path ended on the shore of a little cove. The tide swished a gentle rhythm against the shingle as gulls called in unison from the rocks above. It was the same secluded spot where Felicity had thrown seaweed sticks for Pip and Beetle. It was where she'd met — and scared away — the young fisherman, Colin Reynolds. It was also the same beach upon which she'd come across Martin Granger.

The steep cliffs that hugged the cove and the trees and thickets clinging to them meant there was no view of the village or even the lighthouse. Felicity couldn't remember spotting the cove from the water, either, although there'd been many distractions during her boat trip with the now-fugitive Billy Seddon. The view was limited to the hazy green-grey horizon and the droplets of moisture hanging to Felicity's curls under the brim of her bicorn hat.

The cove was deserted.

It was disappointing. Felicity trudged back over the pebbles towards the path. She would return to the gallery, where she would—

Felicity stopped. A slither of sunlight through grey clouds turned murky waves silver as she waited. She moved closer to the shoreline. Again, she waited.

Yes. She could hear it more clearly now.

Turning, Felicity examined the cliffs and giant tumbled rocks that surrounded the little beach. Her feet sinking into the shingle, Felicity climbed further up the shore, past a line of seaweed deposited by the last high tide.

Again, she paused. The sound was now thoroughly discernible. Crying. Someone was crying, their sobs echoing around the rocks.

Felicity approached a pile of giant boulders from which the sound seemed to emanate. Behind it was an open space not visible from the beach, where the pebbles gave way to a natural formation of vast, smooth stones. The sound of the crying was amplified. In the shadows of the boulders, among the crags of the cliff, was a tall, narrow opening.

A cave.

Felicity advanced with care, her eyes adjusting to the cave's dimness, the sobbing echoing all around her. Close to the entrance, curled into a ball and practically tucked into a crevice, was Thora Dunn. She still wore her oversized raincoat, a wide-brimmed oilskin hat on the rock next to her. With her head on her knees, she was in floods of tears.

Felicity moved slowly. She didn't yet know what ailed Thora, but she would find out and, if she could, help.

"Miss Dunn." Felicity spoke softly, not wanting to startle the girl.

Thora lifted her head and blinked her sea-green eyes. Strands of her thick, wavy hair clung to wet cheeks. She sniffed but said nothing.

Cautiously, Felicity took a seat on a rock close enough that she could speak in gentle tones. "Miss Dunn, forgive my interrupting, but I'm extremely saddened to see you so upset. Whatever is the matter?"

Tears continued to roll down Thora's cheeks. With her unblemished skin and innocent gaze, she looked much younger than her eighteen years. She'd observed Felicity with interest since her arrival in Ottermouth, hadn't she? Felicity remembered the fleeting sea-green gaze upon her on the harbourside.

"You may speak to me in confidence, if you wish," said Felicity. Not all journalists operated ethically, but it was never right to take advantage of someone too emotional to think clearly.

"I shan't even tell your mother unless you want me to. She's rather worried about you, you know. Your aunt, too."

The mention of family made Thora straighten. "I'm all right. I'm just…" She sniffed. "I've made a mistake. I've made so many mistakes." She broke down again into sobs, her shoulders shaking.

Carefully, Felicity placed a hand on Thora's arm. It was agonising to witness such upset, especially in one so young. Felicity could recall being eighteen. It wasn't a terribly long time ago. It was a period when emotions would run wild without one knowing quite why.

"What mistakes have you made?"

Thora wiped her eyes with the heel of her hand. "I've betrayed my family."

Felicity frowned a little. "'Betrayed' is a strong word."

Thora locked eyes with Felicity, a tumultuous mix of hostility and longing evident in her gaze. She'd been raised not to talk to outsiders. Yet both Thora's mother and aunt were counting on Felicity.

"Your family loves you, Miss Dunn. They really do. That won't ever change. Even if times are hard."

Thora looked so deeply unhappy. "Do you really promise you won't tell a soul?"

Thora was preparing to open up, but Felicity's thoughts jumped immediately to Alex. In working together, they shared everything with one another. Making this promise would mean keeping a secret from her friend. Alex would understand, though, wouldn't he?

"I promise," said Felicity. "You may count on me."

Hope glimmered in the girl's gaze. "I was helping Billy. And now he's gone." Her face creased with dismay. "And I'll be next." Tears spilled from her eyes.

"Helping him how?" Felicity suspected she already knew.

"I would bring his… I would carry Billy's goods. I would bring them to the art people."

Felicity nodded sadly. Margaret had said the artists in

Ottermouth were nothing but trouble. As Officer Marshall had highlighted, tea and tobacco were one thing. Illegal intoxicants were quite another.

"Which art people? Miss Lawson?"

Thora put her head back on her knees. "I didn't know what would happen to him," she sobbed, her voice muffled. "I didn't know. I promise."

"You didn't know what would happen to Billy?" Was Thora talking about the near-sinking of the little motorboat?

Thora heaved a breath. "Mr Granger said he cared for me. He said he'd help me leave Ottermouth. He was going to take me to London. And then he… And then he…"

Felicity shivered. It was the connection she'd been looking for. "You were bringing Billy's packages to Mr Granger?"

Thora met Felicity's gaze, her face full of pain. "It's my fault. It's all my fault."

Felicity gave Thora's arm a gentle squeeze. "How is anything your fault?"

The girl wiped at her tears. "I shouldn't have agreed to help Billy. Col said it was wrong, but I didn't listen."

"Colin Reynolds?" Felicity recalled how the young fisherman had clammed up when Felicity asked him about Ottermouth's artists. The players in the sombre drama were being rapidly revealed.

Thora nodded somewhat bashfully. "Col works on my father's boat. But Billy was my brother's best friend. They went to war together, only Stan never came back. Billy says Stan was lucky." Thora sniffed. "He pretends to get on just fine, but Billy only does what he does because he can't find work at anything else. No one wants a man with one hand, your ladyship."

The picture was becoming clear. Thora had aided her brother's best friend out of loyalty to her deceased sibling. It remained a struggle to sympathise with Billy, but a run of awful luck could change a person for the worst.

"What is it that Mr Seddon does, exactly?" Felicity kept her tone soft.

Thora sat up straighter. "Dope, your ladyship. Billy smuggles dope." She wasn't remotely naïve on that point.

"And Mr Granger?"

"He bought it. And sold it."

A ripple of excitement passed through Felicity. With more than one source confirming it, Martin's double life was now something for the paper, but Felicity's work wasn't done. How could she help Thora?

"If Mr Seddon and Mr Granger got into a disagreement," said Felicity carefully, "it wasn't your fault, Miss Dunn. You aren't to blame for what happened to Mr Granger. I hope you see—"

Thora cut her off. "Billy didn't do it. That's not how things work."

Felicity paused. "How do things work? Would you be willing to tell me?"

"Mr Granger was an outsider. We would never… It's just not how it works, your ladyship."

"I believe you, Miss Dunn." Felicity's understanding of the situation was solidifying. As Margaret had said, the fishing people solved their own problems. Martin wasn't part of their community. He didn't fall under their jurisdiction. But did Billy still abide by the fishermen's rules? "Do you know where Mr Seddon is now?"

Outside, the rain resumed, hissing as it hit the rocks, the scent of damp seaweed sweeping into the cave on the breeze.

Thora shook her head. "He's on the continent and he's safe. That's all I know. He has friends in Belgium and Spain and all over. He says he'll stay away till the customs men forget about him."

Was a man like Billy easily forgotten? Might he ever return to Ottermouth? Felicity certainly had no objection to never seeing him again, and it was likely better for Thora that way, too. And while Felicity wished no man dead, it was probably also better for

Thora that Martin was no longer around. Who knows how far he would have dragged her into his tangled web?

"You mentioned Mr Granger wanted to take you to London. Was the plan for you to continue your work as his model?"

Thora looked confused, even shocked. "I never posed for Mr Granger, your ladyship. Mother would never have forgiven me."

"My apologies, Miss Dunn." Felicity had felt certain she'd seen the girl in several paintings. Her art appraisal skills were clearly lacking. "Is it still your wish to relocate to London?"

Thora set her hands flat on the rock upon which she was sitting. "I just... He just..." She shook her head, growing tearful again. "I suppose I clung too much to what Mr Granger told me. Col said I ought to stay away from the lot of them. But I've never even been to a gown shop." She looked down at the rough, unshapely dress under her bulky raincoat. "I've never been to the cinema. Martin said I deserve to enjoy myself." She looked with hope at Felicity. "What do you think, your ladyship?"

While Felicity was loath to agree with a peddler of drugs, Martin had a point. Thora had been born into a traditional community where responsibilities and roles were imposed when one was young. The pleasures she pined for were relatively simple by modern standards. "Every person deserves enjoyment in life. Have you spoken to your mother about your desires?"

Thora was quiet. She shook her head.

"I believe that would be a good place to start," urged Felicity gently.

Thora blinked, then nodded. "I'll talk to her."

The tension within Felicity eased. There was still a way to go, but she'd hopefully helped put Thora on the right path.

Their discussion having been open and honest up till now, was it possible to return to Felicity's original motive for chasing after Thora?

"You came to the gallery today and spoke to Miss Audrey Lawson. May I ask why?"

Thora gave a little sigh. "She asked me to contact Billy. Give him a message. I tried, but I came to tell her I can't."

"What message did Miss Lawson have for Mr Seddon?"

"She wanted her dope," replied Thora with some disdain. "She used to get it from Mr Granger."

The role of another player in the dark spectacle had been unveiled. Felicity had encountered dope fiends before. Audrey hid the signs of her addiction well. The desperate need for money she had expressed in the gallery was no doubt a symptom of the tragic affliction. "Was that the basis of Mr Granger's relationship with Miss Lawson?"

Thora shrugged. "Mr Granger had different relationships at different times." Her eyes darted to the cave floor. "He was like his father in that respect. As I understand it."

The comments echoed what Audrey had said about Martin's other women.

"I shouldn't like to make trouble for anyone," ventured Felicity, "but I'm keen to understand what happened to Mr Granger. Might you know with which other women he associated himself?" The list in Ottermouth was rather small. "With Miss Prothero, for example?"

Thora frowned. "Who?"

Felicity was perhaps clutching at straws. "The daughter of the art dealer, Mr Harold Prothero. The man in charge of the exhibition."

"Oh." Thora smiled for the first time. "The woman who brings the baskets of food around for us. As though we're paupers."

Felicity had seen Elizabeth with just such a basket. The do-gooding explained her bustling about the village and matched with her concern about the smuggling. Why Lawrence had warned Felicity off the art dealer's daughter remained a puzzle.

"Mr Granger wasn't close to her," said Thora. "There's only one woman I know for sure he saw often."

"Oh?"

"He'd go out at night with her, on her boat."

Felicity frowned. The rain was coming down hard again, its echo rattling around the cave. "On Mrs Mountvernon's yacht, you mean?"

"Yes. The lady from the big house. He'd go out with her. On her yacht."

Felicity's stomach dropped. Isabella had lied.

Chapter Thirty-Two

The sense of betrayal coursed through Felicity's veins like hot lava. She'd trusted Isabella. She'd worked hard to please her. Isabella had sworn she'd told Felicity the truth. But she hadn't told her everything, and not only that. Isabella had lied to her, hadn't she?

Felicity powered along the path towards the village, not caring a jot about the wet plants soaking her skirt and ankles or the rain blowing under her umbrella. When Felicity asked Isabella about Martin's other women, what was it she'd said? That it wasn't the kind of business she saw it fit to pry into?

Wanting to be doubly sure, Felicity had checked with Thora. How did she know Martin spent time at night on the water with Isabella? Had Thora seen them taking Xantho out together? Thora had seen the boat and Martin aboard it. In their discussions together, during which Martin had made promises of London and frock shops, Thora had asked him who he spent his nights at sea with. Mrs Mountvernon had been his answer.

Had Jasper known about Isabella's true nature? Felicity sincerely hoped not. Had he known, then he wouldn't have sent Felicity to Ottermouth.

Feeling the sting of betrayal and flames of anger rising within her, Felicity had backed away from the topic in the cave. Her goal had been to help Thora, so she ended her interaction with the girl by urging her to speak more openly with her mother. Thora seemed keen to try to improve her relationship with Margaret, and Felicity remained calm and gracious until the girl was out of view. Felicity's mild expression had then become a deep frown, and she stormed up the path towards Ashdene, the rain lashing at her back.

Isabella's comfort and happiness had been a frequent lens through which Felicity had viewed and acted upon events in Ottermouth. Yet the woman clearly could not be trusted. But as angry as Felicity was at the idea of being lied to, she was also angry at herself. She'd been naïve. Too trusting. Should she not know better by now?

The path flattened out in the section leading to Ashdene's garden gate. Felicity was moving so fast she practically broke into a run, sloshing through puddles in her T-strap shoes. Upon hearing the splash of footsteps behind her, her heart skipped. The last thing she needed was another run-in with Officer Marshall. Or with anyone else.

"Felicity!"

It came as an enormous relief to recognise Alex on the path behind her, a hand on his dripping hat, his overcoat belted tightly against the wind and rain.

At Felicity's invitation, he joined her under the umbrella. The angry pounding in her chest slowed as he eased the umbrella's handle from her grasp with one hand, shaking and then replacing his hat with the other.

"I've been dashing about the place trying to find you," said Alex breathlessly, "but from that look on your face, I'm betting your information trumps mine."

"Isabella lied to me."

Alex's brow shot up. The wind whipped through the trees, flinging a barrage of heavy raindrops onto the umbrella.

Felicity filled him in on what she'd heard from Thora. She

should perhaps have calmed herself before explaining matters to Alex, but she was too emotional to hold back.

"And you can't say who you heard this from?"

Felicity shook her head.

Alex let out a long exhale, which gently and unintentionally brushed the inside of Felicity's collar. "What I have pales in comparison."

"What do you have?" Though Isabella's betrayal still stung, Felicity already felt calmer. The rain seemed also to be easing.

Alex shrugged. "That gallery lot much isn't any easier to talk to than the trawler crew. I got Audrey on her own and asked her outright: was Martin involved in the supply of dope? She laughed. The very idea of it, she said. Then she gave me the slip. Had a train to catch, apparently. So I set about cornering Elizabeth. None of them would stop their work hanging paintings or dusting ceramics or whatever else. The daughter wouldn't even look at me, and her father kept getting in the way." Alex shrugged. "Then I came looking for you. You're usually always onto something quite revealing." He smiled. "Sounds like I missed out."

Felicity smiled back at him. They were an excellent team, but they had their individual strengths. Had Alex been with Felicity, Margaret might not have invited her into her cottage, and Thora would likely not have opened up.

As the heat of her anger continued to subside, Felicity told Alex about Margaret's apology.

Again, he raised his brow. "It was someone from within the fishing community who sabotaged Billy's boat?"

"That's what I understood from Mrs Dunn."

"But we still don't know why."

"Not exactly."

The rain eased to a slow patter.

Alex narrowed his eyes. "You've a theory?"

"I've a hunch," she said but couldn't say more. There were

details of the conversation with Thora that had to remain confidential if Felicity was to keep her word.

"And what about who did for Martin?"

A hot rush of indignation returned to Felicity's chest. "I'm on my way to speak to Isabella."

"Do you plan to confront her about having had a relationship with the dead man? Or about having killed him?"

Alex's tone was mildly provocative, but he had a point. One didn't simply storm up to a murderess with an accusation.

Isabella was certainly capable of hiding the truth. Was she capable of murder? What would have been her motive?

"I want to know why she lied to me," said Felicity. "I don't like to be taken for a fool."

"No one does." Alex folded the umbrella, shaking it into the bracken at the side of the path. "Shall I accompany you?"

Felicity believed she could handle Isabella alone, and Alex's offer didn't imply he thought differently. However, if Isabella had been involved in Martin's demise, and if Felicity's confronting her were to prompt a desperate reaction, the presence of Felicity's quick-thinking and courageous friend would be highly desirable.

She nodded at Alex. "Yes. Let's talk to her together."

The young footman answered the door to Felicity and Alex. Without warning, Pip and Beetle came careening into the hall, ears flapping, fur flying, and barking with joy at Felicity. As Alex returned the umbrella to its stand, Felicity scooped Pip under her arm, unable to bear the mayhem of the two dogs dancing about on their hind legs.

"I'm not taking you out, if that's what you're thinking," she said firmly as Beetle barked at Felicity, first in a friendly, playful manner, then in a more commanding tone.

Mrs Rawling arrived in the hall, providing an opportunity for the footman to retreat from the canine chaos. "Beetle! Please. Where are your manners?"

The Briard's ears and tail dropped. He whimpered. Being reprimanded by someone who adored you was a most difficult thing.

"Where might I find Mrs Mountvernon?" enquired Felicity of the housekeeper as Pip wriggled under her arm.

"I believe you'll find Mrs Mountvernon in the salon, your ladyship. She's preparing to go down into the village for the exhibition opening."

The sound of laughter filled the hall. Alex turned his gaze up the main staircase, his still-damp hat held at his chest.

James Halliday was descending the stairs in the company of two young women, both with neatly cut bobs, elegant dresses, and long strands of precious-looking beads around their necks.

"Lady Felicity." James smiled. "What a pleasure to see you again. Perhaps you already know the Countess of Eavesham? And her sister, the Honourable Miss Underhay? They've come from London for the exhibition. I was just giving them a tour of the place. Might you like to interview them for the paper?"

Felicity blinked. She didn't know the girls, and while they seemed perfectly charming, she had no interest in getting to know them. Not at that precise moment in time.

As James and his companions reached the bottom of the stairs, Mrs Rawling clasped Beetle's collar, preventing the Briard from surging enthusiastically towards the guests.

Alex approached and introduced himself. "Alexander Cooper, reporter with the Western Daily News." He gave James' hand a firm shake. "I'd be delighted to get some quotes for the paper."

Felicity's heart soared with gratitude for the sacrifice her friend was making. Alex had no more interest in speaking to a pair of society girls than Felicity did.

"But I'm afraid we shall have to start with the matter of Mr Granger's tragic passing," added Alex.

The countess and her sister looked rather dismayed.

The American art buyer drew down the corners of his mouth. "Of course. Tragic, absolutely tragic. Mrs Rawling? Might there be a room for us?"

"Certainly, Mr Halliday," said the housekeeper, still stooped to keep control of the Briard. "The morning room would be a suitable venue. Shall I bring a tray of refreshments?"

As Alex turned to follow James and his entourage, he whispered to Felicity, "Go." A quiver across his brow added, *And be careful.*

Felicity gave a discreet nod. She was always careful, and Alex wouldn't be far away. It was time to confront Isabella.

Chapter Thirty-Three

The salon's balcony doors opened onto a view over the paved terrace and Ashdene's lush gardens. Beyond, the slate-grey sea was topped with a steely sky. A gramophone in the room's corner was playing a romantic waltz. A small bouquet of lily-of-the-valley scented the air with a creamy floral perfume.

Isabella stood before the large mirror above the fireplace. She was attending to her hair, adding further pins to an elegant chignon, and twisting her slender neck to admire the effect in the reflection. The draped sleeves of a striking peacock-blue gown hung from her elbows. Her beloved works of art surrounded her, adorning every wall and surface.

Was this woman a liar? Was she a murderer?

Pip shivered in Felicity's arms. It didn't feel right to leave him with Mrs Rawling when she was already struggling to control Beetle. The Yorkie was, however, nervous, perhaps sensitive to the indignation that had once again begun pulsing through Felicity's veins.

As Felicity closed the salon door behind her, Isabella's warm brown eyes met hers in the mirror.

"Cici, darling." She spoke through a pair of pins held in her teeth, which she swiftly added to her hair before turning away from her reflection, her eyes shining and her cheeks pink. This was a different woman altogether to the one Felicity had encountered earlier upstairs in bed.

"Excellent timing, as usual. I was hoping to see you before the opening." Isabella swept forward, giving Pip a scratch under the chin before clasping Felicity by the hand. "Listen. I want to apologise again about hiding that awful drugs business from you. I honestly didn't think it was important, but clearly, I was wrong. I should have been more open with you."

Felicity drew a steadying breath. "So you've now told me everything I ought to know?"

Isabella closed her eyes for a moment and nodded. "Yes. Everything, and I feel so much better for it. Jasper was absolutely right about you, Cici. You're a fine young woman, awfully intelligent. Some might say too intelligent for a woman, but I would disagree. The world needs more of your sort."

Felicity couldn't help but smile a little. If Isabella was being sincere, as it so often seemed, then Felicity was touched by the praise. Sharing encouraging words with one another wasn't a typically British inclination. When words of sincere encouragement were spoken, the effect could be rather magical.

But how far could Isabella be trusted?

"Oh!" Isabella drew a hand up to her mouth. "Wait. I didn't tell you everything. Not yet." She squeezed Felicity's hand. "The detectives from Torquay have interviewed my staff. They've also been through all my things. Made a terrible mess, but of course, they've found nothing untoward. And now they have the word of everyone in the house that I never left Ashdene the night of Martin's passing. The nice young detective I spoke to is fairly confident they'll have me cleared of any wrongdoing, even if the incident took place on Xantho, which is something I still can't quite believe. They've asked me not to leave Ottermouth, and not to board Xantho, which rather scuppers my plans for a little celebration I was hoping to hold on board after the opening — a small private affair, you understand. You and the charming Mr

Cooper would naturally have been invited. But I suppose complying with the police's wishes is the least I can do out of respect for poor Marty."

As she spoke, a twist of her chestnut hair escaped her chignon and sprung onto her forehead. With a sigh, Isabella let go of Felicity's hand and turned back to the mirror. "So, in summary, things are looking up. At least in my case. The police say they still have no idea who did the deed, though."

"Mm-hmm." Felicity's response was little more than a mumble. Her resentment was quickly cooling. Isabella's claims could be checked with the authorities, and if her alibi for the night in question was solid, what did it matter if Isabella had carried out a liaison with Martin? Even if she'd kept the information from Felicity, it wasn't a crime in itself.

"Anyway, I wanted to thank you, Cici." Isabella held pins in her mouth as she fiddled with her hair, eyes flicking to Felicity in the mirror. "You've been an absolute rock. And you've been through so much. The awful discovery on the beach. That horrible boat incident. Mrs Rawling keeps me advised of everything, thank goodness. Because you didn't say a thing about it to me this morning."

It was true. Felicity hadn't made an effort to keep Isabella well-informed. It was maybe unfair to hope for better treatment in return.

Isabella added the last pin to her hair. "What a soldier you are."

Beetle could be heard barking in the corridor. Pip whimpered. He was desperate to get back to his friend.

Felicity stroked the Yorkie to calm him. "About Mr Granger," she began, but she was losing the will to press ahead.

Isabella turned away from the mirror. The wind swept through the terrace doors, making the delicate fabric of her blue dress ripple like water. "Marty would have wanted us to carry on, you know. He was immensely proud of his father's work and so modest about his own."

Felicity nodded. She followed Isabella's gaze towards the paintings adorning the walls of the salon. Though she was far from being an expert, Felicity could now tell the difference between Eustace's and Martin's work. While the son's paintings were evocative and emotional, his father's creations were captivating in a more subtle, masterful way.

"I could stare at all of them for hours," said Isabella dreamily.

The longer Felicity remained in Isabella's presence, the calmer and less irritated she felt. Major Mountvernon's widow was a charming woman who seemed so genuine. It was no wonder Jasper had an urge to care for her. Had Isabella really lied to Felicity? Felicity had been wrong about people before. She recalled her discussion with Thora. Martin had told the girl he'd been on Xantho with Isabella, but Thora hadn't seen them together herself, had she? Could Martin have lied to Thora? If so, why?

Felicity cleared her throat. "About your relationship with Mr Granger." She wanted to be sure.

Isabella's brow lifted. "My relationship with him?" She thought for a moment. "We were artist and patron to start with, I suppose. Then we grew to be friends."

"Were you ever more than friends?" It was perhaps a blundering way to approach things, but Felicity wanted the doubt cleared from her mind.

"For setting up the exhibition, we were business partners, I suppose you could say. And as friends, we were incredibly close." Isabella paused. Her brow wrinkled. "Or perhaps I don't quite follow what you mean?"

But Felicity's focus had shifted. A painting beside the mantelpiece had caught her attention.

"Cici?"

Felicity approached the canvas in question. Pip's ears tickled her cheek as she bent to look more closely at the corner of the painting. No. Felicity wasn't just imagining things.

Her stomach tightened.

"What is it you want to know exactly?" continued Isabella. "I'm not sure I follow."

But Felicity had no more questions for Major Mountvernon's widow. What she'd noticed had the power to change everything. To change everything completely.

Chapter Thirty-Four

The transfer of Pip to Mrs Rawling's care was seamless, the Yorkie having no objection to being left behind at Ashdene with Beetle. From the morning room's open door, Alex looked up from his interview with the American art collector and society girls, his pencil paused on his notebook, as he raised an eyebrow.

Felicity couldn't stop to explain.

At Ashdene's front door, she glanced at the painting of the figure on the beach. The resemblance to Thora was uncanny, despite the girl not having been born when the artwork was made. Yet even with Thora's role now clear, there'd still been something hidden in the paintings all along.

Hurrying down the garden path, thin rays of sunshine sparkling on the dripping foliage, Felicity's senses tingled with excitement and apprehension. She had to get to the gallery before the exhibition opened. What Felicity had noticed on the wall in Isabella's salon could be critically significant, but she had to be sure before telling anyone. Even Alex.

The rain held off long enough for Felicity to arrive in the village. She weaved through groups of chattering, well-heeled art enthusiasts and the odd rival reporter to reach the old boat shed. A ribbon had been strung across the wide opening of the doors, presumably to be cut during the opening ceremony. Felicity ducked underneath.

Catering staff in black-and-white livery were already serving drinks to a clutch of art buyers with early access. Nigel Davies hovered close to them, smiling simperingly. Harold Prothero wasn't present. Nor was Audrey, but that wasn't a surprise. Elizabeth stood nervously beside the drinks table like a novice waitress. Constable Thompson had also apparently been invited for an advance viewing. With his helmet under his arm, he strolled around the gallery examining artworks, twitching his grey moustache, and looking generally pleased with everything.

Felicity took a deep breath and approached Elizabeth.

Nigel acknowledged Felicity with a sneery smile but kept his attention on his customers. The policeman ceased strolling and frowned at Felicity, as if her arrival were an unpleasant interruption. Elizabeth blinked anxiously but didn't move from her position next to the drinks table.

"Lady Felicity," she said, lacking any hint of enthusiasm in her tone.

Felicity nodded a polite greeting. A new and pressing concern had eclipsed Lawrence's warning. "Miss Prothero, I hope you don't mind me addressing you in your father's absence. Might I be allowed to take a quick look around the exhibition?"

Elizabeth swallowed. "Is there something in particular you're looking for, your ladyship?"

Nigel craned his neck in Felicity's direction. "Considering a purchase, Lady Felicity?"

Elizabeth's eyes widened. Felicity followed her gaze.

Alex was ducking under the ribbon in the doorway.

"Lady Felicity." His tone was businesslike, though he was out of puff. "I was hoping I might find you here." *May I ask what on Earth it is we're doing?* a raise of his eyebrows seemed to add.

Indeed, everyone was looking at Felicity enquiringly, but it wasn't time to lay her cards on the table. Not yet.

"It's just..." Felicity turned away from Alex and moved

towards a wall of paintings by Eustace and Martin Granger, the canvasses by the father outnumbering those of the son. All of them captured the lives and the work of Ottermouth's fishing community.

Photos of the two men had been placed among the paintings. Martin had been captured standing beside an easel on the harbour. His father, in a rough old fisherman's jumper, and with a pipe in his mouth, sat aboard a fishing vessel with a sketchbook on his knees.

Felicity leaned in closer.

Alex arrived beside her and bent towards the painting Felicity was inspecting. "Did you speak to Isabella?" he whispered.

"Yes," hissed Felicity, "but that's not it."

"What are we looking at?" Alex's eyes roved over the painting. He was as lost as Felicity had been upon first arriving in Ottermouth.

"It's an exquisite piece." Nigel approached the two journalists. "One of a kind."

Both Felicity and Alex ignored him.

"The brushwork," said Felicity, her heart beating hard. "I need to be sure." She leaned even closer to the canvas.

Felicity might never understand how artists achieved different effects in oil paints, pastels, charcoal, or watercolours. There was, however, one thing about which Felicity had intimate knowledge.

When using Pitman shorthand — in which she was fully proficient — control and awareness of the pen's direction was paramount. A change in direction could alter the meaning of a word.

And pen strokes were exceedingly similar to brush strokes.

The signatures in the corners of the paintings were stylised and striking. Eustace's was bolder and more angular, while Martin's was a flouncy flourish. From a distance, they were consistent between each artist's works. Yet something at Ashdene had caught Felicity's eye, and indeed, in looking closer…

Felicity stood up straight. She turned towards Elizabeth. "I should like to speak to your father, if I may, Miss Prothero."

Elizabeth's mouth hung open for a moment. She looked rather pale. "Yes. I mean, he's very busy. But I suppose I can—" She stepped away from the drinks table but hesitated.

"Officer Marshall." Constable Thompson's voice rang through the exhibition space with a distinct tone of disapproval. "I thought your work in our village was done."

The customs officer didn't seem to notice the ribbon. It broke as he strode through the gallery doors. "Am I not welcome to admire the local achievements?"

The local policeman straightened, though his height was no match for Officer Marshall's stature. "I would suggest you get back on your boat and patrol somewhere else. You got what you wanted, didn't you?"

Elizabeth appeared frozen with panic. Nigel's nostrils flared. The art buyers with him whispered to one another. Alex reached inside his jacket for his notebook.

The customs officer advanced towards the policeman, his chest puffed, the brass buttons on his uniform shining. "Your opinion, Constable Thompson, has no bearing on when my work is done. Especially when you yourself are nose deep in—"

"Officer Marshall." Emerging from a door at the back of the gallery, Harold smiled broadly, his arms extended in a gesture of welcome. "And Lady Felicity is here with the relentless Mr Cooper. What a pleasure to receive you all."

"Mr Prothero." Felicity stepped forward. There was no time to lose. "Might I have a word with you, please? In private?"

The art dealer frowned good-naturedly. "We're on the point of opening the exhibition to the public, your ladyship. Might your business not wait until perhaps tomorrow?"

The policeman held up his hands. "As you know, I'm merely here as an admirer, Mr Prothero. I'm pleased to see our village and its inhabitants represented in the best possible light. As to why Officer Marshall is still loitering around these parts…"

The custom officer folded his arms and smiled with

amusement. "I was actually hoping to speak to Lady Felicity."

Alex narrowed his eyes at the man.

Felicity tipped her head to the side. Officer Marshall was one of the last people with whom she wished to speak, especially at that precise moment. "Can it not wait, Officer Marshall? My business with Mr Prothero is rather urgent."

Alex stepped forward, interrupting the line of sight between the customs officer and Felicity. "Anything you want to say to the paper, you can say to me, Officer Marshall."

Nigel had ushered his art buyers into the far corner of the gallery. The catering staff had also dispersed to the far reaches of the building. Still, they glanced with interest at the spirited interactions between the journalists, the art dealer, and the authorities. Elizabeth watched, blinking nervously. She looked like a trapped animal.

Felicity had to press ahead. She stepped closer to Harold. "If you don't mind, Mr Prothero. I have a very quick question for you." She spoke in low tones to avoid being overheard. A discussion in a separate room was perhaps too much to ask. "I don't want to hold you up and it shan't take long."

Harold frowned, confused. "Y-yes, your ladyship. What is it?"

"It's about the provenance of some of these Granger paintings, particularly the works by Eustace. How did you come about them?"

Harold's mouth gaped. His attention was no longer on Felicity. "Lizzie?"

Elizabeth had approached the policeman. "Constable Thompson." Though loud, her voice shook. "I've a confession to make. It was me. I killed Martin Granger." She thrust forward her wrists, ready for cuffing.

Alex span round.

The policeman's eyes widened with shock. "What? Really?"

"You?" cried Officer Marshall, all trace of nonchalance gone.

Felicity felt suddenly very cold. She brought a hand to her mouth. "No. Oh, no, no, no."

Chapter Thirty-Five

There was no question of it now. Ottermouth's first and only art exhibition had been cancelled indefinitely.

In expanding on her confession, Elizabeth told the policeman and everyone present in the gallery — although Nigel had hurried his art buyers outside as quickly as possible — that she had been invited out onto Isabella's yacht by Martin. Knowing that Martin was an important client of her father's, Elizabeth had accepted the invitation. Aboard the yacht, Martin had made an amorous advance, which she had refused.

When the artist became insistent, even aggressive, being out on the boat alone with the man, Elizabeth panicked. She grabbed something close at hand, which happened to be a pair of binoculars, and struck out. Stunned by the attack, Martin fell into the water. It was too dark for Elizabeth to see what happened to him. So she brought the boat back to the harbour.

"And moored it all by yourself?" Officer Marshall scratched his jaw. "Keen sailor, are you, Miss Prothero?"

Elizabeth straightened. She had a hand on the drinks table to steady herself, the constable having refused to apply his handcuffs. "I was quite terrified. I don't remember the finer details of what happened."

Elizabeth had told her story succinctly and confidently. She seemed far less nervous than when Felicity had first arrived at the gallery. Harold, meanwhile, was white, trembling, and mostly silent.

"I believe the fear I felt made me more capable than normal," added Elizabeth.

The policeman didn't cross-question her like the customs officer did. Alex wrote down every word of what was said. Felicity, too, made notes, but her mind leapt about. What she'd noticed in the paintings' signatures couldn't, for the moment, be addressed. There was also the profound shock of Elizabeth's revelation. Her story didn't add up. Or did it?

Constable Thompson sighed heavily as he led Elizabeth out of the gallery.

"Shall I accompany you to Torquay?" Harold tugged at his shirt collar. He looked like he might faint. "Lizzie, my darling, you need me with you, do you not?"

The constable looked grave but also sorrowful. "I'm sure there'll be sympathy for Miss Prothero's situation."

Elizabeth lifted her chin. "It'll all be all right, Papa. You're needed here."

It wasn't clear whether Harold believed his daughter's confession. The destruction of a young girl's future wasn't how anyone wanted the case to be resolved.

Felicity thought over the moments leading up to Elizabeth's confession. The timing couldn't be ignored. Had Felicity done something to trigger it?

The art dealer's daughter was transported to the police station at Torquay, where she would likely spend the night. After much dithering, and with strong encouragement from Nigel, Harold eventually followed in his own transport. Officer Marshall had slinked away, although his cutter remained moored among the yachts in the harbour.

Still feeling rather stunned by the turn of events, and with the rain still holding off, Felicity raced up to Ashdene with Alex, where they furiously wrote up Elizabeth's confession and arrest, telephoning the story into the newsdesk in time for the evening edition.

It was a huge exclusive for the News, but not even Alex was remotely happy about it. Felicity remained unsettled by the idea she was somehow to blame. She'd wanted to help unravel the case, but not like this.

Ashdene quickly filled with dazed art enthusiasts. They'd been shepherded out of the village by Nigel and were now under the firm and reassuring instruction of Isabella, who swept into action to care for her flock, keeping them entertained and well-fed as the day drew towards its close.

While Alex telephoned his police contacts for updates on the Protheros, Felicity kept herself busy interviewing the bewildered art collectors. The quotes she gathered all followed the same themes. How bizarre and unexpected Elizabeth's sudden confession was, how disappointing yet understandable it was that the exhibition wasn't going ahead, how they wished the Protheros well — everyone being certain Elizabeth's confession was a grave yet fixable misunderstanding — and how, ultimately, the quality of the art stood for itself. Isabella, in particular, was insistent that while Martin was a lot of things, he was not the type to thrust himself upon a young girl.

Whenever Felicity tried to make sense of the information and impressions she'd gathered during her time in Ottermouth, her head span to the point of dizziness. It was far easier to concentrate on her work as a journalist. She was nothing more than a vessel through which facts and opinion could be reported. It wasn't her job to solve things or even to help. Reporting ought to have remained Felicity's focus from the moment of her arrival in the village, but it was too late for that now. The damage had been done.

Mrs Rawling had been swept into the all-hands-on-deck situation with the unexpected influx of guests into Ashdene, and Felicity was in no mood for polite conversation with strangers over dinner. Alex's proposal of a walk into the village with the dogs, followed by supper at the inn, was therefore gratefully accepted.

A chilly wind created choppy waves as they trudged along the clifftop path. Felicity pressed her hands deep into the pockets of a warm, woollen coat. Ahead, Alex threw sticks, whistled, and generally did whatever he could to prevent the Yorkie and the Briard from dashing down sodden paths onto the beaches below.

Alex's efforts meant Pip was only mildly damp when he joined Felicity on the bench seat in their nook at the inn, though he was still too wet to sit on her lap. Beetle was content to lie under the table, his head resting on Alex's cap-toed boots.

Except for the innkeeper, Felicity, Alex, and the dogs, the Dolphin was thankfully empty.

Supper was crab on brown bread and a small tankard of cider. The crabmeat was a mix of brown and white, with lemon slices on the side and no further garnish. Its simple presentation was, however, deceptive. The crab was tender and flavoursome, the brown bread beautifully soft and somewhat warm, and the butter creamy and only slightly salted.

Felicity glanced up at the stony-faced, one-eyed innkeeper as she ate. Was he aware of how delicious his food was? And if so, why wasn't it advertised to visitors? There was no indication outside to suggest the Dolphin even served meals.

A pair of fishermen arrived and ordered pots of ale, which they quietly drank at a table in the corner. Snores rose from both dogs. The salty smell of the harbour came in through the window next to Felicity and Alex's table, which was set ajar. The calm of the inn was far removed from the chaos at the gallery and at Ashdene. The affair that started with Felicity's ghastly discovery on the foreshore was now limited to the art scene. The fishing community was perhaps relieved the artist's death had nothing to do with them, and they would be relieved further still once the customs cutter left the harbour. Elizabeth's confession had been a blow for Officer Marshall, who'd been convinced the murder was connected to smuggling.

Felicity and Alex ate in silence. Initially, because they were both hungry, but even with her hunger sated, Felicity's mood remained sombre. What if she'd met Alex as originally planned, on her first full day in Ottermouth? Would he have reminded Felicity of the importance of focusing on her reporting? Would matters have developed differently? Not that Alex was in the habit of policing Felicity's behaviour. His dedication to journalism was inspiring, yet Felicity always seemed to get too involved in things. She always went too far.

Alex dropped his napkin beside his empty plate. "That was unexpectedly good."

Felicity nodded. She gazed out the window. Not that there was much to see. The glass was dense and mottled, like the window in Margaret's cottage.

Across the table, Alex took a sip from his tankard. "When we were at the gallery, what was it you were saying about brushwork?"

Felicity kept her attention on the blur of the outdoors. "I'd rather not talk about it."

There was a pause. "You don't believe her, do you?"

Felicity glanced at her friend. He had a knack of getting right to the heart of things, and then drilling even further down.

"Does it matter what I believe?" Returning her attention to her plate, Felicity set about finishing her last crabmeat triangle.

Alex waited for Felicity to finish her food before speaking again. "Why did you return to the gallery?" He wouldn't let the matter go.

Felicity looked back out of the blurry window. "I shouldn't have."

Alex sighed. "Whether you were in Ottermouth or not, this would have happened. You're only an observer. That's what we are as journalists." He was looking at her with concern and a little pinch of disapproval.

Felicity looked at her friend. "Then I've not been observing matters well enough."

Alex frowned deeply, the scar on his forehead visible. "We just called in the exclusive of the year. The other journalists have had to dash over to Torquay to get anything like the story we did. And they won't have it in their papers till tomorrow."

Felicity stroked Pip's warm little head. "If I hadn't gone back to the gallery, Elizabeth wouldn't have confessed."

"You can't know that for certain."

"I saw how she was watching me. She was afraid. Lawrence's warning was not without reason. I was the trigger."

Alex shook his head. "I'm sorry. I simply can't agree with you."

Felicity trusted Alex, perhaps more than anyone, but he wasn't beyond saying the odd thing to make her feel better.

She was silent for a moment. "Can a blow to the back of the head be self-defence?"

Alex tipped his head thoughtfully. "It's not impossible."

"But it's not likely, is it? And I hate to agree with the man, but Officer Marshall's point about Miss Prothero handling Xantho—"

"Unlike you to underestimate a woman."

Was Alex trying to rile Felicity?

Glancing at the fishermen, she kept her voice low. "You believe Elizabeth's account?"

"What other credible explanations are there? Isabella's off the hook. That's the most important thing, isn't it?"

Felicity tucked her chin. "You consider Isabella to be my priority here?"

Alex shrugged. "How can I know? You won't tell me what you were looking for at the gallery."

Felicity narrowed her eyes. Alex was a hard questioner, and she loved to watch him at work in interviews. She enjoyed it less when he turned his skills upon her.

Felicity sighed. "The signatures on Eustace's works. They don't match. I don't know enough to know what it means, exactly, but my thoughts went to—"

Bang!

The door to the inn burst open and slammed against the wall.

"You." Lawrence Whitburn marched towards Felicity, his eyes and hair wild, his finger pointing.

Beetle whimpered as Alex pushed back his chair and stood up. Pip growled from the bench, hackles raised.

"Now, now." Alex swiftly positioned himself between Lawrence and Felicity. Recovering from the rude awakening, Beetle now also joined Pip in growling at the artist.

Felicity stood up, but there was nowhere to go. Their table was in an alcove. The innkeeper and the two fishermen looked up but didn't appear concerned. A daily dose of aggravation was likely par for the course at the Dolphin, although Felicity never imagined it would be directed so brutally at her.

"Mr Whitburn." Alex had his palms raised in a placating manner. "I advise you to calm yourself and think carefully before saying or doing anything further."

Lawrence halted his advance and glared angrily at Felicity and Alex.

"Go ahead, Mr Whitburn." Although startled by his entrance, Felicity wasn't afraid. "Say whatever it is you have to say to me." And she rather suspected what was coming.

Chapter Thirty-Six

Fury burned in Lawrence Whitburn's eyes. A lock of dark hair bounced on his forehead. "You," he said to Felicity, still jabbing a finger. "This is all your fault."

"Now, hold on just a moment," began Alex, still standing with his hands raised between the artist and Felicity. Pip and Beetle were also still growling, although the innkeeper and the two fishermen on the other side of the bar had already lost interest in the altercation.

Felicity nodded. "I quite agree with you, Mr Whitburn."

Alex glanced over his shoulder at Felicity, baffled.

Lawrence huffed. The wind had gone from his sails. "You do?"

Alex dropped his hands as though at a loss. Pip was the first of the dogs to cease growling. Beetle soon followed suit. The situation had been quickly diffused.

Felicity nodded again. "My presence at the gallery prompted Elizabeth's confession. I'm certain of it."

"She's innocent." Lawrence again grew animated. "She's spending the night behind bars, and she's innocent."

Felicity nodded. "That's my suspicion, too."

Alex frowned at Felicity and Lawrence. "Then why did she

confess?"

"I told you she's innocent," fumed Lawrence.

"Miss Prothero was with you that night. Was she not, Mr Whitburn?" It was a bold suggestion. Elizabeth had, however, given similarly vague reassurance regarding Lawrence's whereabouts on the night in question, and Felicity was past being careful about such matters.

The artist scowled deeply, his eyes darting around the inn.

Alex sighed. "The Western Daily News isn't that sort of paper, Mr Whitburn. We won't write you up."

"But Miss Prothero's confession has put her neck on the line," continued Felicity.

Lawrence's cheeks reddened. "A confession you say yourself you caused."

Alex watched the artist closely.

"I may have been the trigger, Mr Whitburn," said Felicity. "But I wasn't the cause."

Pip remained on high alert on the bench beside Felicity. Alex caught Beetle's collar and stopped the Briard advancing towards Lawrence, his nose raised in curiosity.

"What was the cause, then?" growled the artist.

Felicity folded her arms. "I was hoping you'd be the one to tell me that, Mr Whitburn."

"Me?" He jabbed a finger at his own chest. "Why me? Just what are you implying?"

"You warned me to keep away from Miss Prothero. Why was that?"

Alex raised his eyebrows at the artist, echoing the question.

Lawrence folded his arms, mirroring Felicity's stance. Threads hung loose from the cuff of his jumper. "Something was worrying her."

"What was she worried about?" asked Alex.

"I don't know." Lawrence's jaw was taut. "I wish I did."

"Might you have a suspicion?" pressed Felicity.

"Look. She didn't tell me everything." Lawrence's anger was

bubbling up again. "But for some bizarre reason, she trusted you." The artist jabbed his finger at Felicity. "Now look where she is!"

"Ho," said Alex, stepping closer to the man. "I won't ask you again, Mr Whitburn. Calm yourself."

Lawrence dropped his hand, but his tone remained desperate. "Lizzie spoke to you in confidence," he said, still addressing Felicity. "She told you what she was worried about."

Felicity's mind whirred. Yes, Elizabeth had shared her concerns about the drug smuggling, but surely that wasn't what had caused Elizabeth to avoid Felicity's eye in the gallery. Something else had happened.

"You're a detective, aren't you?" continued Lawrence. "Haven't you picked up on the clues?"

Alex looked at Felicity. He was ready to jump to her defence if needed.

"I'm a journalist, Mr Whitburn. Nothing more." A wavering in Felicity's own belief in the assertion went hopefully unnoticed by both Alex and Lawrence.

"So that's why you did it?" The artist's emotions were getting the better of him. "That's why you scared Lizzie into confessing, so you could write this whole thing up for the papers?"

"Mr Whitburn, enough!"

Felicity hadn't heard Alex raise his voice before. Lawrence looked stunned. Pip barked, keen to do his bit.

"Then why?" whimpered Lawrence, his anger giving way to defeat. "Why would she do it?"

Alex glared at Felicity. "Shall I escort Mr Whitburn outside?"

Felicity hesitated. She thought back to the paintings. "In your opinion, Mr Whitburn, who might Miss Prothero be trying to protect with her actions?"

The artist frowned. "Who is she trying to protect?"

"Miss Prothero cares about you very much, does she not?"

Lawrence's eyes opened wide. "You're accusing me of being the real culprit?"

"No one's accusing you of anything, old chap." Alex shot a pleading glance at Felicity, as if to say, *Please, don't rile the fellow further, if you can help it.*

"I'm not accusing anyone of anything," reassured Felicity. "It's simply in my nature to uncover the truth, and I'm not quite there yet."

Lawrence shook his head. His shoulders drooped. "I don't know who she might be protecting. I honestly don't know."

Felicity had imagined she'd seen something of herself in Elizabeth, but for whom would Felicity risk the hangman's noose?

She nodded. "Leave it with us, Mr Whitburn."

"Pleasant fellow." Alex smiled wryly as Lawrence slammed the inn's door behind him. "And you all but promised him a solution." Alex's expression turned serious. "What if Prothero's daughter is found guilty? With all due respect to Pip's capabilities as a personal body guard, what's to stop Whitburn from seeking revenge if all goes wrong? He's rather convinced everything is your fault."

Felicity shook her head. "Elizabeth won't be punished for something she didn't do."

Alex narrowed his eyes. "You know what's going on, don't you?"

Felicity was flicking through her memories of the artworks she'd seen since arriving in Ottermouth. "Perhaps." The paintings were often similar, the same themes recurring, but there was one motif that had her puzzled. One image to which she kept coming back. "But I want to be sure." Felicity locked eyes with Alex. "And I know how we can check."

Chapter Thirty-Seven

Still being accompanied by the Yorkie and the Briard meant the search took longer than it might otherwise have done. While Pip and Beetle moved fast, every side shoot of the coastal path had to be explored, their fur becoming soaked and knotted as they disappeared through dense bushes, pretending not to hear Felicity and Alex calling their names.

"About the signatures not matching on Eustace's paintings," began Alex, as they passed Ashdene's garden gate at quite a clip, venturing further along that portion of the coast than Felicity had done since her arrival in Ottermouth. "The fellow was producing paintings for twenty years or more, was he not? Surely a person's signature changes over time."

"It's not just the signature," said Felicity, panting as the path grew steep. "It's the subject, too." To explain herself thoroughly, she would have needed to stop, and there was no time for that. "But I must be sure. There's so much at stake."

"The death penalty isn't off the table," agreed Alex. "If Elizabeth's not protecting Lawrence, there can only be one other person worth such a risk."

Felicity had come to exactly the same conclusion, though she dared not voice it. Not yet. Harold had been genuinely shocked by Elizabeth's confession. If her actions were intended to protect her father, it had not been agreed with him in advance.

Voices drifted down from Ashdene's terrace. It would have been convenient to hand the dogs over to Mrs Rawling, but Felicity and Alex couldn't risk getting drawn into a vortex of discussions and interviews with Isabella and her art-collector friends. There was also the nagging feeling that Lawrence was, to a certain extent, correct. Felicity had triggered Elizabeth into confessing to Martin's killing. If there was a chance she might set things right, then Felicity had a responsibility to take action.

Twilight was almost upon them when Felicity and Alex found their quarry. Pip and Beetle were first down onto the secluded beach, which was nestled into jagged cliffs. The two dogs went flying over to the bare-footed figure wading along the foreshore with her skirts tucked up, dropping clumps of seaweed into a basket on the crook of her arm.

Grace Campbell smiled at the dogs as they danced around her and barked excitedly, tongues lolling. Wiping her wild grey hair from her eyes, her face fell a little as she saw Felicity and Alex approaching. The dogs located a seaweed stick and ran with it towards Felicity. Alex whistled sharply. Finding an alternative stick, he hefted it into the air. Pip and Beetle went flying after it as Felicity continued her approach towards Grace.

"You found Thora, didn't you?" The tide hissed across the shingle at Grace's ankles.

Felicity nodded. "My hope is that she'll talk to her mother now."

Grace smiled. "There's many who care about her. Care about her too much, even."

Although an intriguing comment, Felicity hadn't located Grace to discuss Thora. "Mrs Campbell, there's something I need to ask you."

There was barking as the dogs brought the seaweed stick back to Alex for another throw.

Grace eyed Felicity. "You can ask, but it doesn't mean I'll answer. I've been clear enough on that point, haven't I?"

Felicity wasn't in the mood for games. "Did Mr Granger's father ever paint Mrs Dunn?"

"Did Eustace paint my sister?" Grace's face clouded over. She adjusted her stance at the water's edge. "Why are you asking me this?"

"Miss Elizabeth Prothero has confessed to doing away with Mr Martin Granger. She claims the act to have been self-defence."

Grace's green eyes narrowed. "The gallery man's daughter, you mean? The one who brings us baskets of food?" Her voice was tainted with the same disbelief Felicity felt.

"That's why I've come to you, Mrs Campbell. To ask for your help."

Grace pressed her lips together. Her compassion for Elizabeth alone wasn't enough for her to open up.

"Everywhere I turn," began Felicity. "I see Thora. In practically all Eustace Granger's paintings, she's there. Yet Eustace passed before Thora was born."

Grace glanced down towards the water running over her feet.

"So, if it's not Thora. Then it must be your sister, presuming mother and daughter looked awfully alike at the same age."

Grace was quiet. The dogs barked. Alex asked them to quieten down.

Felicity kept her gaze on the woman. "Please. Help me make sense of matters."

Grace let her basket slip from her elbow to her hand. "Eustace never painted my sister."

Felicity drew in a breath. She immediately began considering the consequences. That confirmed it. The paintings had to be—

"He painted me."

Felicity's thoughts stopped dead.

Grace's hair blew in the wind. Her physique was supple and lean. Her gaze was captivating. She, too, would have looked like

Thora when she was young. Still now, Grace embodied the wild and free spirit of the coast. Her allure would have been beguiling for the artists who came to the little fishing village looking for inspiration for their paintings.

But Grace's admission destroyed the theory Felicity had been working towards.

She had imagined there might be fakes among the paintings supposed to be by Eustace, and that whoever was forging them had become sloppy. Besides bungling the signature, Thora had been used as a model in paintings supposedly painted decades ago.

To what extent Harold Prothero — and his daughter — knew about the counterfeits would have been the next mystery to unravel. But the model wasn't Thora. Felicity would have to start all over again.

"You were Eustace Granger's model?" Her shoulders felt suddenly incredibly heavy.

Grace plodded out of the water, towards a scattering of rocks at the water's edge. Setting her basket beside her, she sat down, tugging at her skirts to cover her bare knees. The seaweed on the rocks intensified the pungent salty scent of the shore.

"I was here when this whole art thing started, and I posed. I posed for any artist that asked." Grace gave a little smile. "It was a thrill. I was young. You know what our community's like. You see the pressure Thora is under. And back then, it was even worse."

Felicity nodded. She was keen to listen and to understand, but her theory being undermined was quite a blow.

"Oh, I may as well say it. I went further than posing, even. That's why they shun me, you know. I was already a widow. Fishing's a dangerous profession. Even then, I wasn't supposed to have my own life. I was supposed to remain a prisoner of my dead husband's memory. He was a good man, don't get me wrong." She shook her head sadly. "And the way I was shunned, my own sister cutting me off, well. I knew what I was in for. But that's not what surprised me."

The wind blew stiffly across the shore. "What surprised you?" asked Felicity.

"The artists. I thought they were all bohemian. Easygoing." A bitter smile spread across Grace's lips. "They weren't. I didn't realise until it was too late."

Part of Felicity wished that Alex was also listening, that two heads rather than one were puzzling over the relevance of what Grace was saying. Then again, such matters were often only discussed between women. Were Felicity's earlier efforts to win Grace's confidence at last paying off? For someone who was by his own admission not a dog person, Alex was doing an excellent job keeping the Yorkie and Briard distracted.

"Too late in what sense?" Felicity asked.

The older woman sighed deeply. "Joe was still painting back then."

Felicity frowned. "Joe?"

"Joseph Ferris," said Grace. "The lighthouse keeper."

"Mr Ferris was an artist?" When visiting the lighthouse, Felicity had asked Joseph about his relationship to Ottermouth's art scene. He'd not been entirely honest, had he?

"When Joe found out I'd posed for Eustace—" Grace shook her head. "Eustace was a widower by then. He was doing his best to be a good father to Martin, but he was an absolute fool for anything remotely pretty. Eustace and I, well…" She trailed off.

The lighthouse keeper's interactions with Grace at the harbour had been familiar enough for a relationship that had spanned the years, but there was no warmth between them. "Was Mr Ferris jealous?"

Grace tucked strands of wind-whipped hair behind her ears. "He was hurt. He loved me. I suppose he still does. And I suppose I love him, in my way. Although it's too late for us. All this happened over twenty years ago now."

Two decades was an exceedingly long time to hold a grudge. Felicity's mind spun with ideas. How did this all fit together?

"Does Mr Ferris still paint?" He'd had paint on his overalls when Felicity visited the lighthouse, hadn't he?

Grace was barely listening. She was somewhere else. "If I could take back the way I behaved, I would. I was so young. So naïve. I see it in my niece. When you're young, you don't understand the value of things. You don't understand how little it takes to shatter a man's heart."

Felicity glanced over at Alex. He was overseeing a tug-o'-war between the dogs. She and Alex were still young, weren't they? Felicity liked to imagine she understood the value of things.

"Joe was so talented," continued Grace. "He was better than any of them. He was a good man, too. But I hurt him. His wound still hasn't healed. And there's nothing I wouldn't do to take it back." Grace looked out to sea, sorrowful at first, then her eyes widened.

The customs cutter had rounded the rocks and was already dropping anchor a short distance from the shore.

Grace woke from her reverie. "Oh, no." Grabbing her basket, she stood up. "I'll not have anything to do with him."

Officer Marshall made quick work of lowering his tender into the water. With powerful strokes, he rowed for shore, the prow of his rowing boat cutting confidently through the steel-grey waves.

With Pip and Beetle still distracted by their seaweed stick tug-o'-war, Alex moved swiftly across the shingle towards Felicity and Grace. He nodded towards the rowing boat as it made contact with the shore. "What does he want, do you suppose?"

"I shan't wait to find out," said Grace over her shoulder, already moving quickly towards the cliff path.

"Lady Felicity!" called Officer Marshall as he jumped out of the little tender, water splashing up his tall leather boots. "I say, Lady Felicity!"

Felicity turned to Alex. "I think I know what's happening. I think I know how to end this."

"Do what you must," Alex said, already advancing towards Officer Marshall. "I'll stop him. Or at least slow him down." Alex drew his notebook from his inside pocket as he intercepted the customs man. "Good day, Officer. Any further news on that drugs smuggler you were chasing? What's the word from your contacts on the continent?"

Grace had already disappeared from view. With their tug-o'-war finished, the two dogs charged gleefully towards Alex and the customs officer, but Felicity didn't wait to see what happened next. With the pebbles swallowing her footsteps and slowing her down, she hurried up the beach as best she could. Felicity had almost given up hope, but the path ahead was now clearly lit.

Chapter Thirty-Eight

Leaving Alex and the dogs to face Officer Marshall at the cove, Felicity rushed along the clifftop path and down into the village. Lanterns had been lit in cottage windows, and the sea was a blueish silver, the water low in the harbour. The big green-painted doors of the gallery were firmly shut. There was no one to hold Felicity up as she dashed along the main thoroughfare.

Only Audrey Lawson was on the cobbles of the harbourside, her suitcase gripped tight. She leaned through the window of an idling taxi, looking frail and upset. It sounded as though Audrey was arguing with the driver about the cost of a fare to the railway station at Paignton. She didn't notice Felicity pass, and Felicity didn't stop. The drugs, Martin's relationships, none of that mattered any more.

Felicity crossed the beach where she'd had the displeasure of getting to know Billy Seddon ahead of their ill-fated boat trip. Where might the young man be now? Perhaps he would retire somewhere peaceful and seek a quiet life. Or perhaps he'd already acquired a new boat fast enough to outrun Customs and Excise. If the latter, then he would hopefully never return to Devon's shores.

Arriving at the cliff atop which the lighthouse stood, Felicity took the steep route that hugged the ragged form of the promontory and avoided the condemned Napoleonic tunnel. Navigating a tight bend at full clip, Felicity ground to a halt. A pile of crumbly red sandstone boulders blocked the path, no doubt brought down in the recent rainfall.

With no time to lose, Felicity put a foot on one of the tumbled stones. It shifted under her weight, and she leapt backwards just in time to prevent a small rockslide landing on her toes. The route was blocked. The forbidden tunnel was now the only way to the lighthouse.

Inside the tunnel, darkness was accompanied by the echoing sound of dripping water. The fading daylight made the opening at the other end barely visible, but from her previous foray, Felicity knew the tunnel to be straight. In hurrying ahead, she nearly broke into a run. A gust of wind almost tore her hat from her head as she emerged out the other side.

Felicity made straight for the small, sturdy lighthouse. Surely, its blinding lights would swing into action at any moment. On the horizon, the sails of a large ship leaned hard in the wind. Perhaps the lighthouse ought to be on already?

Felicity rapped on the door to the little dwelling attached to the lighthouse. She even went as far as peering through the window. It was brash behaviour, perhaps even rude. Was this the person she was becoming?

No. She was fully in control of her actions. This wasn't a normal situation. There needed to be an end to things. There was no guarantee Felicity held the key, but if her suspicions were proved correct, and she'd done nothing…

She rapped on the door again. Still no answer. Where was the lighthouse keeper? Felicity shivered. A man had been murdered. Was she behaving foolishly? Even in an abnormal situation, even with an innocent young woman having placed herself in mortal danger, Felicity shouldn't throw all caution to the wind.

She would go back to the village. She would alert someone to the issue. Constable Thompson was likely still in Torquay. The inn. Felicity would go to the inn. One of the seafarers there would know what to do. There had to be a contingency plan in case the lighthouse failed to function.

She hurried back down the tunnel. The sky was now so dark, the doorway at the other end was hardly visible at all.

Yet there was light. Thin and yellow, in the tunnel's centre. The walls glistened slightly.

Cautiously, Felicity advanced, touching the sides of the passage to steady herself. The cold, wet rock under her fingertips made her shudder. There was only the sound of dripping water and her own footsteps as she arrived in the centre of the tunnel, the dim yellow glow now falling onto the wool of her skirt.

Something felt different. Under her hand was no longer stone. Felicity squinted in the dark. She felt around some more and came across an old-fashioned iron ring latch. Then planks of unvarnished wood. The thin strip of light escaped from a narrow gap between the wood and the tunnel wall.

It was a doorway.

Felicity hesitated, listening. The water continued to drip.

Gngh!

The sound came from behind the wooden door. Felicity's heart pounded. She wasn't alone in the tunnel.

Felicity had been on her way to the village for help. She ought to continue.

But what lay beyond the door? Shouldn't she at least know before returning to the village? Wasn't it best to gather all the information she could?

Feeling for the ring latch, she twisted it gently. Felicity would be as quiet as possible. The door creaked only lightly as it slowly opened. A dim, yellow glow lit the damp floor and walls of the passageway beyond.

It wasn't too late to turn back, but what if retreating was the wrong decision? Elizabeth risked hanging for a crime she didn't commit. Wasn't it Felicity's duty to do whatever she could to make things right?

Felicity crept carefully along the newly revealed passageway. An open doorway off the corridor ahead was the source of the yellow glow. There were voices. Two men. What they were saying wasn't clear, but their strained tones made Felicity's stomach knot. She advanced steadily and extremely cautiously. She had to know. She had to see.

"Say it again. Say it again, and I'll do it. I really will."

"I'm telling you the truth. Why won't you believe me?"

Felicity was quite certain she recognised the voices. She hadn't imagined what the conclusion of her investigations might look like, but as she removed her hat and peeked gingerly into the room off the corridor, it was possible she was too late.

Chapter Thirty-Nine

Carved within the rock upon which the lighthouse stood, the room was windowless. Kerosene lamps cast soft, golden light and an oily smell throughout the space, which was low-ceilinged and intensely cluttered. Tables overflowed with palettes, tubes of paint, pots of brushes, and books bulging with sketches. Works of art hung on the walls, rested on the floor, and leaned on easels.

The paintings were mainly in oils, though a jumble of styles was represented. Some images were angry, dark, and hardly resembled anything worldly at all. Several of the canvasses had even been defaced, either punched through or sliced open.

But some paintings were familiar. Very familiar.

They were the works of Eustace Granger.

Or rather, the paintings had been created using the same style and technique as the man who had founded Ottermouth's art scene. A view of the harbour in Eustace's style even stood half-finished on an easel.

But finding a dead man's paintings still in production wasn't what caused a gasp to escape Felicity's throat.

In the middle of the clutter, standing stiffly, was Harold Prothero. His cheeks were red, and his palms were raised and trembling. His impeccably smart green bow tie and gold pince-nez looked almost comically out of place.

Before him stood the lighthouse keeper, Joseph Ferris. Although lean, his paint-smudged overalls hanging off him, he towered over the art dealer. His long, grey beard obscured the full extent of his expression, but he snarled like a wounded beast.

A short, sharp knife glinted in the lamp light. With his arm outstretched, Joseph aimed the blade at Harold's neck.

Felicity swallowed, her mouth suddenly dry, her heart thumping in her chest. She hadn't yet been noticed. Could she still retreat and get help? Felicity had suspected the forgeries. What had caused Joseph to threaten Harold with a knife? Had Felicity happened upon Martin's murderer?

"Why should I believe you?" The lighthouse keeper barked at the art dealer. "You're no better than that lying little rat Eustace dragged into this world."

Harold whimpered. "You're right. I've done wrong. I'm not to be relied upon. I've made such an awful mess of things." He swallowed. "Just do it. Get it over with. My daughter will be better without me."

Joseph squeezed the knife's handle. "Why, you selfish little—"

There was no time to retreat. Something had to be done.

Felicity's stomach bounced into her throat as she stepped fully into the doorway. For good measure, she cleared her throat.

The attention of the two men was now squarely on Felicity, Harold's mouth opening as Joseph's eyes widened.

There hadn't been time to fully formulate a plan, but Felicity's goal was simple. Violence must be avoided. Harold coming to harm wouldn't help Elizabeth. And committing an act of violence surely couldn't improve Joseph's situation, not that his predicament was entirely clear yet.

If worst came to worst, Felicity knew exactly where her exit was. She would be through the tunnel, onto the cliff path, and shouting for help before either man could catch her. Hopefully, it wouldn't come to that.

"Mr Prothero. Mr Ferris." Felicity's tone was sombre, her hands raised to show she had no weapon and intended no aggression towards anyone present.

"Lady Felicity." Harold sounded relieved. Taking a step towards her, he jerked backwards, his pince-nez flying onto the floor.

Joseph had put a powerful hand on the art dealer's shoulder and yanked him back. With an arm across his chest, he held Harold fast, pressing the knife against the art dealer's neck.

Had Felicity miscalculated? By attempting to help, had she already made things worse? There was no time for self-reproach. Felicity had to think fast. There had to be a way out of the predicament.

Fat tears rolled down Harold's cheeks. "I deserve this. I truly deserve this. I see that now. I've done so much wrong."

What have you done? Felicity might have asked, but digging for the truth couldn't be the priority. There was more than one life at risk.

Joseph shook the art dealer. "Quiet!" His eyes smouldered with rage but also fear. "You." The lighthouse keeper raised his bearded chin at Felicity. "What are you doing here? What do you want?"

"I was hoping to speak to you, Mr Ferris." The words felt thick on Felicity's tongue. Her mouth was parched from nervousness, but she kept her voice steady. "However, I can see I'm interrupting important business between Mr Prothero and yourself."

"Please," Harold sobbed. "You simply must understand. When I first came to Ottermouth, I never imagined—"

Joseph jerked his captive. "Quiet, I said!" The knife bobbed although thankfully did no damage. Not yet. "Turn around and leave." The lighthouse keeper directed the command at Felicity. "Go, or he gets it. This has nothing to do with you."

What if Felicity were to walk away? What were the chances of a peaceful resolution? And what were the chances if she stayed?

Felicity licked her lips. "May I enquire what your disagreement with Mr Prothero is about?" She spoke as though there were no knife, as if she'd happened upon friends engaged in a good-natured argument. "An outsider's point of view can often bring a breath of fresh air." She spoke as though she cared about the outcome. She did care about the outcome. "Perhaps I can help in that regard?"

Joseph chuckled grimly. "If there's one thing we don't appreciate around here, it's outsiders. You should know that by now."

Harold blinked hard as his tears flowed. "It's really too late, your ladyship. It's too late for anything now. Please, don't make this any harder than it already is."

"Mr Prothero." Felicity took a slightly firmer tone with the art dealer. "As I understand it, your daughter is still at Torquay police station. Is it your intention to leave her there?"

Harold shook his head enthusiastically. "My goodness, no. That wasn't my plan at all. I want her freed. I came here by taxi on an urgent basis to advise Mr Ferris of what I must do. Then I was going to go back to Torquay and tell the police—"

Joseph's grip tightened on the art dealer. "You will do no such thing." The knife grazed Harold's throat, and Felicity's heartbeat quickened.

The dripping water in the tunnel echoed in the distance. They were alone. Truly alone. Felicity couldn't give up. Not now.

She addressed the lighthouse keeper. "Am I correct in assuming Mr Prothero has informed you of the situation faced by his daughter?" There'd been a basket of provisions in the cramped dwelling attached to the lighthouse when Felicity had visited. Had Elizabeth made a delivery to Joseph? Might he have compassion for the young woman who'd shown him kindness? "How old is Miss Prothero? Twenty, perhaps?"

Harold sobbed. "She's nineteen. She's just nineteen."

Joseph's grip on Harold released slightly. Might Felicity's plan be working?

The art dealer whimpered. “Oh, it’s my fault. It’s all my fault.”

Joseph’s hold on his hostage grew tighter again. “I can’t believe it. I don’t believe you.”

“But I did it,” Harold snivelled. “I really did it.”

“Did what, Mr Prothero?” Although Felicity strongly suspected what the answer would be.

Chapter Forty

"I killed him," sobbed the art dealer. "I killed Martin Granger."

The windowless studio fell into silence, the glow of oil lamps creating an inappropriately snug atmosphere. The water still dripped in the tunnel beyond.

There it was. Martin Granger's murderer had been revealed. He'd been right in front of Felicity the whole time.

By confessing, Elizabeth had intended to save her father. It was scandalous — unforgivable, even — that Harold hadn't spoken up when his daughter made her false claim to Constable Thompson. But what if Harold lost his life before he could make his own confession to the police? What would become of Elizabeth then?

Joseph's hand shook, the knife perilously close to the art dealer's neck. "You're lying."

Felicity steadied her breathing. "Is that the truth, Mr Prothero? Or are you saying it to relieve your daughter of her burden?"

"It's the truth." Harold had ceased sobbing. He sniffed. "Why won't anyone believe me?"

There was something so unassuming about the rotund, bow-tied art dealer. He seemed the least likely of Ottermouth's men to pose any physical danger. The blow that had done for Martin had, however, been to the back of the man's head.

"He was going to crush me," continued Harold. "Crush everything I'd worked for, everything I held dear. I was in such a terrible muddle over what to do."

The lighthouse keeper shook his head and frowned. "And on top of everything, you now propose to ruin me?"

Harold twisted his head to look at his captor. "But I came here to warn you, Mr Ferris. Don't you see? You can decide for yourself what you want to do." Tears threatened at the corners of his eyes. "I'm trying to right my wrongs. Doesn't that count for something?"

Joseph tightened his grip on Harold, the knife tip trembling. "I can't allow you to tell them everything."

"Mr Ferris, please. Think carefully before you act." The situation was so desperate, Felicity had been reduced to pleading. There must be some way to get through to the lighthouse keeper. But how? "Must we see more lives ruined, your own included?"

Harold snivelled, tears rolling down his cheeks. "I should have spoken up as soon as I heard Lizzie confess, but I was in shock. Complete and utter shock. I tried to say something to her at the police station in Torquay. She was so calm. She said, 'I know the truth, Father. Things are better this way.'"

"Hogwash. Complete hogwash." Joseph's hands continued to shake. Did he really want to go through with things?

"Tell us what happened, Mr Prothero," urged Felicity gently. "Share with us the details of what transpired between you and Mr Granger. Mr Ferris and I shall at least listen. Won't we, Mr Ferris?" Helping Joseph believe Harold was key to diffusing the situation.

The lighthouse keeper scowled deeply at Felicity. At last, he nodded.

"Is there a chance you might remove the blade from Mr Prothero's neck while he speaks?" Felicity kept her tone soft and entreating. Was it a step too far?

Joseph breathed hard through his nostrils and glared at Felicity. He lowered the blade.

"Thank goodness," said Harold, rubbing his neck, his shoulders slumped with relief.

Joseph kept the knife pointed at Harold. "Speak."

The art dealer collected his pince-nez from the floor and produced a handkerchief from his jacket pocket. Wiping his lenses and dabbing at his eyes, Harold glanced at Felicity.

Was he sizing her up for an escape?

She firmed her stance in the doorway to the little room. While Felicity had no wish to keep anyone prisoner, Harold's making a dash for it risked provoking the lighthouse keeper to do something he would forever regret.

Replacing his pince-nez on his nose and his handkerchief in his pocket, Harold at last spoke. "Mrs Mountvernon and I go back many years. She and the Major first came to my London gallery before the war. They were furnishing an apartment overlooking Regent's Park. A splendid place—"

"Get to the point," commanded Joseph.

Felicity raised her eyebrows. She was inclined to agree.

Harold blinked rapidly. "After the Major passed, Isabella moved to Ottermouth. Not long after, she introduced me to Martin. Normally, I wouldn't organise an exhibition outside of London, but I'd just had a run of bad luck. Invested in a series of sculptures I was sure would take the market by storm." The art dealer shook his head, his jowls tightening.

"How did your relationship with Mr Granger develop?" pressed Felicity. Joseph's patience must not be tried.

Harold sighed. "Martin was an artist himself, of course, but he was particularly keen to sell works by his father. He planned to purchase a yacht, as I understood it. He had a great number of Eustace's old works stashed away — or so he told me — and I would earn a generous cut, which I was more than happy to accept. I'd already promised Lizzie she could continue her studies on the continent, and I didn't want to deny my daughter her dream. She's entirely innocent. A beautiful, gentle soul." The art dealer smiled a little through his tears. "It wasn't until the preparations at the old boat shed had begun that I realised some of the paintings Martin had provided were fake. They were exquisite work." Harold gazed at the canvasses around the little room. "Splendid specimens, all of them. Practically undetectable."

Joseph lifted his chin a little. He took pride in his work.

"I wasn't especially familiar with Eustace's style, you see," continued Harold. "I was rather new to Ottermouth, so I hadn't noticed straight away. My first thought was: I have to inform Martin." Harold chuckled with a hint of regret. "How naïve can a person be?"

The lighthouse keeper had lowered his knife. "Get on with it."

The art dealer swallowed. "I wanted to ensure we were alone when bringing up the topic, so I requested a private audience with him. Martin proposed we go out on Isabella's yacht the night before the exhibition's opening. He was expecting it, of course." Harold wrung his hands. "I can recall the words he used. He said he knew. He knew only too well the paintings were fakes. He'd been waiting for a fool like me to make his fortune. There was no way out. He said he'd take it all away from me. Not just the exhibition in Ottermouth, but what I'd built up in London. He would destroy my reputation. My career." Harold was pale, his eyes wide and glinting in the lamp light. "And the day before — just the day before — I'd confirmed to Lizzie that her tuition was settled, her travel and accommodation all paid for. And Martin was laughing. He was laughing at me." Harold pulled at his collar, as if he couldn't breathe. "The rage I felt towards the man. I've never experienced anything like it. I can barely recall what happened, but I remember the weight in my hand. The thud. He stopped laughing. Touched the back of his head and stumbled forward. I just stood there. I didn't push him. He fell overboard. I looked over the side of the boat." Harold stared at Felicity and Joseph, his gaze haunted, the scene replaying itself in his mind. "He was gone."

Silence once again descended on the cramped lamplit room.

"Why didn't you try to save him?" Joseph's brow was drawn low. At last, he was convinced.

Harold shook his head slowly. "It was dark. There was no trace of him. I don't think I quite realised what I'd done. I threw the binoculars overboard. Or at least I thought I did. I brought Xantho back into harbour. Grew up on the Hamble, you see." He smiled a little. "I was hoping I might teach Lizzie to sail while we were in Ottermouth. I only gave her a lesson or two."

Neither Felicity nor Joseph returned Harold's smile.

The lighthouse keeper raised his knife, levelling the blade at the art dealer. "Your weapon was found on the boat. That woman from the big house could have hung. Your daughter still might. You care about no one but yourself."

"What did Miss Prothero find out?" asked Felicity. There was no point focusing on Harold's cowardice, and the atmosphere had to be kept calm. "Why did she offer herself up to the police?"

Harold hung his head. "She's a bright girl. She knew something was wrong. I had to come clean, so I told her about the fakes."

Joseph surged forward. "You did what?"

Harold scurried backward, toppling an easel, until he was pressed against the wall. He held up his hands as Joseph grabbed his lapel and pressed the knife tip above his bow tie.

Felicity's heart jumped into her throat. The situation was escalating out of control.

"You swore you'd tell no one," snarled Joseph.

Harold whimpered. "I know, I know."

"Did you also tell your daughter you're a coward and a murderer?"

Harold squeezed his eyes shut and shook his head. "It wasn't murder though, was it? Was it?"

The lighthouse keeper grunted as though bearing an

incredible strain. He gripped the knife handle tightly but didn't press it any further into Harold's neck.

Felicity swallowed. "You're the forger, are you not, Mr Ferris?"

Joseph stiffened. He turned his gaze towards Felicity.

"Y-you came to me yourself, Mr Ferris. Remember?" Harold adjusted his pince-nez. "I didn't even know who you were. I'd assumed Martin was forging his father's paintings himself. You came to me after his body washed up. You made me a proposition—"

Felicity was about to cut Harold off — the art dealer spoke as if there weren't a knife pressed to his neck — but Joseph beat her to it.

"I didn't know you'd killed the blighter!" The lighthouse keeper gave his captive an almighty shove, sending him almost to the ground, then stormed away, kicking a tin can full of brushes, which clattered across the floor. "You didn't tell me you were a murderer when I made my proposition, did you?" Joseph turned to face Felicity. "I'll not go to prison because this man is a fool and a coward!" His knife was now pointed at her.

"Mr Ferris." Felicity's response was calm but firm. She could turn and run. She still had that option. "No one's taking you to prison." *Not yet.* What was the penalty for art forgery? It was certainly much less than a sentence for running someone through with a knife. "Whose idea was it to create the forgeries? Yours or Mr Granger's?"

The tip of the blade dropped a little. "Mine." Joseph spoke through gritted teeth.

Harold remained wide-eyed and motionless, his back still against the wall.

"I hope you don't mind me observing this, Mr Ferris," continued Felicity coolly, "but it seems your primary motivation was not financial gain."

As an art forger, Joseph must have made money from producing his fakes. In his worn-out overalls and minuscule living quarters, he didn't appear keen to spend it.

He tugged on his beard. "I've never wanted to be rich."

"Why do it, then?" *Keep them talking.* That's all that Felicity could do. At least till the knife had been put away. It wasn't simply a case of keeping Harold from harm. The ruinous effects of violence rippled further than one could fathom.

Finally, the knife dropped to Joseph's side. He rubbed his forehead, turning away from Felicity slightly. "Eustace would tease me for not being as good as him. Said I'd never amount to anything. Then he… Then he…"

Felicity remembered what Grace had told her, about what she had done. What Eustace had done. And how hurt Joseph had been. "It was a long time ago, was it not?"

Joseph's gaze flickered away from Felicity. His anger wasn't for her. It was perhaps not even for the art dealer. It was for a ghost. A tormentor already many years dead.

"Eustace took what I loved. He humiliated me. So I humiliated him."

Harold blinked at the lighthouse keeper. This was perhaps also a revelation for the art dealer.

"I withdrew because of Eustace, but I never stopped painting. The first time I copied his work, it was for my own amusement. I sat on it for years. When I took it to Martin, it was just another way to entertain myself, but he fell for it. Thought it was a forgotten work. He soon realised, though. He knew his father's paintings so well. The suggestion to sell it came from him." Joseph shook his head. "He made a pretty penny from me, all right. Quite a cunning little snake, that one. Knew how to make money. Knew less well how to make art." He tugged on his beard. "But I didn't care. I'll admit I got enjoyment from undermining Eustace."

"And after all those years," said Felicity, carefully, "was it worth it? Did you get what you wanted?"

The look Joseph gave Felicity was stern. His hand was still tight around the knife. "I told you I enjoyed it."

She pressed onwards. "And were you to harm me or Mr Prothero, would you enjoy that, too?"

Joseph frowned.

"What is it you truly want, Mr Ferris?"

A wave of sadness passed through Joseph's eyes. Felicity was getting through to him.

Harold straightened himself, adjusting his bow tie. "If you didn't care about the money, why the blazes did you come to me to sell more of the works?"

The sadness disappeared from Joseph's face. His nostrils flared as he turned towards the art dealer. "You killed a man, and you question my behaviour? I'll not go to prison because of you!"

Harold tried to scamper backwards as Joseph advanced towards him, knife raised, but he had nowhere to go. "I came here to warn you, didn't I?" The art dealer held up his hands. "I have to come clean. Don't you see? For Lizzie's sake. I'm giving you a chance before I tell the police everything. You can leave, go anywhere you want. You must have the money to do so."

The lighthouse keeper kept advancing as the art dealer slid along the wall. "I don't want to leave. My life's here, or it's nowhere at all."

Harold tripped on an empty canvas and lost his footing. Joseph was immediately upon him, grabbing his lapels.

"Don't," cried Felicity. "Please!"

"Joe."

The voice came from the corridor behind Felicity. Everyone turned.

"Stop."

Chapter Forty-One

THE NEXT MORNING

Glimmers of golden sunshine broke through the rolls of grey clouds that surged in from the sea. Patches of blue sky even appeared. The water was calm, patterns from the breeze dancing over its surface. In Ottermouth's harbour, waves sloshed lazily against the hulls.

The Dolphin Inn had become the focal point for police activity in the village. Behind the bar, the innkeeper remained stone-faced, as though it were an ordinary day. In the back room, Felicity had been invited to sit at a worn oak table. A musty, old grandfather clock stood stoically in the corner, ticking softly. A faded painted plate featuring a ship on wild seas turned slowly within its face.

Felicity had told her story in Torquay the night before. Now, back in Ottermouth, she was telling it again to Detective Inspector Sands, a thin man of around forty with tortoiseshell glasses who'd been summoned from the art squad in London to investigate the forgeries.

Seated next to Detective Inspector Sands on the other side of the table from Felicity was Constable Thompson. He continued to eye her with hostility as he listened in on the interview, helping himself to the hot tea and surprisingly delicious ginger snaps supplied by the innkeeper. The policeman's hostility was, however, now combined with a grudging respect.

Felicity had no objection to repeating herself as the sun streamed through the thick, mottled window of the plain little room, picking out the tiny flecks of blue in her grey tweeds. The Quick family's driver, Finnegan, had brought a trunk of extra clothes from Bradley Court, Felicity having spent longer than expected in Ottermouth. She had no problem with prolonging her stay and willingly provided the authorities with nearly all her information. She drew a line only where her sources had requested discretion. And also at matters of the heart with no bearing on the police's investigations.

The London detective requested that Felicity start with her arrival in Ottermouth. They went over her discovery of Martin's body on the beach, her efforts to dig into the smuggling, and her realisation about the fraudulent artworks. Finally, she recounted the showdown in the old tunnel system under the lighthouse and the unexpected conclusion to the stand-off.

The excitement of everything that had happened still buzzed in her veins. Nevertheless, Felicity had to suppress a yawn. It had been an extremely long night. Alex was thankfully on hand to write everything up for the newspaper and was doing a splendid job of it. The first headlines had hit the racks that very morning.

It was another coup for the Western Daily News, although Jasper's reaction had been mixed.

"As long as you're unharmed, Coop's there to write everything up, and Isabella's taken care of," he'd said to Felicity via telephone, somewhat begrudgingly. He'd not berated her for over-involving herself in matters, although that was perhaps on hold till her return to Bradley Court.

As Constable Thompson crunched through yet another ginger snap, Detective Inspector Sands looked up from his notebook.

"What was it exactly that put you onto the fakes, your

ladyship?" The London detective had a nasal voice. In her tired state, he reminded Felicity of a vole.

She reflected for a moment. "I wouldn't say I was entirely onto it, Detective Inspector. It was more of a hunch. Eustace's signature had caught my attention. There was an inconsistency in the direction of one element of the E."

The detective smiled. "You've quite the eye, your ladyship. It's not the only telltale mark, but I would say the signature was the strongest visible hint."

"The subjects rendered in the paintings also attracted my attention," continued Felicity, "but that line of enquiry was rather a dead end."

The detective lifted his eyebrows. "Might you care to elaborate?"

"One model looked rather like a young girl in the village. The daughter of the Maggie's captain."

Constable Thompson frowned, biscuit crumbs hanging in his grey moustache. "Thora Dunn?"

Felicity nodded. "Only it wasn't her. It was simply someone who looked very much like her."

The constable shook his head, confused.

The detective shrugged. "I wouldn't know enough about the local people to comment on that, but we've more than adequate evidence. Very admirable work, really. It's difficult not to be touched by the talent of some of these fellows. Laboratory analysis of paint types may provide further evidence, but Joseph Ferris' activity as a painter overlapped with Eustace's, so there may not be much difference, chemically speaking. We'll go through all the works, of course, and do our best to separate the fakes from the genuine articles. We have the confessions you heard, your ladyship. Not that much can be done in the case of Mr Ferris. At least, not till he's apprehended."

Felicity nodded. "Naturally." Her heart lurched a little as she was struck by a vivid memory from the previous day.

Provoked by the art dealer's questions, Joseph had flown into a rage and pounced upon Harold, his knife still drawn. Felicity had cried out, the situation having flown completely out of control. Then came the interruption.

Felicity had half-expected Alex, but the voice from the passageway had been a woman's.

Grace Campbell strode into the windowless studio, her grey tresses wild, the lamplight dancing in her alert, sea-green eyes.

Joseph's demeanour had changed immediately. He stood up, the knife dropping to his side.

Grace commanded Joseph to accompany her. "Things have gone on for long enough," she said. "It's time for us to leave."

Harold was left gasping for breath on the floor. Felicity took a step back as Joseph raised his knife from the doorway.

"No one is to follow us. Is that understood?"

The pair had not been seen since. The only vessel missing was Joseph's rowing boat. Who knew where they might be? Neither Grace nor Joseph was suspected of smuggling, so His Majesty's Customs and Excise weren't scouring the waves for them. Foraging for food and sleeping in caves, they could move undetected between isolated coves. Joseph had no doubt stashed his earnings from the forgeries. Perhaps they'd already found passage abroad? They could be anywhere.

Witnessing someone evade the law never brought a sense of satisfaction. Even if Joseph had no hand in Martin's demise, the forgeries he'd painted out of hatred and bitterness for the artist's father had played a role in the tragic events. Joseph's decision to threaten Harold with his knife was also ill-judged and thoroughly reprehensible.

Yet somehow, Felicity wished him well. The lighthouse keeper had tortured himself immensely for decades, and there was also Grace to consider. She'd made decisions when young that she now regretted, but did that warrant the rejection of her community? She deserved a chance at happiness, didn't she?

The detective pushed his glasses up his nose. "We at least have Mr Prothero in custody."

Felicity gave a little sigh and nodded. She'd done what she could to assist in that respect, although it hadn't taken much.

With Joseph's and Grace's footsteps receding down the tunnel, Felicity had been left alone in the cramped, lamplit studio with Harold, the man who'd done for Martin. Did he pose a danger to Felicity? What ought to be her next move? Before Felicity could speak, Harold had exhaled wearily and complained of a headache. From there, it was a rather simple matter of gently reminding him of his daughter's plight and of his original plan to confess to the police.

"You're quite right, your ladyship," Harold said as they made their way out of the little room, the art dealer as docile as a lamb. "You're quite right."

With Constable Thompson still in Torquay and Audrey Lawson having presumably settled on a fare and taken the taxi Harold had arrived in, Felicity went with the art dealer in tow to use the telephone at the Dolphin. Besides the innkeeper, the bar had been empty. The fishermen had swung into action up at the lighthouse, having noticed the absence of its light sweeping over the now-dark waves.

It was while standing on the harbourside with Harold, hugging herself against the wind's chill and awaiting police transport, that Felicity was reunited with Alex. His eyes bore a touch of desperation as he hurried towards her, but his gaze quickly returned to its usual dark-blue calm upon realising Felicity was perfectly safe. She delicately explained the situation, mindful not to agitate Harold, who was slumped against a nearby lamppost, as listless as a puppet with its strings cut. Alex did an excellent job maintaining a serene demeanour, though his brow shot upwards when he understood the scoop they had on their hands.

They agreed Felicity would accompany Harold to Torquay while Alex remained in Ottermouth. He would write up the story for the morning edition, taking care not to jeopardise any official proceedings or the Protheros' precarious situation. Naturally, Alex was able to fulfil his end of the agreement with meticulous expertise and even coaxed a few statements from Harold before the police arrived.

Once in Torquay, Felicity gave her evidence, which helped the police accept Harold's confession. Elizabeth was free to go. Felicity offered to escort her back to Ottermouth, but Elizabeth remained at the police station, determined to remain close to her father. Felicity captured a few comments for the newspaper from the police and from the art dealer's daughter, which she passed on to Alex. Elizabeth would say nothing about her confession or what she knew about the forged paintings. "Father was under an enormous amount of pressure," was practically all she offered.

Constable Thompson took a slurp of tea and clattered his cup into its saucer. "Can't say I'm surprised at how it all ended. Far too many outsiders about. It's not good for a place like Ottermouth. Things ought to get quieter here now." He squinted as the sunlight struck his face. "Back to the way it used to be."

Felicity didn't react to the constable. While she hoped for peace in the village, resisting change was like standing on the shore and shouting for the waves to stop.

"What kind of sentencing do you believe Mr Prothero will face?" Felicity directed her question to Detective Inspector Sands.

The detective looked up from his notebook. "The fact the art dealer claims to have been tricked by Granger might cushion him from the worst of it, but there'll be a jury to convince. Prothero was on his own with Granger on the yacht, remember. We only have his word."

The difference between the verdicts of manslaughter and murder was vast. The court case would be highly emotionally charged and garner a great deal of attention.

Felicity pressed on. "What about the selling of the forgeries?"

"Again, we have only Prothero's word that there was a period during which he had no idea the fakes were fake, so to speak." The detective glanced down at his notebook. "There's also the collaboration between Ferris and Prothero to consider. Although without Ferris to testify, Prothero might claim he never knowingly sold a fake. He could say he believed the paintings supplied by Ferris were genuine." The detective shrugged. "Again, it's down to the jury and how sympathetic and believable they find him. I think it's safe to say he'll be looking at a rather long time in jail in the very least. Any proceeds from the sale of the fakes will also need to be recovered."

Felicity spared a thought for Elizabeth. No wonder she had tried to defend her father. What future did Lizzie have without Harold to support her? The best a young woman in her situation could hope for was a rich relative ready to take her under their wing.

Constable Thompson seemed no longer to be listening, having returned his attention to the ginger snaps.

"Will there be any consequences for Miss Prothero, judicially speaking?" asked Felicity.

The detective shook his head. "I don't think so. She lied to the police, but she's been through quite enough. And it's not over yet."

Felicity nodded sadly. When the excitement of the events in Ottermouth had died down, she would send a letter to Elizabeth, offering her support. It was a precarious situation for a young woman to be alone in the world.

The grandfather clock showed it was nearing midday, if its timing could be trusted. It certainly hadn't been dusted in rather a long time.

"If you've no further questions for me, Detective Inspector, I should like to return to Ashdene." Felicity had agreed to lunch and a catch-up with Alex. He'd remained dedicated to the reporting side of things and had been carrying out interviews at the big house, both face-to-face and via telephone.

"Of course, your ladyship," said the detective, tucking away his notebook as they all stood up from the table. "Thank you again for your help. It's not exactly my side of things, but it seems fortuitous you arrived in Ferris' studio when you did. Who knows what might have happened otherwise?"

It was a comfort to Felicity to imagine she'd helped. "It's, of course, not possible to say what the outcome might have been otherwise."

Detective Inspector Sands frowned with a touch of disbelief. "It's quite clear matters would have been much worse."

Constable Thompson rolled his eyes. "If Detective Inspector Sands has no further use for you, Lady Felicity, then neither do I."

"Thank you, Constable." Felicity smiled politely. It wasn't exactly a fond farewell, but she was becoming rather immune to disapproval, especially from those she would never hold dear. "Good day to you both."

As she reached for the handle, the door to the little room flew open. Felicity took a step back. A frown of disappointment flashed across her brow. This was a most unwelcome interruption.

Chapter Forty-Two

Officer Marshall of His Majesty's Customs and Excise took up the entire doorway of the inn's little back room. "Constable Thomson," he boomed, his chest puffed, the brass buttons on his uniform gleaming in the sunlight. "I've a bone to pick with you."

Felicity stepped aside, relieved the unpleasant-natured customs officer had no bone to pick with her. She wanted as little to do with the man as possible. He radiated frustration and dogged determination, his narrowed eyes glinting at the local constable from where he blocked the doorway with his bulk.

Officer Marshall's investigations had indeed been thwarted at every turn. Billy Seddon had slipped from his grasp. Martin Granger's demise had nothing to do with smuggling. Officer Marshall was the type who couldn't stand to be proved wrong. He struggled to accept defeat and likely felt compelled to have the last word.

Constable Thompson seemed unmoved. He grumbled something inaudible as he slid the last ginger snap from the plate on the interview table.

"What did you say?" fumed Officer Marshall. "Come on, man. Speak up."

Detective Inspector Sands stepped forward. "I don't believe we've been introduced." He offered a hand to the customs man, but the interaction was stilted. Officer Marshall wasn't in the mood for making new acquaintances.

"Listen, Thompson," boomed Officer Marshall. Had he not been blocking the doorway, Felicity might have slinked out of the inn. Then again, she was curious about how the conflict between the two men and their respective areas of responsibility might be resolved.

"I know you're nose deep in whatever's going on around here," continued the customs officer. "You're just like all the other coppers along the coast. Turning a blind eye for a bottle of whiskey and a pouch of tobacco. Maybe more. And you might have got away with this one. But believe me, I won't forget Ottermouth. I won't let this one go."

The constable crunched on his biscuit, watching Officer Marshall as though he were a hand puppet in a seaside theatre show.

The London detective blinked in disbelief. "Excuse my ignorance on the matter, Officer Marshall, but you appear to be making some rather grave accusations towards my colleague here from the Devon County Constabulary. May I suggest a different approach? A meeting without raised voices and with the relevant superiors present might be more appropriate."

Constable Thompson chuckled, his bushy moustache lifting slightly. "No, no. You carry on, Officer Marshall. You hang around Ottermouth for as long as you like. It shan't be any bother to me. I'll be retiring next month. Moving to Cornwall. Although I must say, it's been a true pleasure working with you."

The customs officer's jaw fell slack. Felicity did her best not to smile. So that's how their rivalry ended. Would the absence of Constable Thompson allow Officer Marshall to move on from Ottermouth? Only time would tell, and Felicity had a lunch to attend.

"Do please excuse me, gentleman," she said as she slipped out of the room. Nodding to the innkeeper as she traversed the bar, she stepped onto the cobbles outside. There was still a pinch of spare time ahead of her meeting with Alex. Felicity would make a quick detour to the gallery. The chances of Elizabeth being back in Ottermouth were slim, but Felicity was keen to see her if she was.

Gulls called in chorus from the rooftops as a pair of cats weaved among shellfish crates, tails linked. A briny seaweed scent danced on the breeze. The arrival of sunshine and blue skies had helped reinstate the picturesque and peaceful mood of the village, although life hadn't quite returned to normal. The streets were teeming with journalists, all striving to keep pace with the Western Daily News, which was the undisputed authority on the events in Ottermouth.

Aboard the Maggie, the fishermen and their families were busy preparing for the next trip. As expected, they gave the press short shrift. The only interviewees available for the freshly arrived reporters were the dazed art buyers who hadn't yet returned to London. There were also boatloads of day-trippers already coming in from the bigger coastal towns, the ferry companies being eager to cash in on Ottermouth's newfound notoriety.

As Felicity made her way along the cobbles, she came across the tall, thin journalist who'd arrived in the village shortly after Martin's death. He lifted his hat and gave her a hopeful, gap-toothed smile. "Don't suppose you'd be willing to give an interview for the Empire Examiner, your ladyship?"

Felicity smiled in return. Funny how he recognised her now. "I don't suppose I would." She spoke only to the Western Daily News.

The reporter shrugged. He'd expected her refusal. "The police are still in the Dolphin, are they?"

"They are. It might not be an opportune moment, however."

The journalist touched the brim of his hat in thanks and hurried onwards, undeterred by Felicity's warning.

While the Empire Examiner might make a story of the ill will between Officer Marshall and Constable Thompson, it wasn't a piece for the News. The local policeman's complicity in low-level smuggling fitted with what Felicity had observed of the constable. But the only source of evidence was Officer Marshall. For the sake of exposing unpaid duties on tobacco and alcohol, it perhaps didn't benefit public interest to encourage the impression that the authorities keeping law and order along Britain's coast couldn't work together.

At the old boat shed, the bunting had been taken down, but the gallery's wide doors were open. Where paintings had been hanging the day before, there were now bare walls. A detective Felicity recognised from Torquay was in attendance. He was speaking to Harold's assistant, Nigel Davies, although Nigel was perhaps not to be considered the art dealer's assistant anymore. A couple of confused art buyers hovered nearby, Nigel watching them closely, his arms tightly folded over his pinstriped jacket. No one seemed to notice Felicity's approach.

"Lady Felicity Quick."

Lawrence Whitburn had arrived behind her.

Standing in the gallery's doorway, he wore a grim expression, his hands positioned somewhat aggressively on his hips. "I've something to say to you." His tone was anything but friendly.

"Mr Whitburn." Felicity's manner was bright, but she braced herself for whatever might come next. She'd had Alex and two dogs to protect her during the last encounter. "Please, go ahead. What is it you have to say to me?"

Chapter Forty-Three

Lawrence's glare was stern and his legs planted wide, the sunshine through the boat shed doors casting his shadow onto the gallery floor.

"Thank you," he growled. "For everything you've done."

Felicity's brow jumped with surprise towards the brim of her grey cloche. "Well. I'm not quite sure—"

"For everything you've done for Lizzie. And for her father. It all could have been much worse." Laurence gave an odd little scowl. "So thank you." The artist seemed incapable of softening his expression.

Felicity smiled a little sadly. "If I've helped, then I'm glad to have done so." It had been a long night, and the outcome was far from ideal, but it was highly possible Felicity's actions had indeed averted something more terrible. "Where's Miss Prothero now?"

"Still in Torquay. They'll be taking her father to the prison at Exeter soon. Lizzie wants to support him." Lawrence's face showed a flicker of softness. "Her heart is so pure."

"Pardon my prying, Mr Whitburn, but might you know who will support Miss Prothero in the absence of her father?" While there were many victims of the drama in Ottermouth, Elizabeth was perhaps the only one who could be considered fully innocent.

Folding his arms over the chest of his ragged jumper, Lawrence flung a glance in Nigel's direction. "He's sold three of my sketches this morning already. And he hasn't even offered the paintings yet. If Lizzie wants to continue her calligraphy studies, I'll make sure it happens."

Had it been Elizabeth's specialism in calligraphy that had allowed her to notice the forged signatures and take action to protect her father? She might never talk about it. It was, however, gratifying to know Elizabeth had someone to care for her.

"Will Miss Prothero continue with her plan to study abroad, do you think?"

Lawrence was quiet for a moment. "She's not yet decided."

Felicity smiled gently. Lawrence and Elizabeth were both creative, passionate, and idealistic. It seemed a good match. "Let's hope the court case is smooth and quick. Miss Prothero has been through so much already." Despite his cowardice, Harold's commitment to his daughter was clear, and he now seemed willing to be honest about everything.

Lawrence nodded gravely, his gaze darting away as Nigel called his name. The gallery assistant was leading the two art buyers towards the artist, their eyes gleaming with admiration.

Lawrence frowned. "Excuse me," he said to Felicity before turning his back on his admirers and leaving the gallery.

Felicity folded her arms as she watched him cross the cobbles of the harbourside. Only individuals with substantial wealth or exceptional talent could engage in such behaviour without consequences.

"Oh," said Nigel as he reached Felicity, only slightly disappointed by Lawrence's departure. The gallery assistant turned to the art buyers. "Artists can be extremely volatile characters. Mr Whitburn especially, but his temperament is part of what makes his art so appreciated and so valued. The artist and his work are utterly unique."

Nigel's potential customers nodded with enthusiastic agreement, the gallery assistant having successfully turned a disappointment into a benefit. Adjusting his purple bow tie, Nigel advised the pair against pursuing Lawrence, but the art buyers weren't to be dissuaded and toddled off after the artist, no doubt keen to glimpse his studio.

Nigel tutted. "They're worse than children." It wasn't clear whether he was talking about the artist or the buyers.

"Are you continuing where Mr Prothero left off, Mr Davies?" enquired Felicity, fishing her notebook and pencil out of her pocket. Although rather weary, Felicity wasn't entirely devoid of the drive to collect news.

Nigel regarded her obliquely. "If you mean selling forgeries and delivering deadly blows, then certainly not, your ladyship."

Felicity smiled. "I meant running the art dealership. Minus the forgeries, naturally."

Nigel glanced around at the gallery. He narrowed his eyes. "I've been allowed by the authorities to look after the interests of the art owners unaffected by the fakes. Only works by Eustace Granger are under suspicion of being forged. Anything owned by Mr Prothero and Martin Granger is also frozen for the time being, as the authorities attempt to recoup the profits from the forgeries as they were sold." Nigel gave a little shake of his head. "But I now have Mr Whitburn eager to sell, and with the attention of the press on Ottermouth, and the forger on the run…" He straightened, the hint of a satisfied smile on his lips. "It's all amounting to a rather tantalising opportunity. I had a telephone call from a buyer in Paris just this morning. And Isabella, as you know, is still keen to support. I believe we'll have an exhibition in London before the summer."

Felicity nodded as she wrote it all down. Joseph had gone on the run only the night before. News travelled fast, although that ought not to have been a surprise. "I'm sure the art buyers and sellers are in capable hands, Mr Davies. I wish you the very best with your endeavours."

Nigel held up a palm, his face suddenly grave, his eyes darting to Felicity's notebook. "Make no mistake, your ladyship. I don't revel in Mr Prothero's misfortune — although he certainly brought some of it upon himself — and it's not my intention to profit from his situation. It's simply the position in which I find myself. I have always strived to be of service to artists, their admirers, and to the art itself." He spoke these last words as though concluding a speech to a captivated audience.

Felicity nodded with a little smile. *And the money*, she thought, although it wasn't necessarily a bad thing to regard finances as an important part of the equation. Harold had perhaps not been as astute in this area, which left him exposed when Martin pulled his trick.

"Might you know what has become of Miss Audrey Lawson?" enquired Felicity, out of personal curiosity as much as interest on behalf of the paper.

Nigel snorted. "The police seized the watercolour she wanted to sell, pending evidence of ownership. She said she was keen to cut ties with Ottermouth, anyway. Too many bad memories." He quirked an eyebrow. "Or so she informed me on the telephone."

Nigel was likely shrewd enough to understand the broader context. If Audrey was indeed a misuser of drugs, she was better off in London, where she wouldn't attract the attention of the likes of Officer Marshall, and where she would likely find a new supplier for her habit. She might also have friends in the city, who would hopefully help her get back on the right path.

After jotting down a few more details about the processing of the artworks and the preliminary plans for a London exhibition, Felicity wished Nigel well and set off towards Ashdene. It was surely about midday by now, the sun high in the sky and sparkling on the water, giving the coastline an almost Mediterranean feel, even though it was only just spring and still not that warm.

But as Felicity walked quickly along the harbourside, having perhaps lingered in the village a little too long to be precisely on time for lunch, her progress was interrupted. Thora Dunn came sprinting towards her, her brown linen pinafore catching around her shins as she ran. Looking rather nervous, the girl thrust a small package into Felicity's hands. It was about the size of a small loaf of bread.

"What's this?" said Felicity, surprised.

Thora barely met her gaze. "It's for you, your ladyship."

"Really? A gift isn't necessary."

Thora nodded. "Please, your ladyship."

Gingerly, Felicity set about loosening the string around the brown wax paper. As the aroma rose from the package's contents, she regretted not waiting to be somewhere more private before opening it.

Chapter Forty-Four

The tobacco leaves under the brown wax paper of the package were of a remarkably high quality, as evidenced by their flaked and moist texture. Not that Felicity herself smoked, but her brother was rarely without a pipe.

Thora smiled a little, the sun catching the thick waves of her reddish hair and creating a copper halo. She seemed pleased by Felicity's reaction, able to tell Felicity was impressed by the quality of the goods.

"From us Dunns, your ladyship. To say thank you."

Felicity smiled but wasn't comfortable. She glanced around the harbour. No one beside Thora and the gulls swooping above them had seen the contents of the package, but that didn't make the transaction any less illegal.

However, to ask about the provenance or, worse still, to refuse the gift was out of the question. Felicity had come a long way, from being spurned by Ottermouth's fishing community to being trusted and thanked. She wouldn't jeopardise that progress.

Felicity re-tightened the paper and string back around the tobacco. She had no bag to place it in, so she put it inside her jacket and pressed it to her side with her arm. It felt rather cloak-and-dagger.

"My brother will certainly enjoy this very kind gift." Gratitude was an important part of the transaction if relations with the fishing folk were to continue on good terms. "But I'm not sure what I've done from your family's perspective to earn your gratitude." The Dunns, after all, had nothing to do with Martin's demise.

Thora looked back over her shoulder. The harbour arm against which the Maggie was moored was abuzz with activity. Margaret was carrying provisions on deck while Captain Ned oversaw work on the trawler's winches. The sandy-haired young fisherman, Colin Reynolds — whom Felicity had encountered fishing alone what felt like weeks ago now — was also busy aboard the Maggie. Tourists dotted the harbourside, watching as though the scene were a tableau in a museum.

From across the harbour, Margaret gave Felicity a discreet smile, a gentle wind loosening strands of hair from the prim bun at her neck. Even the captain nodded in Felicity's direction, although his expression remained impassive. Colin's face reddened with embarrassment as his gaze met Felicity's. His eyes then went to Thora. She stared back at the young fisherman, a little blush reaching her cheeks.

Officially, the identity of whoever sabotaged Billy Seddon's boat remained unresolved, at least outside of the fishing community. Felicity had, however, a strong inkling.

"I'm thankful you took the time to listen to me yesterday, your ladyship," said Thora, sweeping her wind-blown hair from her cheeks, "and to guide me. I was so confused. You helped me see what I must do." She glanced over at Colin. "Col was rather lost as well. He's awfully sorry, you know, your ladyship. He'll never do such a thing again. It was silly, and he was so angry at Billy."

As Felicity understood it, it was Colin who'd put the hole in Billy's boat. Perhaps it was frustration at Thora's collusion with the drug smuggler that drove him to it. Or maybe jealousy at the time Thora and Billy were spending together. Whatever the reason, the altercation Felicity had witnessed between the two young men on her first visit to the inn had been a rather big clue.

"It's quite all right, Miss Dunn," reassured Felicity. "If you say Mr Reynolds shan't do anything similar again, then I have no reason to disbelieve you."

The girl smiled. She looked uncannily like Grace had done in her youth, as captured in the paintings by Eustace. And by Joseph.

"Ma is also pleased you helped my aunt," added Thora.

Felicity frowned a little. "Your mother's pleased Mrs Campbell left Ottermouth?" It was sad to imagine Grace's own family celebrating her departure.

Thora tucked her hair behind her ears. "It wasn't a nice situation for anyone. Ma wishes she'd done things differently, but it's likely better this way." It was a wise, measured view of things. The girl seemed to have matured considerably in a brief span of time.

Felicity was mindful of the need to keep her appointment with Alex, but she couldn't brush aside how she'd grown to care about Thora and her family. "Do you expect everything to return to the way it was?"

"Oh, no, your ladyship. It's all going to be different from now on. Ma and I will start a seafood stall here on the harbour, seeing as there are more tourists about. Pa is considering selling the Maggie to focus on mussels. And Col's applied to become the new lighthouse keeper."

Felicity lifted her brow. Would the package under her arm be among the last? Ending an old way of life was a form of loss, but traditions ought not to be blindly upheld, especially when not sanctioned by the law.

"Have you heard anything from Mr Seddon?" Felicity had to ask this. If Billy returned to Ottermouth any time soon, there would likely be trouble. He didn't seem the type to peacefully run a seafood stall, although Felicity had been wrong about people before.

Thora's forehead creased. "Not for the foreseeable, your ladyship. He's awfully far away."

Felicity nodded. It was enough reassurance. "Shall I put word about the new seafood stall in the newspaper?"

Thora's sea-green eyes glowed. "Oh, would you? That would be lovely. We might get a few more customers that way."

That was Felicity's hope as well. She wanted a bright future for Thora and the rest of Ottermouth's residents.

Thora threw a look towards the other side of the harbour. "Got to get back to work, your ladyship. Please excuse me." She gave a little curtsey, pinching the sides of her brown linen pinafore.

Felicity smiled. The curtsey was an unnecessary but incredibly well-meaning gesture. It was also a distinct contrast to Felicity's initial interactions with Ottermouth's fishing community.

"Of course, Miss Dunn. I've also somewhere I must be." Felicity had likely already left Alex waiting too long. What if he'd been dragged into some kind of society-style interview with a dreadfully boring art collector and needed rescuing?

On the coastal path towards Ashdene, Felicity breathed in great lungfuls of sea air as her Oxfords made light work of the loose stones underfoot, the package of tobacco still pressed to her side. Her time in Ottermouth was nearly at an end. How different the experience had been compared to her expectations. Had she been asked upon her arrival in the village, Felicity would not have been able to predict any of the dramatic events she'd witnessed and even played a part in.

There had been lows, and there were still challenges to come — the fates of Harold, Joseph, and even perhaps Grace hung in the balance — but there were also benefits for the community that could not have been foreseen.

It was with this sense of optimism that Felicity climbed the trail towards Ashdene. She and Alex would discuss the events in Ottermouth as they continued to unfold, but might they, too, consider what lay ahead on a personal level? Alex's path was perhaps easier to envisage than Felicity's. He'd not wavered from his dedication to reporting. Still, Felicity felt positive about her own prospects, even if the route ahead wasn't entirely clear.

Felicity's cheerfulness was reflected in the fluttering bracken fronds, the dancing heads of the pink pincushion flowers, and the white clouds tumbling through the bright blue sky above. Waves crashed over the rocks below with enthusiastic white sprays. She was even genuinely grateful for the tobacco pressed to her side. Jasper would surely enjoy it, and there was no one to search her luggage between Ashdene and Bradley Court.

The ambiance was disrupted by growling and barking coming from ahead, where the trail curved and vanished from view. Felicity recognised the dogs' tone as aggressive rather than playful.

"Beetle! Beetle!" The shouting that added to the commotion was Isabella's. "Stop it, I say. For goodness' sake, let the poor fellow go!"

Her stomach tightening, Felicity hurried ahead. After everything she'd been through, there was little use in shying away from trouble at this late stage. Had it been wishful thinking to imagine everything would be rounded off peacefully?

Chapter Forty-Five

Following the clifftop path around a sharp bend, Felicity stopped to appraise the scene before her.

The Briard, Beetle, was present, shaking himself with vigour and looking more like a tangled mass of fur than a dog. Isabella, in a relatively demure dark purple jacket and skirt decorated with a jewelled brooch, stood with her knuckles on her hips, chastising her hound. Pip was also in attendance, his little teeth bared and his nose wrinkled in a growl directed at his dear companion, Beetle.

James Halliday stood with his arms folded in a relaxed manner over the breast of his well-tailored brown jacket. He looked both perplexed and amused. Alex also stood to one side, his hands in the pockets of his dark blue three-piece suit. He raised an eyebrow at Felicity. *I would like to assist, but I'm not sure where to start*, his look seemed to say.

"Beetle, enough!" Isabella continued her admonishment of her dog. Between vigorous shakes, it was possible to see a limp form hanging from the Briard's jaws. A torn leg lay on the coastal path, multicoloured innards strewn about the place.

"Beetle, please! Mrs Rawling will be so very upset."

The Briard stopped shaking for a moment. The victim in his

maw was a rag doll stuffed with remnants and decorated with an eye-patch and a cutlass on its belt. It was perhaps intended to look like a pirate, though it rather resembled the innkeeper at the Dolphin. The pitiful effigy had been quite decimated by Beetle.

While Felicity suspected the still-growling Yorkie to have also been involved in the destruction, her heartbeat settled upon realising no living creature was in danger.

"Oh dear." Felicity bent to scoop the leg from the path as Isabella attempted to snatch the forlorn-looking doll from Beetle without success. "The poor thing does look rather worse for wear." Felicity held up the dismembered and slightly soggy leg between finger and thumb and pulled a face.

Alex smiled.

Isabella continued to try to trap the Briard and retrieve the toy. Pip was also snapping at what was left of the rag doll pirate, but Beetle was too fast for any of them. He was enjoying himself immensely.

James looked on, shaking his head a little.

"My darling housekeeper made the toy for them," said Isabella between lunges. "Put rather too much time and effort into it for these two sharp-teethed scoundrels, if you ask me."

As Beetle attempted to outmanoeuvre his mistress by dashing behind her, Alex reached down and deftly snatched the half-destroyed toy from the dog's jaws. Beetle sat and whimpered, his ears sinking. Pip barked bossily. In his mind, it was now his turn.

James offered a round of applause. "Well played."

With a lift of his homburg hat, Alex gave a little bow and handed the toy to Isabella, which she accepted by pinching its rather generous earlobe, from which hung a little gold hoop. The toy had been lovingly made, with care and attention to detail. It was perhaps more suitable for the love and attention of a child than for two half-wild dogs. It was clear Mrs Rawling cared for Beetle and Pip very much indeed.

James stepped forward and collected the soggy severed leg from Felicity, which she gladly handed over.

"Do you suppose it might be repaired?" asked Felicity.

"Mrs Rawling might work her magic," said Isabella, examining the damage. "But I shall advise her that if she wants the dogs to have toys to play with, then there must be two pirates and not one. They've fought over it all morning. We only came out for a walk to distract them, but the little rascals somehow smuggled it outside."

Beetle whimpered on as Pip continued to emit the occasional demanding bark. They were indeed a pair of scoundrels, yet somehow still lovable.

"Will you join us for lunch, Cici?" Isabella asked, with a glance at James.

Felicity's agreement was to meet with Alex. She'd expected their lunch to be private, so they could exchange information freely. She looked at Alex questioningly.

Before he could respond, Isabella continued.

"Don't worry," she said, perhaps misreading the concern in Felicity's expression. "The collectors and buyers are all gone from Ashdene. At least for now. They're rather keen to make acquaintance with Mr Davies, who's apparently doing a roaring trade in Lawrence Whitburn's works. They're also eager to get a glimpse of Mr Ferris' underground art studio."

Felicity blinked. "The police will surely have locked it all up."

Again, Isabella glanced at James, and they both smiled. "That won't stop them from trying," she said. "Perhaps it will become some kind of tourist attraction. Who's to say?"

Felicity looked again at Alex. He shrugged. It seemed there was no objection to the lunch from his side.

"Yes, we'll join you," said Felicity, "but shall Mr Cooper and I first take the dogs for a run? To tire them out and allow them to forget about the toy while he's taken in for repairs?" She was resolute in her desire to have some time alone with her friend. There was much to catch up on.

"Enjoy your time alone together," called Isabella as she

returned along the path to Ashdene, cradling the damaged rag doll and with James at her side.

Felicity had to scoop Pip up and hold him under her elbow to prevent him from bounding off after the pirate. Alex skilfully distracted the Briard with a stick, throwing it into a thicket, into which Beetle dived without hesitation. With the new toy at a safe distance, Felicity set Pip back on the ground, and the dogs set about tumbling around with one another, their growls back to sounding as playful as ever.

The wind blew in gently from the sea, making the leaves rustle. Felicity took a deep breath. She was only mildly embarrassed by Isabella's parting comment, which carried an undertone of extra implication. A woman could be friends with a man, couldn't she? It was 1922, after all.

"There's a bench nearby with a marvellous view. Shall we sit for a spell?"

"By all means," replied Alex, and they started off side by side towards the headland. "I say. Isabella and James. More than friends, are they?"

Felicity felt her cheeks flushing. She frowned.

"I'm sorry," said Alex quickly. "That was indiscreet of me."

"Not at all." Felicity's reply was just as fast. "It's natural to wonder about such things." She didn't want Alex to think there were topics that couldn't be discussed between the two of them, although the idea of others pondering the nature of her friendship with Alex created a tension in the pit of Felicity's stomach.

"I believe we would both wish for Isabella to be happy," she continued, dismissing her own uneasiness. "Whether she finds that happiness with Mr Halliday or with someone else or with no one at all, I don't suppose it matters."

Alex nodded, his eyes on the path ahead. "Not from our perspective."

They were nearing the bench, which was nothing more than a plank of wood atop two sawn-off stumps. It was, however, perfectly placed to appreciate a sweeping view of the sparkling sea dotted with boats and the dramatic, rugged coastline as it stretched off towards Dorset. A large patch of sloping, scraggy grass encircled by dense foliage lay before the bench. It was the perfect spot for the dogs to run riot together, with growls and yaps and clumps of turf occasionally flying into the air.

Alex gestured for Felicity to sit down first, then took a seat beside her, a respectable distance away. He removed his hat and ran a hand over his slicked-back hair.

With relief, Felicity took the package from under her jacket and set it on the bench between herself and Alex.

Alex frowned at it. "Am I allowed to ask?"

"You can open it if you like."

He did so, giving the contents a sniff. He raised his brow. "This will help keep your brother sweet, but who imagined you to be a pipe smoker?"

"It's from the Dunns."

"The fishing family?"

Felicity nodded. "Everyone seems awfully thankful and friendly towards me all of a sudden. Perhaps I should have intervened the first time I saw a knife drawn in the village."

"Say, Cici." Alex looked suddenly rather serious. "I owe you an apology. Perhaps even several."

Felicity tilted her head. "I don't see why."

"I didn't follow you. Not straight away. It took me a while to shake that customs chap. Then there were the dogs to deposit back at the house." Alex gripped the edge of the bench. "I realise they're poor excuses, and I moved as quickly as I could, but I must admit, the whole time I was telling myself that you know how to handle things." Alex winced as he said this. The sunlight made the blue of his eyes shimmer like the sea. "Was that awful of me?"

Felicity gave a little frown. "Why would it be awful to trust in my judgment? And it was actually probably for the best that you didn't follow me directly. The situation was so delicate." *Although I would, of course, have been very pleased to see you,* she wanted to add but for some reason remained silent, aware of her own quickening heartbeat.

"You've been through the mill on this posting." Alex's tone was still sombre. "But you've made a success of it." He smiled a little. "You always do."

"Thanks to you," said Felicity in all seriousness. "I wouldn't have been able to write things up as thoroughly and as quickly as you have. The newspaper would have been quite neglected."

Alex looked amused. "So, you're at last becoming honest with yourself about where your priorities lie."

Felicity hadn't quite realised what she'd said. "Oh." She frowned, the awareness throwing her off balance despite being seated. "I see." Felicity had indeed neglected her duties as a reporter to a certain extent in favour of a more active role in matters. "You won't tell Jasper, will you?"

Alex shook his head. "Never." He smiled again. "You know, your brother gave me an awful hard time for not taking better care of you."

"Did he now?" Was that why Jasper had been so reasonable with Felicity on the telephone? Had he already taken out his frustrations on Alex?

"That's what got me thinking I'd behaved terribly," continued Alex, "by not dashing after you."

Jasper chastising his little sister was one thing, but giving Alex a scolding was something Felicity wouldn't stand for. "It was only thanks to you distracting Officer Marshall that I could do my bit." Felicity blinked. "Wait. Is that why you came to Ottermouth? Because Jasper wanted you to keep an eye on me?"

"Heavens, no." Alex's forehead creased deeply, his scar prominent. "I came here to help. To be part of the team." The corner of his mouth hooked sheepishly upwards. "And to get the scoop."

Felicity laughed. "Of course, the scoop. You're a newspaperman, after all."

"I've never attempted to hide my true nature from you."

They sat in silence for a moment, watching the wind make patterns across the sea and listening to the rustling of the leaves. Felicity's curls danced about under the brim of her cloche. The dogs continued their play, growling good-naturedly. Felicity had developed such an effortless rapport with Alex. There was no one else with whom she felt so at ease. Not even Jasper or Lady Henrietta.

But they were definitely just friends. Felicity recalled attempting to put her hand through Alex's arm under the umbrella they'd shared. He'd pulled away, preferring to walk in the rain. That was a sign, wasn't it? The boundaries of their relationship were quite clear.

Later, they'd no doubt write up copy and call in articles together. Alex was returning to Exeter that evening. Felicity would travel to Bradley Court the next day. After Ottermouth, they'd likely be given different stories to cover, but they could always plan for a meet-up. A bun and a pot of tea in the city. They even had their regular table in the tea rooms. It was a pleasant feeling to have a friend like Alex. To know that even if they weren't always together, they were still on the same team.

"Cici." Alex's tone was once again serious.

She turned to him. "Yes?"

"I've a proposal I'd like to make to you."

Felicity's heart jumped. "What is it?"

Claim your free Lady Felicity Quick ebook!

Sign up for my email newsletter and you'll get **Murder at Afternoon Tea** absolutely free!

As a newsletter subscriber, you'll also receive writing updates, special offers, and behind-the-scenes exclusives...

Use this link to sign up and claim your copy today:
https://BookHip.com/XMGPNZC

Read the next in the series...

Murder at a Boarding School

A Lady Felicity Quick 1920s Cozy Mystery
Book 6

Liverton Ladies' Academy teaches Britain's finest young women etiquette, deportment and ... murder?

England, 1922. At a sprawling Devonshire estate, surrounded by wealthy girls targeting excellent marriages, Lady Felicity Quick has abandoned her exciting, hard-won career in journalism to teach letter-writing and table manners at an exclusive finishing school...

Except nothing is as it seems.

Answering an irresistible plea for help, Felicity is undercover, hunting a Great War spy who betrayed the British and cost countless lives. Between lessons in dance, French, and flower arranging, Felicity edges closer to unmasking her foe, but then chaos erupts: a body is found. Are more sinister schemes afoot than first thought?

With the students' futures under threat and a promise made to loved ones to fulfil, Felicity is more determined than ever to make daring strides to uncover the truth — even if dodging deadly perils was never part of her lesson plan.

Delve into the secrets of Liverton Ladies' Academy in this completely gripping 1920s English mystery! Full of twists, humour and unique characters, Murder at a Boarding School is perfect for readers who love the bold lady sleuths of Verity Bright and Magda Alexander, the historical English settings of Downton Abbey and classic Agatha Christie, and the twisty period puzzles of T E Kinsey and Rhys Bowen.

Murder at a Boarding School will be available soon!

The Lady Felicity Quick Mystery Series

Murder at Afternoon Tea

(Novella | Exclusive for Newsletter Subscribers)

Murder on the Village Green

(Book 1 | Available Now)

Murder at a Country House

(Book 2 | Available Now)

Murder at the Tea Rooms

(Book 3 | Available Now)

Murder at the Ball

(Book 4 | Available Now)

Murder on the Coast

(Book 5 | This Book)

Murder at a Boarding School

(Book 6 | Coming Soon)

About the Author

Rosie Hunt is a British author of cozy mysteries both puzzling and historical. Her books include the Lady Felicity Quick mystery series set in the green and pleasant countryside of southwest England in the 1920s.

A history addict and former journalist, Rosie grew up immersed in the worlds of Poirot and Miss Marple. This early exposure to baffling murder mysteries rather coloured her outlook on life, and it was only a matter of time before she began writing her own.

Rosie loves clotted cream, knitting, and Golden Age crime fiction, and she'll never miss an opportunity to visit a National Trust property. She lives with her husband and their four-pawed overlord on a river in Northern Europe.

Join Rosie's mailing list
bookhip.com/XMGPNZC

Follow Rosie on Facebook
facebook.com/RosieHuntAuthor

Printed in Great Britain
by Amazon

38877485R00164